SUSAN

THE INDIAN HOMEMAKER

An Epitome of Motherhood and Woman Empowerment

SUVASISH MUKHOPADHYAY

INDIA • SINGAPORE • MALAYSIA

ISBN

Hardcase 979-8-89066-828-8
Paperback 979-8-88935-959-3

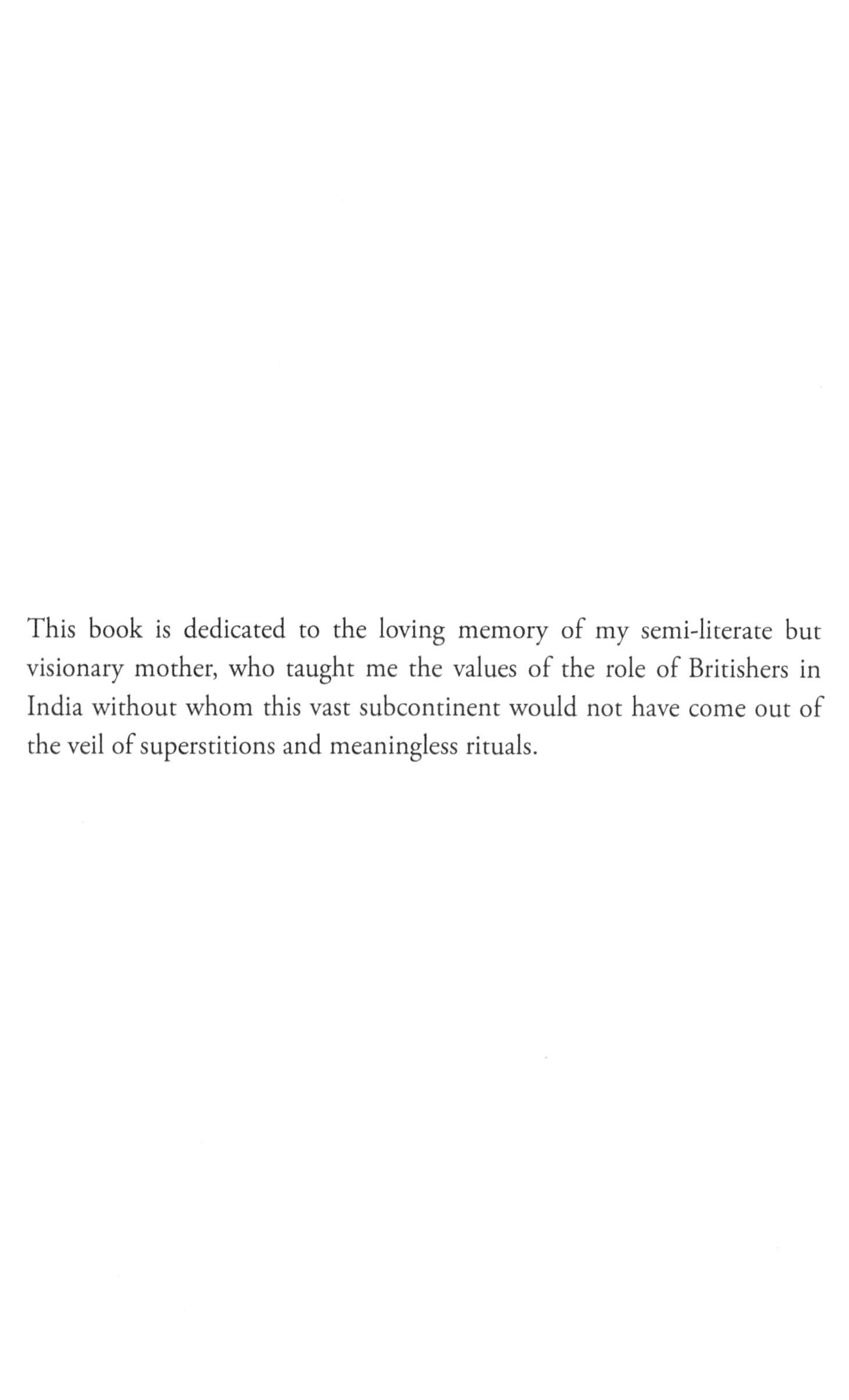

This book is dedicated to the loving memory of my semi-literate but visionary mother, who taught me the values of the role of Britishers in India without whom this vast subcontinent would not have come out of the veil of superstitions and meaningless rituals.

Contents

Other Books by Suvasish Mukhopadhyay

Fundamentals of Fluid Mechanics

My Students of Far and Near

Tsunami the Biggest Bane

You Can Score More

How to Study and Succeed

The Happiness Code

Motivating School Kids

An Eternal Quest for Peace

My Students My Love

The Rise of the Setting Sun

Choose Your Correct Career

Pune: The Preferred Destination

Managing the Management in Corporate

Scoring High

Your Mind is Your Prime Power

Comparison - The Highest Form of Insult

Change Your Life in One Hour

The Art of Living

My Beloved UBER Drivers! The Best Managers of the World

MY NIT! MY LOVE!

Philosophy of Prof Mukhopadhyay

A Game Lost and Won

"The best thing is to track the progress of a sapling."

– Suvasish Mukhopadhyay

Foreword

"Women hold up half the sky."

People rarely quote Mao Zedong any more. But, that was a statement made by him. Gender biases have a long history in many countries, not just in India. Among other things, UNDP's annual Human Development Report documents such gender biases. In India, had female work participation rates in the labour force been higher, the GDP (Gross Domestic Product) and the growth in the GDP would both have been higher. Economics apart, assorted metrics bring out the male/female differential. Preference for son and foeticide/infanticide exist, and the catalogue of crimes against women is long. So, as to not sound completely negative: (a) across metrics, there have been improvements and (b) laws and their enforcement have improved. However, since the backlog of discrimination is significant, these incremental improvements have still not made a sufficient dent in prejudices and proclivities that go back several centuries.

Most people have heard of Gandhiji's famous talisman. "I will give you a talisman. Whenever you are in doubt, or when the self becomes too much with you, apply the following test. Recall the face of the poorest and the weakest man whom you may have seen, and ask yourself, if the step you contemplate is going to be of any use to him. Will he gain anything from it? Will it restore him to control over his own life and destiny? In other words, will it lead to swaraj for the hungry and spiritually starving millions?"

As originally stated, the gender in Gandhiji's talisman was male. But, it is more pertinent for women. If one thinks of Rawlsian's original position behind a veil of ignorance and contemplates possible future scenarios of being born in India, the worst-off situation will be that of being born as an

SC/ST girl in one of India's "backward" districts. This unsatisfactory state of affairs is ascribed to patriarchy and male mindsets.

While that is undoubtedly true, as depicted in films and TV serials, women often suffer at the hands of other women, the mother-in-law versus daughter-in-law relationship being the cliched example. Paraphrasing Kipling, the female of the species can be deadlier than the male. Unfortunately, it isn't always the mother-in-law. Contrary to what one might expect, a mother often makes daughters a lot worse. And, extrapolating to posterity, if a daughter's lot improves, that is because of the mother.

William Rose Wallace's poem is now remembered only for a couple of lines. The other lines are no less significant.

Infancy's the tender fountain,
Power may with beauty flow,
Mother's first to guide the streamlets,
From them, souls un-resting grow —
Grow on for the good or evil,
Sunshine streamed or evil hurled,
For the hand that rocks the cradle,
Is the hand that rules the world.

This contour finds shape in Professor Suvasish Mukhopadhyay's novel *SUSAN – The Indian Homemaker.* The novel isn't only about a mother-daughter relationship, but it's also about Susan who faces several adversities in life. There is also a strand of the relationship between Susan's mother (an unnamed Mrs Mazumdar) and Susan and between Susan and her daughter, Andria. The choice of names is intriguing. Susan is typically a Christian name, as is Andria, though not invariably so. All said and done, Christian women (assuming the family is Christian) are relatively better placed than many other women. Be that as it may, we follow Susan's life, through the words of Professor Mukhopadhyay, and it is a life full of calamities and adversities — her father's death, a marriage that flatters to deceive covetous relatives and in-laws, her husband's illness and death and HIV.

These are successive tests foisted by destiny. None of these breaks her spirit. For a while, she lives for her daughter. Then, when her daughter is settled, Susan finds her own destiny. This is a novel about motherhood and women's empowerment, and the author's familiarity with geography, culture and the educational system shines through. More importantly, there is the important message of triumphing against adversity.

– Prof Bibek Debroy

Preface

This book talks about an Indian woman who went through a lot of struggles for raising her daughter and making her successful academically and professionally. The central character is a Christian lady named Susan. Her father was an Assistant Professor of Mechanical Engineering at NIT, Rourkela. Susan's childhood was quite rosy. There was a trend of gender bias in her family, and she felt the same at her tender age.

Everything was going on very smoothly, and they were quite well off due to her father's job. But, no one can predict destiny. It was 1974. She was just a kid of seven years. Her father was detected with gum cancer, and within six months, he left the world. He left behind his widow and three tender children, among whom Susan was the eldest. The days of struggle started. As a replacement, at the institute, her mother was given a position of a lower division clerk in the accounts section of NIT Rourkela. Overnight, the earning of the family became one-fourth. Rock-bottom poverty started, and with the salary of a lower-division clerk, Susan's mother had to manage the whole family.

Gradually, time was running. From the second standard, Susan reached the tenth standard. She had very few friends. It was 1983. Susan passed ICSE, and her mother forced her to go to Jalpaiguri to her maternal uncle's place for her higher secondary education. She did not have any other option and could not protest. After the Higher Secondary examinations, Susan returned to Rourkela.

An NIT student named Sanjay used to tutor Susan's brother and sister. Sanjay was a scholar and a whimsical boy. Susan's mother requested Sanjay to teach mathematics to Susan for her Joint Entrance Examination. Sanjay started teaching her but realised in the very beginning that Susan was not made for science. However, he was keen on Susan for her paragon beauty.

Gradually, his attraction intensified, but truly speaking, it was a one-sided affair. But, time is the best judge of everything. Slowly, Susan, too, realised that Sanjay had developed a massive weakness towards her, and with each passing month, their relationship as a teacher and a student took a sharp turn, and they became passionate lovers.

Susan's mother did not want their relationship to flourish. Secretly, she was trying for Susan's marriage with a farmer from Jalpaiguri. When Susan came to know that, she was shocked and narrated everything to Sanjay. Sanjay was crestfallen, and to stop Susan's mother, the only solution was to get married. By that time, Sanjay had completed his graduation but did not have any job. He was pursuing his post-graduation. In November 1986, they got married in the office of the marriage registrar in Rourkela.

In March 1987, Sanjay visited Rourkela, and while entering Susan's house, he faced staunch resistance from Susan's mother, but without caring for it, he entered forcibly. On seeing that, Susan's sister expressed that they had gotten married. It was not known to Sanjay or Susan that her sister was aware of their marriage. Her wretched mother told Susan to leave the house. Sanjay was not at all perturbed.

On that very day, Sanjay returned to Serampore along with Susan at midnight, and his father accepted them. At the age of nineteen, Susan had to take complete responsibility in the kitchen. Sanjay had tremendous mental pressure. His post-graduation was not complete. With the scholarship being stopped, there was no hope of completion.

In the mid of 1988, Sanjay had a severe nervous breakdown. Then Susan was only twenty years old. When her other friends were enjoying a namby-pamby college life, she was rotting in the kitchen under the feudal nature of her father-in-law. She was nothing but an unpaid domestic maid in the house of Sanjay's father. Since Sanjay was not ready for any other profession except teaching, he was sitting idle at home. Sanjay was addicted to alcohol and tobacco, and his maternal side possessed a rich history of mental illness. Due to this untimely, premature and unceremonious marriage, Susan was internally depressed, and the major setback was the discontinuation of her graduation.

Sanjay was very stubborn as far as his profession was concerned. He was not ready to go for any job. One day in the year of 1989, Susan requested Sanjay to complete his post-graduation at least. After a gap of one year, he went to meet his guide in BE College, Shibpur (presently known as IIEST), and this time, without any discontinuation, he successfully completed his post-graduation with distinction in December 1989. But, his fate did not change. In earlier days, he was an unemployed youth with a graduation in Engineering, now he became an unemployed youth with a post-graduation in Engineering.

Feeling helpless, Sanjay's father contacted his uncle in Nagpur. He came and listened to the problem and wanted Sanjay to move to Nagpur to get a teaching job because, in Maharashtra, even in those days, there was no dearth of private engineering colleges. As per his uncle's advice, Sanjay applied to ten colleges and ultimately was selected as a lecturer of Civil Engineering in a private engineering college in Khamgaon. The duo was relieved from the tentacles of the house of Serampore.

In December 1990, Susan noticed signs of the arrival of a new member. It was good. Since it was their first, the duo wholeheartedly accepted it. Their daughter was born in September 1991.

The teaching profession could not help Sanjay to get rid of depression, and the closest family members are tortured the most by a depressed person. Susan could read the message in his eyes. While working in Khamgaon, Sanjay's uncle sent him an advertisement, which was published in local newspapers, for the recruitment of lecturers in Civil Engineering in Government Engineering Colleges in the state of Maharashtra. Sanjay casually applied and got selected. His initial posting was in Pune. Just for the whims of a scholarly husband, the good lady had to face all these odd situations. After a couple of months, Sanjay got government-allotted quarters in Yerawada.

The main problem of Sanjay was that he was overreactive and hypersensitive. Gradually, Susan realised that she could not change Sanjay due to his rigid frame of thinking. So, she decided to shift her attention to her small daughter, and she took an internal oath to make her daughter's life successful as far as academic and professional careers were concerned. Now, she abandoned her past and dreamt of a new life. She became the sculptor of her daughter's career.

Susan started her initial assignments for Andria. She wanted Andria to be fluent in English and sharp in Mathematics. Truly, these are the only two aspects that rule the academic world. Gradually, the caterpillar years of Andria were over, and she went to the middle grade from the primary grade. In her school, her grades were consistently good, and her academic achievements were marked by all teachers, though she was never pampered for her scholasticism, and her parents never wanted their daughter to be a trophy child. Gradually, she completed her tenth standard, and obviously, she opted for the science stream. After her twelfth standard, she opted for Mechanical Engineering at a reputed college in Pune and successfully graduated with good grades.

After continuously staying with Sanjay, Susan had forgotten the normal behaviour expected from a person. Periodic assault by Sanjay was a regular phenomenon in Susan's life, but she never shared her feelings with her neighbours.

The year was 2011. Sanjay was suffering from swollen lymph nodes and fever. After investigation, it was found that he was infected with HIV. It was a bolt from the blue. Susan did not bow down; for her life was a war field, and there was no scope of going back. She was ready to face all the consequences.

Before the declaration of the result of her graduation, Andria was placed in a Japanese MNC located in Pune through her college. Susan wanted Andria to be smart on all fronts of life, so she decided that Andria must learn to drive. Susan realised that half an hour of training in a driving school was not enough. A learner had to practise in their own car. She managed to purchase a second-hand Maruti 800 for Andria. People in their society used to coax Susan for Andria's wedding, but it was a firm decision of Susan to not arrange Andria's wedding before she became academically stronger and financially more successful. She did not want Andria to suffer like her. She always tried to give the best life to her.

Some of the neighbours suggested Susan file a case against Sanjay and get a divorce and alimony. But, Susan was never an opportunist. She remained the same lady who left her house permanently with Sanjay within a fraction of an hour. She did not express her opinion, but except for her, no one knew that her love and affection had not changed over time. She did not believe in showcasing it. Love is not a matter to exhibit. Susan remained as introverted as she was. The neighbours and friends distanced themselves from her on not getting any reaction. Susan's life was followed by a bunch of worries. She used to have sleepless nights, and at midnight, she used to go to the terrace of her apartment and gaze at the star-spangled sky.

Due to an unceasing and unending struggle, Susan forgot that sex was a part of married life. Truly speaking, the personal life of Susan and Sanjay was far better before their marriage. A sweet kiss was far better than brutal intercourse. The aroma of sex does not lie in meeting each other; it lies within the feelings of the partners. That aroma was lost from her life for many years.

In her dictionary, the word peace was not there. Susan was an ideal mother who executed women's empowerment in the true sense. She did not have a service record in any government or private office, but her service was reflected in each and every successful step of Andria's career. The rest of the book talks about how Susan placed Andria in the proper place and position as a global expert in Environmental Engineering through her hard work, vision and smart decisions. Susan was a lady who always supported ladies because, in today's context, ladies are the biggest enemies of ladies. In our society, a mother-in-law wants a grandson, not a granddaughter. This is the crux of the truth. That's why truth is stranger than fiction.

Gradually, Susan's dream took its final shape. But, as far as her duties were concerned, she thought that she had finished all of them, and unlike other people, she did not consider the marriage of her daughter as her duty. She thought that Andria's marriage was her personal liberty. So, instead of sitting at home, she decided to join an NGO to help the HIV-infected children on the outskirts of Pune. She did not even know that she was the epitome of women's empowerment and women's liberty. For Susan, women's empowerment did not mean arranging some kitty parties for snob ladies of the society, for her women's empowerment meant preparing an independent woman. She could not create a garden, but she took care of a sapling.

Susan's life could be compared to a tragedy. During childhood, she lost her beloved father and best friend, Jenny; during the prime of youth, she had to leave her studies and face ruthless insults from her sadist and crooked father-in-law. Being Sanjay's personal choice, his father was not happy with Susan. The only fault of her was that she could not bring money and ornaments through her marriage. Though afterwards, only to give a tight slap to her father-in-law, Susan not only completed graduation but also went for post-graduation and successfully completed it. She was not even a Hindu, while her father-in-law was an orthodox Brahmin. He was obsessed with the caste system and religion, but that dunce did not realise that God created man, and man created caste. During married life, in the first fifteen to twenty years, most couples achieve their desired dreams step by step, but Susan had witnessed the gradual metamorphosis of a man from a scholar to a lunatic.

After serving an NGO for four years, Susan heaved a sigh of relief. She completed her basic duties and decided to leave the NGO and provide honorary service for a vagrant home where poor girls were taken care of. It was in Alibag. She shifted her base from Pune to Alibag.

Andria wanted a comfortable living for Susan, at least at her advanced age, but Susan was made of a different material. Andria was a flower for her. It was her duty to bloom the flower, but a huge amount of work was still pending. Now, she decided to take care of a garden that comprised many poor girls from different pockets of the city. History repeats itself. Susan started teaching them, starting with A, B, C, D. She could be compared with the sun, which never sets. When one observes the western crawl of the sun, it rises in the opposite hemisphere. For the vagrant home, Susan was a blessing in disguise. Sometimes, she felt very lonely, mainly in the evenings. She would think of her sweet childhood spent in Rourkela, the hazy memories of the father-daughter relationship, Sanjay's love, anxieties, depression, severe bout of insanity and lastly grooming and blooming of Andria. Society would not know this silent and selfless contribution of a lady for her family; she would not get any award; she would not be noticed, but somewhere through her daughter's good work, people of the world would realise the true meaning of women's empowerment and women's liberty.

– Suvasish Mukhopadhyay

Praise for the Book and Author

I am really impressed by the central theme of the book. The chapters are aligned in a very proper way and the book narrates the story of the struggle, devotion and determination of an Indian homemaker who fought till the end to give shape to the career of her daughter, and in spite of all odds and torture from her spouse, she never vented. Right from beginning to end, the central character of this fiction, Susan, gave maximum importance to her self-esteem. Ladylike Susan is rare, and she can be the perfect character for an ideal mother, and the whole womanhood of the world can be described through her character. I appreciate this noble theme, which is the brainchild of Mukhopadhyay, whom I have known for the last three decades. I wish him scintillating success for this marvellous project, and the whole book will be an inspiration for the generations to come, and it is proved by the writing that a homemaker can contribute more than a working lady, but sacrifice, devotion, determination and dedication of a homemaker is rarely counted and considered.

I compliment Mukhopadhyay for this unparalleled project undertaken by him and wish him the best of luck in this undertaken project.

– Ashwin Moghe

(Vice President, UltraTech Cement Ltd., Mumbai)

Unputdownable spirit of a woman through the journey of her life.

– Rajib Chattaraj

(Superintending Engineer, PWD, West Bengal, India)

The world is not a bed of roses. But lesser so for women. *SUSAN – The Indian Homemaker* is a novel about the myriad junctures in a woman's life, is a complete book. The storyline of conflicts and resolution steers the boat of a woman's life as it navigates across the uncertain waves of life. Every turn has a lesson; every lesson has a meaning, and every struggle has a reason. Susan's courage that she instils in her daughter, the bitter-sweet familial relationships that are not dramatic or 'filmy' but very real and feels personal! Relevance, a sweet cordiality that other women must resonate with, takes the cake! The backdrop of a tumultuous time in West Bengal paints an accurate picture of the society she grows up in. The author does his best to bring forth the minute intricacies of a woman's mind and, more importantly, her strong yet delicate heart. A beautiful read!

– Tithi Mukherjee

(Content Architect, Quantum Leap Learning Solutions, Bangalore, India)

Professor Mukhopadhyay's writing style is unique in the sense that it is a literal narration from a first-person perspective. I have been a student of the professor and can attest to his teaching and writing style. He has a taste for the most controversial subjects and speaks with us in an unreserved manner. The contents of the book should stimulate the reader's interest and should be a very good read.

– Anand Gorthi

(AECOM, New Jersey, USA)

The novel is an excellent narration of the journey of a woman through the tremendous adversities in life, never give up attitude, inspiring her child to work for the greater cause of society and finally achieve the greater pursuit of life. The book makes the reader identify themselves with the characters they experience in life. My congratulations to the author for this life-enhancing experience in the book.

– Sanjoy Ghosh

(GM, A reputed oil sector in India)

Susan, the main character of this book is the epitome of the magical power of an Indian woman, who can overcome all obstacles by her sheer willpower and devotion to life. She is almost like the new incarnation of the divine Indian mythical female characters like Sita, Draupadi, Shaibya or Sati. The interesting thing about the book is that it is depicted in a lucid manner like a real-life story and readers may feel acquainted with some character or the other in this book. The story flows like an unhindered river until it meets the ultimate sea of happiness. Another marvellous work of Suvasish Mukhopadhyay keeps the readers enthralled.

– Sanjeeb Kumar Paul

(Chief General Manager (Bio Fuel), Bharat Petroleum Corporation Limited, Mumbai, India)

Mukhopadhyay is known to me for the last two decades and, right from the beginning, I keenly observe his association with English literature. In 2001, I wrote the Foreword in his first non-technical book entitled 'My Students of Far and Near'. This present book entitled *SUSAN – The Indian Homemaker* has a very heart-touching theme, where a homemaker, Susan, had to absorb all the shock and tantrums of her schizophrenic, depressed and HIV-infected scholar husband, Sanjay. The main characteristic of Susan is that she didn't run away from the problems she faced. On the contrary, she sustained and tried to resolve all the problems very boldly and didn't care for this sad, bad and mad society which can contribute only to criticism. She brought up her only child, Andria, in spite of all odds and became successful in making her a global citizen in the true sense. There lies the contribution of her motherhood. According to my view, Susan is a true symbol of motherhood and women's empowerment. If there would have been a Susan in every family, the thought process of the country would have been changed in a positive direction, and the country would have gotten rid of gender bias. I am truly impressed by the theme of this noble creation.

– Dr Ashok A Ghatol

(Former Vice Chancellor of Babasaheb Ambedkar Technical University First Director of College of Engineering, Pune, India)

Let me first congratulate the author Mukhopadhyay for coming up with an excellent novel, portraying a silent but challenging journey of a woman in West Bengal, India. What I feel is, it's more important that the book shows the brighter side of her life rather than collecting sympathy by depicting only the darker side of her life. The author unwinds the story in a lucid style and makes you read the book from start to finish.

– Prof Shreenivas Londhe PhD PDF
(Professor in Civil Engineering, Vishwakarma Institute of Information Technology, Pune, India)

The narrative proposed in the book is pretty interesting and adheres to the real-life situations that many women are facing. After going through the synopsis, I am really touched by the subject Mukhopadhyay is proposing in this upcoming book. Indeed, with great confidence in his writing skills, personally, I am looking forward to his valuable contribution in the form of this book, addressing the mental/physical stress nearly half of the population is going through in this walk of life and showing them a path to overcome their struggles with the example of the character drafted in this book. I congratulate Mukhopadhyay for this immensely important issue being addressed in this upcoming book, and I am confident that it will positively work for women's empowerment. Best wishes.

– Dr Makarand Ghangrekar
(Professor of Civil Engineering, IIT-Kharagpur, India)

Mukhopadhyay has written an extremely gripping story about the life of a woman who courageously handles the mental illness of her husband and its consequences in her own life as well as that of her daughter. A must-read book in the current circumstances where the pandemic has exposed mental health vulnerabilities in the community at large and the shocking ignorance and neglect of this subject till now.

– Dr D M Dhavale
(Eminent Psychiatrist)

I have known S Mukhopadhyay for the past seven years as an excellent teacher and a kind and humble human being. I have also read his previous book on the path to happiness. After reading the synopsis of his new book *SUSAN – The Indian Homemaker*, which depicts the courageous journey of Susan, I found it highly inspirational and optimistic. I would like to strongly support and endorse this book.

– Dr Amit Sangle

(Eminent Maxillofacial Surgeon)

Writing has become a passion for Mr Suvasish Mukhopadhyay, and his creativity in portraying instances that relate to life is simple yet conveys a message for mankind. Suvasish's habit of concentration, acquired through long years of self-discipline, has resulted in the complete manifestation of this wonderful piece of work.

His journey as an engineering faculty and wholesome quality-filled rings in his writing treasures to the fore like a "Management Guru." I wish the readers an absorbing, stimulating and joyful reading.

– B B Ahuja

(Former Director, College of Engineering, Pune, India)

SUSAN – The Indian Homemaker is a delightful and compassionate book crafted with refined pathos and piercing wit to unfold the deepest recesses of our souls. In this book, Mukhopadhyay with his compelling narrative style weaves a rich collage of details that appear so real that you readily identify the situations with your own lived experiences and draw inspiration from the choices and actions of the protagonist. You're sure to love this book because it's your story in print.

– Dr Sarbani Banerjee

(Author and reviewer

Proprietor, Editio Princeps Publishing Services, Mumbai, India)

I had the opportunity to know Mukhopadhyay from a close angle being his student, and I am associated with his writings for the last two decades. I went through a few of his books, i.e., 'The Happiness Code' and 'My Students! My Love!' Mukhopadhyay possesses an unparalleled passion for English literature, and he has authored many books. The speciality of Professor is his simple and lucid narration.

I was deeply touched by the book entitled 'My Students! My Love!' Except for Professor, no other faculties in this world authored a book about his students with such a lovely passion. The book entitled 'The Happiness Code' is the epitome of motivation, and lakhs of people are motivated by this book. Through his lectures and live sessions, Sir has helped a great cross-section of the world to know the meaning of happy living. I want Sir to author more books in the genre of self-help and motivation. I am deeply moved and motivated by his writing.

– Dr Shivaji G Patil

(Former Executive Engineer, MIDC, Pune, India)

Acknowledgements

I had an opportunity to read people over the last five decades. I am deeply grateful to a person whom I could not provide with a humdrum domestic life coupled with a comfortable living due to my moody nature and obsessive-compulsive disorder with academics.

My special thank goes to Steven Mascarenhas, Smita Varade, Dr Sunil Kute, Sumit Mitra, Arjita Biswas, Sanjeeb Paul, Ashwini Damle, Pankaj Dhende, Mayur Bhujbal, Koushik Ghosh, Sameer Dutta, Kumar Manibhusan, Oluabukola Esho, Usha Kategaonkar, Sanchit Joshi, Param Juneja, Monika Mane, Suman Jain, Asmita Manna, Niranjan Deshpande, Jhilmil Bhalwar, Digvijay Mali, Sagarika Joshi, Gopal Sikdar, Jayesh Charthal, Rajib Chattaraj, Hariba Sonawane, Dr Shivaji Patil, Anil Dhoble, Abhineet Kumar, Neelima Jha, Srikrishna Swaminathan, Dr Rajaram Dhole, Shramik Shevate, Kalpesh Patil, Sahil Salvi, Yash Gavankar, Abhishek Mishra, Suhas Gandhi, Gaurav Handa, Tushar Chaudhuri, Anand Gorthi, Sonal Patil, Pratap Bhosale, Ratnambar Singh, Subhash Deshpande, Rajarshi Aich, Prof. N.S.Shinde, Dr. Atul Patil, Sanjay Basu, Abhiman Bhosale, Ashwin Ranna and Prafulla Bhabekar. My very special thanks go to my student Vishal Dalal who is always by my side to motivate me for all my literary creations.

I would like to convey special thanks to my student, Sufi Shahi, who is pursuing his research work in Italy and is always in touch with me for any kind of help related to my book writing projects. I thank the complete team of my publisher for their relentless efforts to publish the book on time. I do hope and trust that, in the near future, I will be in a position to create more books for my readers.

I am thankful to the readers of the books authored by me before this one. Their constant support, motivation and inspiration made my path easy for going ahead in this field of literature and writing. Until they are present, my existence is there. I, therefore, owe all my success to my readers and do hope that I will be in a position to author more books for them.

My special thank goes to the complete team of Notion Press and especially Ms. Sukanya Narayan (my publishing manager) for their advice and guidance during the complete process of publishing this book.

– Suvasish Mukhopadhyay

1

Sweet Childhood Memories

It was 1971 when Susan was only a four-year-old child. She was emotionally attached to her father and had beautiful days in her childhood. Her father was an Assistant Professor at NIT Rourkela. Susan also had a younger sister. Since she was the eldest of the two, she was naturally closer to her father. Her father was an extraordinary scholar. He had a chequered bio-data. Right from matric, he had been a rank holder. In BE from Jadavpur University, he secured distinction and stood first in Mechanical Engineering. In ME, too, he stood first in the stream of Thermal Engineering at Jadavpur University. Despite his busy academic schedule, every day, he used to devote two hours to Susan and would allow her to express herself freely during that time. He used to talk less and completely allow Susan to speak at ease. He used to purchase chocolates and doughnuts for his daughters. The doughnut was her favourite food. He used to return home from college at 5:00 pm after which he used to accompany Susan to a nearby park at the NIT-campus. There used to be many other children of other professors and staff members. All the children used to assemble in the park, and like Susan's father, many other parents used to accompany their children.

At the age of four, Susan was admitted to a school. The school was four kilometres away from the campus. There was a school bus for commuting. Many children were admitted to the same school. In the morning, her father used to accompany her to the bus stop at the campus.

Susan was fond of circuses, and in those days in the circus, a variety of animals was used and, truly speaking, cruelty to animals was much less. When people became aware of the cruelty to animals, by that time, lakhs of animals had become victims. Susan's father took Susan and her younger sister to the nearby circus for the evening show. Any circus must be enjoyed after sunset to enjoy the effect of light.

At that time, Susan was six years old and her sister was four years old. Her father went with both his daughters to the circus while their mother didn't show any interest. There was a variety of foods in different stalls, and ice cream was an inseparable part of their menu. Both Susan and her sister enjoyed *jhalmuri* (an Indian snack) in newspaper cones followed by vanilla ice cream. They were well-dressed. Their father used to purchase dresses for them every month. There was no dearth of comfort. As an Assistant Professor, he used to get an excellent salary in those days of the early seventies, and he didn't have any liabilities. For that, he was able to spend on both his daughters, and they used to have new dresses, shoes, and basic cosmetics at periodic intervals.

Susan had her very initial teaching from her father. After returning from the playground, Susan used to sit with her books and notebooks at the dining table, and her father used to teach her for thirty to forty-five minutes. She had good grasping power. She was an above-average student and intelligent, too. When the result of her second standard was out, her father accompanied her, and she stood second in the class. She still remembers the sentence told by her father. He said, "Always be second in the class, never try to be in the first position. Mind that the student who occupies the second position in the class is more intelligent than the student who gets the first rank." All may not accept this statement, but I, being an experienced professor, totally support it.

Childhood is like ephemeral beauty. It comes and goes and leaves behind a mixture of memories for the future. In life, once a day goes by, it can't return, but the sad and good memories remain. Susan's father-centric childhood memories are quite sweet.

2

The Daughter of a School Teacher Who Died Prematurely Due to a Sudden Heart Attack

It was a very sad incident. Susan was studying in junior school along with kids of other professors, and many children used to come to the school from different zones of the city of Rourkela. There was a lovely girl in her class. The girl's father was a secondary school teacher in one of the famous schools of Rourkela. Her name was Jenny, and she had a very close intimacy with Susan.

Even on holidays, Susan used to visit Jenny's house, or sometimes, Jenny used to visit the NIT campus with her father, and both of them used to play for a long time in their quarters and the garden adjacent to Susan's quarters. Since ample space was available on the campus, the principal decided to construct big double-storied bungalow-type quarters. The front side of the quarters used to be a garden of flowers, and even in the backyard, ample space was available along with a servant's room, and many professors used the backyard for growing different kinds of vegetables.

Everything was going very smoothly, but suddenly, in the month of March, everyone noticed that Jenny stopped coming to school. In those days of the early seventies, the telephone was not affordable to a common person. It was considered a luxury item. So, despite a thousand wills, no one could know what happened to Jenny. Susan was mentally disturbed beyond measure.

After three to four days, Susan's father decided to visit Jenny's house along with Susan. It was evening time. Both Susan and her father went to Jenny's house by a cycle rickshaw, and after reaching there, both of them were shocked beyond measure. They spotted Jenny's father from a long distance, and when they got closer, they found the gentleman sobbing.

Susan and her father came to know that, four days ago, when Jenny's mother tried to wake Jenny up in the morning to go to school, she didn't get any response. Initially, her mother thought that Jenny must be in deep slumber. But still, she had some doubts. So, when she touched Jenny, she found out that her body was needle cold, and there was no pulse. She died in sleep due to a heart attack. People say that the basic cause of heart attack is smoking, diabetes, stress, lifestyle disorder, junk food, and so on and so forth. But, what was the mistake of this six-year-old Jenny who didn't have any of the reasons stated above? It was sheer bad luck.

After knowing that, Susan's father couldn't move, and little Susan started weeping. At the age of six, Susan probably couldn't realise the depth of the meaning of death, but that much she understood that Jenny would never come back to play with her. The evening was enveloped by crepuscular darkness.

Jenny's family used to stay in a small quarter of 1-BHK. In the front room, over the table, Jenny's photo was placed with a garland around it. She was a single child. Her mother was nowhere to be seen. Their neighbours took her. The neighbours were trying to console her.

Susan and her father stayed there for nearly one and a half hours. After that, they took leave from Jenny's father and started walking towards the NIT campus. Susan was holding her father's fingers, and after a few steps, her father took her in his arms. Little Susan was the most comfortable in her father's arms, and she felt the warmth of her father's affection. No force or money in this world can replace it.

Around 8:30 pm, they reached home. In the drawing room of their quarters, a beautiful painting was displayed, which was painted by Jenny just two weeks ago. Suddenly, Susan's father approached the painting and, with a coloured sketch pen, wrote at the bottom of the painting, "Jenny, we will miss you, but won't forget you."

3

Love for Gardening

Susan possessed immense love for gardening, and she was equally interested in flowers and vegetables. Right from the tender age of five, she used to help her father in gardening. Her father purchased several books for her loving daughter, and all those books were full of information on various flowers of the world. Both father and daughter performed innumerable experiments for the growth of various kinds of flowers. All the flowers are not available everywhere. They need special weather conditions, special types of soil, and particular temperatures. For example, you cannot grow apples in West Bengal and strawberries in Bihar. But, you can very easily grow apples in Himachal Pradesh and strawberries in Mahabaleshwar. So, climate and nurturing, both play important roles in the growth of a plant.

Susan's quarter was very big. In the front area, there was a garden of flowers. Right from roses to marigolds, a lot of varieties were present. Apart from that, on the window sill, a lot of nine o'clock flowers could be seen. In the backyard of the house, they made a garden of vegetables. Various vegetables were planted, e.g., cauliflower, cabbage, brinjal, tomato, chilli, etc.

Susan used to enjoy watering plants daily. In the morning, before going to school, she used to water the plants, and in the evening after returning from school, her hobby was to check the growth of the saplings and plants along with her father. The greatest pleasure lies in tracking the progress of a sapling. Susan never used to pluck any flowers. Even if the flower was very big and mature, she allowed it to be separated from the plant on its own. Because, at that tender age, she realised that a plucked flower was a dead flower. Common people use flowers for worshipping but seldom do they realise that flowers that are offered as a tribute to

God are nothing but dead flowers. But, little Susan understood this harsh reality at that tender age.

She was mature, and her mental age was more than her physical age. She was sharp, intelligent, caring, loving and passionate. Unless one becomes passionate and emotionally attached, one cannot be creative. By calculating hours, you cannot be creative. When your work becomes your passion, you become engrossed and work becomes your hobby. Unless one is obsessed, one cannot have a hobby. Gardening was Susan's obsession, and only for that reason, on holidays, she used to work for hours together with her father in the garden. She was much attached to her garden.

Even after thirty years of leaving Rourkela, the memory of the garden was vivid in her memory. But after marriage, due to poverty, she was distanced from her first love gardening and confined within a small seven hundred square feet flat in Pune. From her life, the garden was detached thirty years ago. Now, she looked at the garden of other people and thought about what her fault was for which she was distanced from her first love. It was not her fault. Her only fault was that she loved a half-mad person, Sanjay, and married him at the age of nineteen, and Sanjay was stubborn with her obsessive-compulsive disorder of reading and writing and never respected or bothered about Susan's feelings. He never even tried to understand what she wanted. The poverty and aggression of Sanjay ruined Susan's married life.

4

Historical Influence of West Bengal on Her Father in 1971: The Dreaded Naxal Period

The Naxal Movement of 1971 in West Bengal is an all-time headline in the history of India. College students were mainly involved and many of the faculties gave them passive support. Even in NIT-Durgapur, there was tremendous turbulence, and one of the very close colleagues of Susan's father was very much involved in the Naxal Movement of 1971. He was a professor of Economics at NIT-Durgapur.

West Bengal has always been different from the other states of India due to its forward-thinking. That is why, there is a saying, "What Bengal thinks today, India thinks tomorrow." There used to be cultural, linguistic, religious and political differences among the people of Bengal. The thinking pattern of Bengalis was totally different. In an intellectual plane, they are placed in a stratum, which is much higher than the stratum where other Indians are placed.

Susan's father was a very student-friendly professor. He had been to NIT-Durgapur for some research work. He was accompanied by Susan, and they stayed in the quarters of his colleague on campus. Susan still remembers the ghastly tragedy. It was late evening. Someone knocked on the main door. Her father opened the door and found that there were two students. One of them was writhing in pain because he was caught by the police and mercilessly beaten for his link with the Naxal Movement.

Her father asked them to sit and then nursed the boy who was injured, although the two boys were not known to him. They had come to her father's colleague, but he had gone to the market. Susan's father knew the art of befriending students. Within a fraction of a minute, both the students became comfortable with her father. Little Susan was a witness to the whole incident. Since her father was an NCC cadet in his college days, he was familiar with all kinds of first-aid activities. He washed the injured parts of the boy and bandaged them after applying an ointment. Then he told them to take rest for at least two hours and prepared coffee for all of them. These kinds of student-friendly professors are an extinct community in today's world where all are busy participating in the rat race for publishing meaningless research papers.

5

Father's Death, Barren Teenage and Wretched Mother

The year was 1974, and Susan was in the first standard. Suddenly, her father became ill. He used to have a high fever, and in spite of all sorts of medications, the temperature did not subside.

He was a chain smoker, and one day, he observed a tiny cyst kind of thing in the upper gum. He consulted the resident doctor of NIT Rourkela. The doctor was a full-time government employee of the college hospital. The concerned doctor treated him for three months but in vain. On the contrary, the size of the abscess started increasing. Then, he consulted a reputed doctor in Rourkela. That doctor smelled something odd and recommended him a biopsy.

The biopsy report changed the complete destiny of the family. The report was positive and Susan's father was diagnosed with an advanced stage of gum cancer. In those days, chemotherapy was not available; the only treatment was radiation and operation. He was shifted to Thakurpukur Cancer Hospital in Kolkata. He was operated on more than once. He lost his speech, and the right jaw was removed after the operation.

It was the month of May, and Susan's seventh Birthday was on the doorstep, but the man who used to arrange her birthday was fighting with death. The days were numbered. Gradually, all the hopes oozed out, and on 18th June, he left the world and left behind his uneducated widow along with their three innocent children. Susan's life was shattered that day. After that, the life she had was nothing but a life of compromise. Gradually, she reached her teenage and little Susan lost her childhood on the very day she lost her father.

The complete experience of Susan's teenage years was very pathetic. Before the completion of her childhood, she lost it due to rock-bottom poverty and her mother's cynical nature. Susan was never close to her mother right from day one because her mother was an uneducated rustic lady with all the inbuilt vices in her mind. One of the most crucial vices was gender bias. She could never love any of her daughters but always used to pamper her only son, James, who was five years younger than Susan.

Susan's teenage was like a barren afternoon of summer. There was no rejoicing, no merriment. She preferred to have solitude and used to confine herself in her bedroom on the first floor of the house. When her other friends were enjoying themselves beyond the limit, Susan did not even get five rupees from her mother to go to the school picnic. As long as her father was alive, she had a very comfortable life. Her father could be compared to the Rock of Gibraltar for her. But, after her father's untimely demise, her life took a complete U-turn, and the shoddy past started from that moment. The death of her father squeezed the whole essence of her life.

Her relationship with her mother never sprouted. Even her mother was frustrated as she had to accept her widowhood at the age of thirty-two. When the spouses of other professors used to enjoy a kitty party, her mother used to take care of three children with a very minimal salary of a lower division clerk. The family income practically became one-fourth overnight, and the only solution visible was to compromise with their lifestyle. To be on the safer side, her mother used to think twice before spending a single rupee, and due to that, always there used to be a *khit-pitty* relationship between Susan and her mother. Susan used to protest, but her sister and brother used to sustain the dominating nature of their mother.

6

A Staunch Hater of Gender Bias

Since Susan faced gender bias right from childhood, she developed a staunch hatred for gender inequality. Susan used to feel exasperated by seeing the gender biases of her mother. She possessed profound regard for those parents who believed in gender equality. Gender bias and male child obsession are national obsessions throughout the country, irrespective of caste, creed, religion and qualification. There are even lakhs of highly qualified people who are having gender-bias and prefer a male child. For not having a male child, lakhs of people are depressed at the core. Actually, their qualification is not proper. They only have paper degrees; they are qualified, but internally they are not truly educated. The beginning of care is the start of affection. If a father cannot accept his daughter, how would bonding or affection grow? Self-introspection is very essential for being genuinely educated.

Susan used to have self-introspection and self-talk. Self-talk is very beneficial for the proper blooming of a mind. Due to her modern thinking, Susan broke through all the shackles. She knew how to give a proper shape to the career of a girl. The first and foremost thing was whole-hearted acceptance. Wherefrom a girl would be educated unless she is accepted?

There is so much to be done, so much to be seen and so many fresh avenues to be explored. However, we are lagging behind in social aspects. People from all walks of life need thorough counselling for their obsession with a male child. The most important fact is that girls are more caring than boys. A father is his son's property and a daughter is her father's property, provided she is given care and love from day one. Since Susan was affected by the gender bias attitude of her mother, she did not allow history to repeat itself.

7

Introduction with Sanjay

Susan was introduced to Sanjay at the NIT Rourkela campus. Sanjay was a student of Civil Engineering, and Susan used to stay in the professors' colony on the same campus. Sanjay was then in his final year of Engineering and used to stay in Hall 4. He used to take private tuition within the campus; his students were the children of supporting staff. One of the staff members was named Mr Sushil Mazumdar, and Sanjay used to take the tuition of his daughter. His daughter and Susan were in the same school and the same class. The first meeting of Sanjay and Susan took place in the house of Mr Mazumdar.

One day, when Sanjay was teaching Mr Mazumdar's daughter, Susan came to their house for collecting a notebook. That was their first meeting and for Sanjay, it was love at first sight. Susan was famous on campus for her paragon beauty, but she was very reserved.

After that, Sanjay was appointed as a private tutor of Susan's sister and brother. Mr Mazumdar introduced Sanjay to Susan's mother because she was trying to find a good private tutor for his younger daughter and son. Mr Mazumdar was in the examination section, and Susan's mother was posted in the accounts section. After that, months passed and there was no second meeting. Sanjay used to go to her house for teaching her sister and brother thrice a week, but he never had an opportunity to meet Susan at their house.

After a couple of months, one day, Sanjay went to a shop on the campus for purchasing cigarettes, and luckily, Susan too was there to buy some knick-knacks for her family. Sanjay mostly used to roam alone; he did not have the quality to befriend others very easily. Right then, Susan invited Sanjay to their house for a cup of coffee. Susan was well aware of the scholasticism of Sanjay from the feedback of her sister and brother about his teaching quality. Sanjay possessed a winning personality, and he knew how to exhibit himself. He was recognised for his showmanship among his friends and even among the professors. The whole periodic table of Chemistry was at his fingertips, and in hundreds of places, he had chanted the periodic table to impress the audience. His scholastic attitude was well accepted by all, but at the same time, he was famous for his erratic attitude, mood swings and sour tongue. As far as English is concerned, he had very good fluency in English, and his presentation was nothing but a presentation of flowery and ornamental language. One can say, he used to have ornamental English.

Sanjay came to Susan's house and had a seat. After a couple of minutes, Susan came with a tray, and Sanjay was impressed by the colour of the tea cosy. She served him tea, biscuits and sweets. He had been there for nearly one hour. After a couple of minutes, Susan's mother went to the kitchen. In the drawing room, only they were left, and there was a discussion about many topics, right from Chemistry to Chemotherapy.

After a couple of minutes, Sanjay took her leave and assured her that he would meet her again. While seeing him off Susan became slightly emotional, but she controlled herself.

8

The Beautiful Years of Their Affair

Susan was famous for her reticence, and since she was so beautiful, whatever fashion she adopted used to suit her. She was famous for her retro fashion and orthodox view. Like her other friends, she never used to have the ultra-modern style, and her mother was also very conservative because, being a widow, she had to take care of both daughters. The slightest mistake can defame you if you are not rich. Everyone attacks the poor because it is easy to attack a poor person. That's why she was reserved.

Within three to four meetings, Susan realised that Sanjay had a crush on her, and she, too, accepted Sanjay because he was good-looking and a scholar, and he was going to be a very successful engineer. Susan's mother was not aware of the development of their affair as they used to meet outside the college campus. Susan was a graduation student and was in the girls' college. Sanjay used to meet her in the afternoon, and they used to sit in the park near the college. While gossiping, they used to sit side by side and Sanjay used to lace Susan's fingers with his. They were never bored. Because in this world, no one feels bored while sitting with their boyfriend/girlfriend. It is a universal truth. Within six months, they had a passionate affair.

One day, they went to a nearby cinema hall for watching a movie, and after enjoying the movie, they went to a nearby Chinese restaurant. It was vividly etched in Susan's memory that on that day, Susan scribbled the name of Sanjay on one of the tissue papers many times. While chitchatting, hours used to flee like minutes. In the company of Sanjay, Susan felt an incandescent love for life.

One day, they decided to meet around 11:00 am. The road to the girls' college went through the professors' colony. Sanjay was going slowly with his cycle, and suddenly, he found Susan near the water tank at the second gate of the college. She looked very fresh. Hair clung to her head after her bath. Sanjay was deeply moved by Susan's beauty but did not express it. With each passing day and month, their affair became more and more solid, and it intensified beyond limits. But, the saddest part was that the time of Sanjay's exit from the college was at the doorstep. It was April 1986, and Sanjay was supposed to be graduated in June 1986. After that, it was not possible for him to be in Rourkela despite his thousand wishes. This was a matter of deep concern and grief for both of them. Sanjay was planning to pursue ME from BE College, Shibpur. How to stay separately was a great question for both of them, but at that time, there was no answer.

Gradually, the day of departure came closer and closer. It was 28th June 1986. The entire batch graduated in Engineering, and Sanjay was one of those 260 students of NIT Rourkela. Truth is stranger than fiction and time could not hold them together. Sanjay had to leave for B. E. College, Shibpur for his post-graduation. His sweetheart remained in Rourkela. He might have passed from NIT but his mind was not separated from the campus of NIT Rourkela.

Sanjay graduated from NIT Rourkela in 1986, but in his mind, the memories of NIT Rourkela were vivid, whether it was Guptaji's kiosk outside the main gate of the college, the college canteen or the big playground of NIT Rourkela. Susan still remembers when Sanjay used to put on his favourite song of Tagore *'Dnariye aacho tumi aamar ganer opare'* in an old tape recorder in their house. There was a local florist outside the campus. Sanjay used to purchase fresh red roses for Susan from that shop. After Sanjay's departure from the campus, whenever Susan saw that shop, she remembered the beautiful moments shared with Sanjay in their short-span affair. Those moments are to be treasured forever.

9

Unconsummated Marriage

The starting of the affair was perfect and smooth, but in their married life, Susan could not be happy with many bad qualities of Sanjay, and with each passing month, those bad traits of Sanjay's character unfolded to Susan. It was a very simple marriage. Every lady dreams of the day when she would be carried in a palanquin for her marriage, even Susan had that dream, but it remained a dream only; never was it materialised into reality. Sanjay was her fiancé, and Susan was his fiancée, but they did not have any formal engagement before their marriage. They had a marriage in the office of the marriage registrar of Rourkela and it was not known to Susan's mother.

After marriage, Susan was continuing her college life, and Sanjay used to visit Rourkela once a month to meet her. The whole day, they used to spend together, and at night, Sanjay used to stay in a nearby hotel. Everything was going smoothly. But suddenly, there was some turbulence in March 1987.

Sanjay went to Susan's house. Her mother prevented Sanjay from coming inside the house, but Sanjay forcibly entered the house. Seeing that, Susan's younger sister loudly disclosed that Susan and Sanjay got married. Knowing that, her mother became furious. It was 19th March 1987 and, the day was Thursday. Without thinking of the future consequences, Sanjay told Susan to come with him, and within no time, just believing in Sanjay, Susan left her house for a lifetime. It is not so easy for a girl to leave her family for a lifetime for someone whom she loves. Susan was one in a million. She left the house permanently, just leaving her memories behind. She only took her SSC and HSC mark sheets and certificates and the medals of her father.

Since Sanjay was a post-graduate scholar, he did not have any earnings apart from the scholarship of rupees one thousand per month, and his father's retirement was at the doorstep. Both of them reached Serampore at midnight via Kharagpur, and luckily, Sanjay's father gave a cold welcome to Susan. Then the struggle started. The domestic worker started embarrassing Susan by taking Sanjay's father in confidence, and one day there was an allegation made by the domestic worker that Susan had stolen milk from the kitchen. Upon knowing that, Sanjay became furious and immediately drove the domestic worker away. But, his father played dirty politics. He did not appoint any new domestic worker and imposed the responsibility of the kitchen on Susan who was just nineteen then. When Susan thought back about this shady past, she became traumatised. The euphemistic approach of Sanjay's father was never accepted by Susan. Just because of the unemployment of her husband, she had to sustain all those tortures. Sanjay's future was linked with precariousness, and he practically used to spend his whole day in Ravi's kiosk who was a local tea vendor on the road adjacent to Serampore station. Sanjay did not have adequate money to purchase a dress for Susan, so he would just look at the mannequins in different showrooms in the city of Kolkata and used to imagine his first and last love, Susan, in the place of those mannequins. In the evening, Sanjay used to visit the river Ganga with Susan. They used to sit silently and witness many cremations along its banks. In the same river, Susan witnessed the stink of floating carcasses many times. For Susan, the river Ganga was nothing but a dark mirror, which reflected the lights coming from the industries located by its bank on the opposite side.

10

The Diplomatic Relatives in Her Maternal Family

All the relatives of Susan's maternal family were very diplomatic and professional in their behaviour and deeds. Neither did they support Susan's mother nor Susan. After marriage, Susan visited her maternal uncle's house along with Sanjay but received a cold welcome.

They preferred to be in the seat of a distant spectator and never wanted to be involved in any kind of litigation related to Susan. For them, juicy gossip was more important than Susan's mental peace. Basically, they couldn't come out of their rustic core, and truly speaking, they were uneducated. They were quite rich, but they didn't have the pompous attitude of showing off.

In the night, there was a sumptuous dinner. In the presence of Sanjay, they used their dinner set made of glass. Susan still remembers the clinking of glasses while serving water to all the people. Middle-class Bengali families seldom use glass dinner sets for dinner. They consider it a luxury item. For middle-class Bengalis, a dinner set made of glass is a thing for displaying and showcasing. They arrange it within a wooden shelf, and people can see it through the glass which covers the shelf.

The speciality of the maternal side of Susan was their diplomacy. They became neutral. They were enormously rich. They possessed hundreds of acres of land, but their lifestyle was very ordinary, and all the family members were very thrifty. They always treated Susan as an outsider only. For this quality, gradually, Susan distanced herself from them.

11

No Financial Security

The main problem of Susan was her identity crisis due to her unemployed husband. This jobless condition can be portrayed in a pathetic way if someone goes for the autobiographical narration of Susan and Sanjay. Due to this poverty and uncertainty, Susan lost her icy snobbishness, which she used to possess as the daughter of a professor. The icy snobbishness was converted to meek submissiveness due to rock-bottom poverty and dependability on her father-in-law for just two square meals.

Sometimes, Susan used to get rid of the claustrophobic atmosphere of Sanjay's house by visiting Kolkata along with Sanjay with minimal amounts for spending. She still remembers the Kolkata sidewalks where they used to purchase *Jhalmuri* in newspaper cones. Once, they visited Kolkata, and Sanjay had only one crisp new one-hundred rupees note in his purse, and he wanted to spend on some good food in a restaurant in the Esplanade area, but Susan prevented him from doing that.

They were roaming in the arcade of the Grand Hotel. Gowns were being sold, and the price was only seventy rupees, but they didn't have the capacity to even purchase a gown even. They had to satiate themselves by window shopping. While returning from Kolkata, Susan would look at those beautiful gowns, which they couldn't afford. She still remembers the blurry glimpse of those beautiful gowns. Today, it is very easy to afford those dresses, but the zeal to have them is no more.

12

Unceasing Struggle Due to Husband's Bibliomania and Whimsical Attitude

Sanjay was a bibliomaniac right from his school days, but it was not known to Susan. Sanjay was obsessed with the brimming bookshelf in his house. During their affair of one and a half year, they used to meet for a few hours, and all the traits of Sanjay's character were not known to Susan. But, after marriage, she had the misfortune to stay with an extremely capricious and bibliomaniac person. Sanjay was unsocial, and he didn't have a mingling nature. He used to be confined to his study table for hours together, and apart from engineering, he used to read various subjects. He even used to go through the dictionaries of Physics, Chemistry and Mathematics. His life was not like a straight channel. His life had many meanderings, and he was totally unpredictable. Even he was not sure of his activities for the next moment. Many irrelevant ideas used to creep into Sanjay's mind, and he used to discuss them with Susan, though Susan had zero interest in those ideas. Just to make him happy, that innocent girl used to nod positively.

The whole day, Sanjay used to smoke, and every morning, Susan's first work was to clean the spilling ashtray, which used to be placed at the corner of Sanjay's study table. Sanjay's bibliomania crossed all limits, and he used to act in such a way that the terms dictionary, glossary and thesaurus could be very authentically used with his name. Once, Sanjay decided to purchase some books and went to College Street in Kolkata with Susan. He went to a bookshop, which was famous for its collection of old books. To date, Susan remembers the muffled voice of the shop owner. Sanjay used to behave like a madman whenever he used to visit College Street due to his obsession with books. Susan used to sustain Sanjay's whimsical and mad attitudes just because she loved him and she had no place to go. Her relationship with her mother was completely sealed on the very day she left her home. She was never supportive of Susan for her upright attitude. This world is very cruel. Whenever anyone becomes the whistle-blower, they are side-lined, tortured or even murdered, depending on the situation. Susan was a lady who never compromised with any wrong thing, and that's why she was avoided by her mother.

Sanjay practically spent all the money on purchasing books, and after that, they visited College Square and sat by the edge of the water. On College Street, in front of the kiosks, which used to sell old books, Sanjay used to shamble at a very slow pace because he was attracted by all those kiosks. Susan didn't get anything from Sanjay or his family except poverty, rude behaviour, bad temper, anxiety and stress. She had to face an unceasing struggle due to Sanjay's bibliomaniac and whimsical attitudes. Whenever Sanjay was asked any question about his impractical expenses, he used to wiggle his eyebrows, and Susan never liked that attitude of Sanjay.

13

Since Her Husband Wanted to Be a College Professor, He Did Not Join Any Other Profession

During the days of post-graduation, Sanjay clearly announced that he would not join any other profession apart from teaching. But, in those days, in the state of West Bengal, there were no private engineering colleges and only four government engineering colleges, and Sanjay had never inquired about the scope of teaching outside West Bengal. A chance to be a faculty in any of the four government engineering colleges of West Bengal was very slim. He got offers for more than one job but did not join. His father used to force him to appear for different interviews and written examinations to get selected at a PSU (Public Sector Undertaking). However, Sanjay used to go for those examinations and interviews with half-hearted feelings, and he had already made up his mind that except for teaching he would not go for any other job. He went to some schools for being selected as a teacher, but school authorities clearly stated that they wanted candidates with BSc and BEd, not BE and ME.

Sanjay's father was retired and extremely tense about Sanjay's attitude. There was only a big interrogative mark for their uncertain future. They were married, but there was not even an iota of conjugal pleasure in their life. Sanjay and his activities were an ever-escalating tension for the whole family. Susan missed the bubbling life of the contemporary girl she was, and all the time, she was accompanied by Sanjay who was morbidly melancholic. In college life, Sanjay was famous for being magniloquent, but Susan could not even understand his other side. After marriage, it was excruciating to pass bleak afternoons with a person who had a psychiatric disorder. Gradually, Susan was affected by induced depression. If anyone is put with a depressed person 24X7, they are bound to be affected.

Sanjay was interested in artificial neural networks, and he used to draw complex networks that could be only compared to a labyrinth. Susan just used to look at Sanjay's activities but failed to understand what Sanjay wanted to do with his whining talent. Sanjay was famous for his mood and mood swings since his college days. Addiction was a part of his life. Right from smoking to drinking, everything was present on the list. In one corner of his room, there used to be a stash of alcohol. No one liked it, but it was difficult to overpower him.

Despite so many offers, Sanjay did not join any job, and his father used to fume for this deed of his son. His father generally used to spare Sanjay, but in his absence, he used to insult Susan for no fault of hers. Susan had to bear those insults for her imbecile husband. In our society, man is always what his designation makes him. Sanjay was marked and known as an unemployed engineer in the locality, and even class-IV staff of the area used to laugh at him. For the neighbourhood, he became a laughingstock. Susan used to feel ashamed of accompanying Sanjay publicly. She knew that Sanjay was a person who could never separate himself from literature, engineering and mathematics, but it was not possible to make society understand the obsessive-compulsive disorder of her husband. Susan's life was just like a slow death, and it could be compared to wilting of a glossy leaf due to lack of water, sunlight and nourishment.

14

Doesn't Have Any Ornaments

Ornaments are not required daily, but for certain occasions, they are needed. When Susan left her home, she had been wearing a set of earrings. Sanjay told her to leave that too. Susan listened to Sanjay. After their marriage, Sanjay did not have the capacity to purchase any ornaments for his sweetheart, and from Sanjay's father, there were no expectations. Susan was very beautiful, but she did not even possess a ring. During the famous occasions of Durga Puja, all Bengali ladies used to decorate themselves with different shades of *sarees* and matching gold ornaments, whereas Susan did not have anything to wear. She used to wear ornaments made of stones and bronze. After nine years of their marriage, Sanjay was able to gift her a necklace. This was her struggle and sacrifice for the person whom she loved and whom she relied on without testing his nature. It was the simplicity of Susan for which she suffered throughout her married life.

Curiosity is a feminine vice. Whenever she used to attend any programme, other Bengali ladies used to ask her about her ornaments and would politely tell them that she was not fond of gold ornaments. Although it was a diplomatic lie, she had no other option. Whenever any person gets a good spouse, that spouse is exploited beyond limits. The same thing was done by Sanjay. He did not care for Susan's sentiments. He was only obsessed with his own studies, bibliomania and very high self-aspirations. Rarely did he care for Susan's emotions and sentiments. He took her for granted because he knew that Susan did not have a place to go, and Susan was not of that nature.

Susan was well-known for her tongue-tied attitude. She never disclosed her problems to others. Generally, most of the ladies vent their problems by discussing them with neighbours and relatives. But, Susan was not of that nature. She digested all the grief, insult and torture. Never did she criticise Sanjay or his father, though due to this duo, Susan's complete youth was destroyed.

15

Parasite

Sanjay's elder brother got married soon after Sanjay's marriage. He was seven years elder to Sanjay. When Sanjay married Susan, he was twenty-four, and his elder brother married at the age of thirty-three. Both Sanjay and his father did not attend his marriage for some reason, which is beyond the scope of this book. His elder brother was well placed in a fertilizer company in Durgapur, and his wife also belonged to the same city. After around seven months of their marriage, both of them came to Serampore. It was February 1989. Sanjay was pursuing his thesis work for post-graduation, and his scholarship had stopped long back. For pocket money, he used to take a few private tuitions.

His sister-in-law came to the house and silently and minutely observed everything. Sanjay was unemployed and his wife was confined to the kitchen. Society used to consider Sanjay as a ludicrous fellow. Being a sister-in-law, she observed everything and reserved her comments. After returning to Durgapur, she wrote a letter to Sanjay's father in which she described Sanjay as a parasite. It was highly insulting both for Sanjay and the family, but we cannot amputate someone's feelings. Sanjay had to accept this pungent comment from his sister-in-law. She even insulted Sanjay's father too. His father was red with rage and anger. His ego of feudalism was hurt, and he could not tolerate that. But, he made a mistake. Instead of suppressing the matter, he started talking about it to everyone that he was insulted by his daughter-in-law. For the common public, it was a matter of time-pass, and it became a topic of gossip among neighbours and relatives.

In spite of such an insult, Sanjay was equally sluggish and static. Susan never liked his lackadaisical nature, but she had nothing else to do. She became a victim. She was nothing but a passive spectator of all the wrong and whimsical deeds of Sanjay, but she did not have the right to protest. She used to be morose in the atmosphere of their damp house, which was full of a pall of silence. The untimely death of her father and choosing the wrong person ruined her pre-married and post-married life. Sometimes during the evening, she used to stand by the acrid *Tulsi* plant on the balcony of the house, submerged in thoughts of the days she had left far behind.

16

Addiction and Hallucination — Treated as a Parasite — Schizophrenic and Mentally Ill Maternal Uncles

Susan was cheated by her destiny. With each passing month, it was becoming practically impossible to stay with a half-mad husband. If a person becomes fully mad, there is a benefit. He can be sent to a mental asylum, but the problem becomes severe with this kind of partially mad person like Sanjay. They are anxious; they suffer from stress; they suffer from acute depression; they attempt suicides; they do vilification and they have nexus with drugs and psychiatric medicines. Their temperament is never steady and their moods swing. No one can guarantee their temperament and next steps. These kinds of people are highly unpredictable. They whimper when they feel uneasy. For a normal person, it is practically a punishment to stay with a mentally ill person.

Due to heavy doses of medicine, Sanjay's speech used to be slurred, and while sleeping, there used to be drooling. Sanjay's maternal clan was vicious. There was more than one abnormal person in his clan. Even Sanjay's mother was a critical patient of depression. She was no more, but Sanjay inherited the complete history of mental illness from his mother. The speciality of such diseases is that one may not get property from parents but one can inherit diseases from parents with a hundred per cent guarantee. In India, to date, most mental illnesses are suppressed by family members. Society accepts all physical disorders very normally, whether it is blood pressure or kidney failure. But, to date, mental illness is a social taboo and society does not accept mentally ill people. They are given the tag of mad. Only for that reason, right from the patient to his family members, everyone goes into denial mode, and they are not ready to take any kind of treatment or counselling. Still, nowadays, gradually people are coming out of their shells and have started visiting psychiatrists.

Sanjay's maternal clan had a very close nexus with psychological disorders. One of his maternal uncles was mad, and he was kept at home only. Due to his bouts of insanity, other members of the family got disturbed, but his maternal grandfather did not send his mad son to the asylum. Another maternal uncle was highly schizophrenic. Patients with schizophrenia are famous for their suspicious activities. It is practically not recommended to stay with an insane person or a schizophrenic. It affects the life of normal human beings to a great extent. For psychiatric drugs, Sanjay was not allowed to drink alcohol by his psychiatrist. But, he was wayward and stubborn. He was famous for his grandiloquent nature. Keeping the doctor's advice at bay, he used to consume a lot of alcohol. He was a regular and heavy drinker. Due to this drinking habit, medicines failed to give the desired result. He used to have hallucinations from time to time. Initially, the psychiatrist thought he must have been attacked by paranoid schizophrenia, but afterwards, it was ruled out by the psychiatrist. Sanjay had a severe anxiety disorder, bipolar disorder, depression and acute neurasthenia (weak nerves). Even his mother was a patient of depression and neurasthenia.

Susan observed Sanjay's many abnormal activities. In the uncanny silence of the winter noon, Sanjay used to count some unsoiled notes again and again. She found him counting the same bunch of notes eleven times. This was due to the repetition of thoughts, or more precisely speaking in medical terms, it is called fixation of thoughts. Only for this particular symptom, Sanjay regularly used to take a tablet named Ridazine-10. In spite of his daily intake of the tablet, sometimes it became difficult for him to have control over his thought process. Then he needed to double the dose. Sometimes, it was difficult for Susan to talk to Sanjay because he used to give asinine logic. It was not at all acceptable to Susan. Both were helpless. Neither of them could influence the other even by one per cent.

Many times, Susan stepped gingerly into their room, and Sanjay was not even aware of her presence. Susan came across Sanjay's insane attitude frequently like gnashing his teeth, twirling a straw or pouring a blob of wax on his forehand. All these incidents were very shocking, but there was no one with whom these incidents could be shared. Sanjay's father was on the safer side because of their love marriage. There was no chance for Susan to make him responsible. She had to sustain all these mad activities of Sanjay day after day. Sometimes, she used to ask herself, "Am I normal like before?"

17

Husband's Father Was Brought up in a Mining Area Near Bihar

Susan did not have an opportunity to see her mother-in-law because she died when Sanjay was in the eighth standard. Generally, girls face problems from the side of their mothers-in-law, but for Susan, the picture was exactly the opposite. Sanjay's father was more notorious than any notorious mother-in-law. He was effeminate, cynic, jealous, angry, greedy, proud, a person with sexual displeasure, and he had the wrong idea about himself. He was a spike in the boot for Susan.

Susan came to Sanjay's house in March 1987. His father retired in September 1987. Since June, he took a long leave for three months. He used to sit in the chair in the drawing room just like a watch dog. He was a man without any friends. His only recreation was to irritate Susan. Since Sanjay and Susan were completely dependent on him for their survival, he exploited Susan like an octopus. Everything was under his control.

There was no gas connection in their house. Susan used to cook in conventional *Chula*, and for that, she needed coal, cow dung cake and kerosene. Sanjay's father was such a thrifty person that he used to give the daily quota of coal, cow dung cakes and kerosene from his inventory, which was always kept under lock and key. Every day, in the morning, he used to give Susan only three cow dung cakes. Once Susan demanded an extra cow dung cake. He vehemently refused her request and advised her to manage with newspapers. Susan's father-in-law was a sadist.

He was born in the state of Bihar, and his birthplace was Giridi. He was brought up in Chinakuri, West Bengal, which was located at an approximate distance of two hundred kilometres from the border of Bihar. Right from his school days, he was egotistical, and everyone used to avoid him. He was famous for his sarcasm. He was not highly qualified. He was a graduate of the pre-independence era when education had its true quality. He was an Arts graduate from the famous institute KN College of Bharampur of Murshidabad district of West Bengal. When he went to take admission to KN College, he fell in love with the gothic architecture of the college building. The college was good. He was a good student too. But, only for his clustered ego, anger and wicked attitude, he failed to design his career, whereas his other friends completed their post-graduation very easily. They were far less brilliant than him, but they had a normal mode of thinking.

18

Left Graduation, Sustained Insults and Did Graduation and Post-graduation after Marriage

Due to her marriage, Susan's graduation was discontinued. Initially, because of her mother's enormous pressure, she admitted herself to BSc with pure science and her subjects included Physics, Chemistry and Mathematics, but with the passage of time, Susan realised that pure science was not her cup of tea. So, in 1986 she discontinued her BSc and admitted herself to BA and her main subjects were History, Political Science and Economics. But, due to the change of her coordinates from Rourkela to Serampore, her graduation remained incomplete. Just before the examination of the first year, she left Rourkela. Since she was not a graduate, she had to sustain insults from her father-in-law, and he passed pungent comments that Susan would never be able to complete her graduation. Susan took this comment very seriously.

In 1987, her graduation was discontinued. After eight long years, in 1995, she took up BA at Indira Gandhi National Open University (IGNOU). It was a correspondence course, and by 1998, she cleared her graduation with History as a major. After that, she did not inform her father-in-law. She was admitted to MA History at Pune University in distance education mode, and in 2001, she completed her post-graduation with second division and sent a photocopy of her MA certificate to her father-in-law. However, the unsporting father-in-law denied the receipt of the photocopy of the certificate.

On her next visit to Serampore, Susan took a colour photocopy of the certificate for her father-in-law, and when it was shown to him, that scoundrel did not praise her. On the contrary, he passed a sharp comment, "Oh. It is the second division!"

These are the cultural vultures of society. He was famous for his supercilious nature. He had esoteric knowledge of literature, but he was only a graduate. He became jealous of Susan for her post-graduation. These types of people are social carcasses. They only produce social stains and pollute society. They have no leadership quality, but they consider themselves uncrowned leaders of the world, and their main problem is their clustered ego for which there is no solution. Only his pungent remark made Susan complete her graduation and post-graduation. Susan always possessed the scion of aristocracy, and that was her only capital.

19

Cheated by Mother, Sister and Brother

Susan's mother was famous for her euphemism. She literally had an allergy from her elder daughter for no fault of Susan. Her mother was known for her desperation. She had a sordid nature, and she was sly enough to cheat others. After Susan's departure, she wanted to sell out some ancestral property, which belonged to Susan's father. However, for selling that ancestral property, her mother needed Susan's permission and written approval with her signature. But, to bypass Susan, her mother made a false affidavit where she declared that she had only one daughter and one son. In the affidavit, she straightaway denied the existence of Susan. The word philoprogenitiveness was not applicable to that wretched lady. Even if she had gone for a truce with Susan, that would have been better and more significant. But instead of doing that, she clearly amputated the relationship in black and white with the certification from the side of the court. This was a criminal offence, and her mother did it despite being a government servant.

When Susan was there at her home, there used to be fierce quarrels with her mother, and her sister and brother both were passive supporters of their mother. When Susan thinks about this sad episode of her life, tears spring from her eyes. But, she was helpless. In a country like India, even a rapist is punished after twelve years of the crime and ninety per cent of the rapists get off scot-free just because of inadequate evidence. So, in this country, wherefrom Susan would expect her mother to be punished for her cheating and forgery? Truly speaking, she was not only cheated by her mother but by all. Even her sister and brother cheated her because they were passive supporters of their mother's deeds.

One evening. Susan was looking at the setting sun. The setting sun was feverishly beautiful. After a couple of minutes, the scarlet disk sank into the tree-lined horizon. Susan became speechless. The loneliness of a barren evening grasped her mind for the time being.

20

Used by Selfish Father-In-Law for Four Years

Susan's father-in-law can be compared to an octopus for his blood-sucking attitude. Since Sanjay was unemployed, for her father-in-law, it was a great opportunity to use Susan as an unpaid domestic worker. Her father-in-law was the sheet-anchor of the family, he was never apologetic for his wrong deeds, possessed a feudal nature and denunciation was his regular habit. He was famous for his sanctimonious nature. He was highly megalomaniac, and he used to confiscate the independence of all the family members for his vicarious pleasure.

Susan never liked the note of sarcasm in his voice. But, he did not bother. He used to cackle very often at others. He used to coerce his family members for doing jobs they did not like. He used to canalise his sadistic attitude through his behaviour, and his family members were his soft targets. He was famous for his venomous behaviour. He used to mimic others, and Susan never liked this bad gesture of her father-in-law. He was a cynic and used to chuckle at others' failures. Seeing these odd behaviours of her father-in-law, Susan used to be startled. Throwing tantrums was a regular affair. In those days, Susan did not have an articulate nature, otherwise, there was enough chance to protest, and basically, her father-in-law was a coward person. But, at the same time, he was famous for his squabbling and coaxing nature.

His only demand was blandishments. Most of the time, his mood used to be ghoulish. He used to coax Susan for doing many things. He was very selective about food, and early in the morning, he used to fix the menu of lunch, and there used to be at least four-five items. Susan had to cook all those items one after another, and it was a routine irritation for her.

Her father-in-law was not a person to bequeath his property to his children. He was of the nature to keep his property in limbo. Though

Sanjay already decided to refuse his father's property. His vision was very clear. He said, "Since I hate my father, I hate his property too. The question of taking his property does not arise."

His father had a nasty habit of eavesdropping, and once, he was caught red-handed by Sanjay. Truly speaking, his father was also a mentally derailed person, and he was perverted. In office life, he was a head clerk, but on the domestic front, he was a Rasputin. His Czarist approach ruined the peace of the family, and he practically destroyed the complete bonding between all his family members. He used to do spineless politics, and he had the habit of clipping the wings of those who were dependent on him so that he could suck them more.

Susan possessed a wide human outlook in spite of crushing routine and rock-bottom poverty. But, in the presence of her father-in-law, it was not possible to implement good things in the family. Her father-in-law's most preferred hobby was quarrelling with anyone. He used to search for the slightest reason for fighting and quarrelling. The atmosphere of the whole house could be compared to Czarist Russia. While quarrelling, he used to open floodgates of hatred and go for heated discussions.

Among the two brothers of Sanjay, he already created a gulf with his divide-and-rule policy and soft discrimination. He was on the side of his elder son because he was obsessed with his good looks and fair skin. Sanjay knew everything. That's why he had cemented all the relationships just for the sake of survival. He used to act, and he used to have minimum interaction with his father. It was not possible for Sanjay to go for blatant flattery. He used to hate his father, who was a chauvinist person.

In the afternoon, after lunch, Sanjay used to go to his friend, Abir, who used to stay on the other side of the railway track. The other side of the railway track was famous for its leafy lanes. Abir used to stay at the corner of a leafy lane, and his house was a stone's throw away from the railway station.

Sanjay had at least a vent, and he used to spend maximum time with Abir, who was his classmate in school life. Abir was also an unemployed youth. But, for Susan, there was no vent. She didn't have any friends in the locality. Firstly, Susan was reserved from day one, and secondly, Sanjay's unemployed status was a social taboo. That's why Susan had no other option than to choose captivity within the four damp walls of the age-old rented house. Hope and vitality both were oozing out gradually.

Freedom is dear to all but most of all to those who have been deprived of it. Susan experienced the same thing in the initial four years of her married life. She used to engross herself in day-to-day housework like a domestic maid. She had to do the dishes in the morning as well as evening. It was a peculiar house. Just due to the wickedness of her father-in-law, there was not even a single basin in the washroom or kitchen. In the washroom, there was a water connection from the municipality. The wicked father-in-law closed it and diverted it to the kitchen. In India, women are nothing but unpaid domestic workers. Her labour was taken for granted by her father-in-law because people never take anything seriously unless they have to pay for it.

21

Loneliness and Isolation

Loneliness and isolation are very closely linked. When a patient becomes quarantined for some contagious disease, they feel lonely. Loneliness intensifies depression and grief. In a government-run hospital, I personally found wailing patients, but they were not taken care of due to inadequate staff in the hospital.

Once I went for training from my college to a famous hill station of Panchgani. I had an opportunity to see lush green fields through the window of my room. We were put up at the Asia Plateau of Panchgani. It was a nice resort. To date, I vividly remember the pristine purity of the atmosphere. Loneliness and aloneness are not the same things. In loneliness, you feel bored but aloneness can be enjoyed. Even within a crowd, you can be alone. Aloneness is totally different from loneliness. Loneliness comes into the picture when you miss others and aloneness comes into the picture when you enjoy yourself. These are totally different things. Love, prayer, life, death, aesthetic experience, blissful moments — they all come when you are alone.

But, it needs a special art to enjoy aloneness. It is not possible overnight. For Susan, life was full of loneliness. With her mother, the relationship was cemented on the very day she left the house. In Sanjay's house, most of the time Sanjay used to be at Abir's house, and Sanjay's father was not a person worth talking to. In the local neighbourhood, there was not a single girl of her age with whom she could gel. So, she was very alone, and isolation was an inseparable and integral part of her life.

Forget about others, even Sanjay was not in a position to understand Susan's problems. He was obsessed with his study and gossiping with Abir. Is it a crime to love someone? Is it a crime to emotionally depend on someone? Certainly not. But, you cannot rely on a person who has psychiatric problems. They are not dependable. They are not sure of themselves and their next activity, so wherefrom you will get the guarantee to depend on them?

Susan used to think of her childhood, and she concluded that after her father's death, her life became a river with a dry bed. Nothing was left. At the age of seven, her fate was sealed. Her initial life was damaged by her wretched mother, and her married life was tarnished by an erratic and mentally imbalanced husband. If Sanjay would have been mentally healthy, her father-in-law would not have come into the picture. It was Sanjay who could not earn. More precisely speaking, didn't earn. People with a diploma in engineering have a humdrum domestic life. On the contrary, with a post-graduation in engineering, Sanjay was unemployed. Truly speaking, he was not unemployed, but he declined all the job offers, and he was only obsessed with teaching. But, for teaching, in those days, there was no scope in West Bengal due to the absence of private engineering colleges. All his friends joined jobs. Some were in government and some were in the private sector. For men, two things are very true. The first one is that a man must have a job, otherwise, he does not have any position in society, and the second one is that they are only interested in getting physical. They seldom possess the patience to read the mood of their partners. Most men behave like bulls because the surge and urge of sex convert them into one.

22

Unemployment of Her Husband

Unemployment of Sanjay was the only problem in Susan's life in her post-married days. Being a post-graduate in engineering, Sanjay was not ready to do any job except teaching and there was no scope for teaching jobs in West Bengal in the early nineties. It was a great problem and a big question for the entire family. If Susan had known Sanjay's attitude before marriage, she would have thought twice before taking the final decision to marry an irresponsible and capricious person.

Susan was feverishly beautiful even in those days of struggle. But, Sanjay did not value her. He did not realise what he got. Rarely any person gets such a loving and caring spouse in this era of cut-throat competition and a materialistic world.

Susan had no liaison with her mother, but she had some connection with her maternal side. Susan's intelligentsia was underestimated by her father-in-law, and Sanjay was only obsessed with his own mad reading habits and thoughts. In the name of a husband, Susan possessed a semi-lunatic person.

Sanjay had a tremendous interest in English literature apart from pure science, and for that, he used to be absorbed in his Shakespearean thoughts on most days. In the evening, Sanjay used to go to the local market to have some knick-knacks for his evening tiffin, and he was fond of fast food. That bad habit was inherited by him from his mother. Sanjay possessed all the good and bad qualities of his mother. One of the major ones was her madness. His mother was a critical patient of neurasthenia. It means she had weak nerves.

Sanjay had a tousled hairstyle, and he never used to comb his hair, and it seemed as if he was carrying a nest on his head. He was haggard and vagabond. Susan was very good-looking and known for her paragon beauty. On the other hand, Sanjay was no match for her. There is a famous English adage, 'Made for each other.' This adage was not at all applicable to Susan and Sanjay. Sanjay was famous for his mood swings, and since he was an unemployed youth, he had no value in society. His condition was like a sick lion who was being kicked by an ass. He was sad, depressed and a full-blown alcoholic, and all the while, he had an anguished soul. He was always perturbed beyond measure, and it was literally difficult for Susan to stay with this half-mad husband 24X7.

Sanjay's father was not affected because he was not attached to his son. The problem was with Susan. In the name of wife, truly speaking, Susan became a caregiver of Sanjay. At the tender age of nineteen, Susan had to do all caretaking of a semi-lunatic husband and a wicked father-in-law. Can there be any bigger punishment than this? And that too for no reason.

Sanjay's father was an unsocial person. Still, he had some very nasty colleagues just like him. Those caustic visitors used to visit his father once in a blue moon, and Susan's work was to obey the orders of her father-in-law and do the basic hospitality for those wretched guests.

One evening is etched in Susan's memory. Sanjay gave her an envelope, and when she opened it, she found a cheque signed by Sanjay. The cheque was in the name of Susan, and the amount written on the cheque was one million rupees. Sanjay did not have even one thousand rupees in his account. This spoke of Sanjay's mad love for Susan. He wanted to give her many things. No man is a hundred per cent bad. This loving gesture of Sanjay could be compared to the flickering of a tube light in the lonely corridor of a government-run hospital. In her pathetic life, Susan sustained much sorrow. Though nineteen years was an age for enjoying, flourishing and blooming. But, for Susan, it was an age for wilting. Susan realised that sorrow was nothing but a shadow of unfulfilled desires.

Many times, Susan found Sanjay rifling through cupboards and searching for some books. His bibliomania was the prime cause of his madness. Sanjay had a true affair with academics, and that was lethal for the whole family. People opt for professional degrees for earning more, but in the case of Sanjay, his earning was zero but the bonding between academics and his inner mind was solid concrete, which could not be segregated. Whenever Sanjay used to face difficulty in solving mathematical problems, he used to twist his hair and find solutions. His favourite hobby was solving higher-order differential equations when he used to feel bored. Can you imagine it? If a normal person feels bored, he goes for relaxing, gossiping and watching television or movies, but in the case of Sanjay, the scenario was totally opposite.

23

Several Visits to Psychiatrists

In 1988, Sanjay was suffering from rock-bottom depression, and he was practically bedridden. He was supposed to complete ME by the end of 1987. But, he failed to do so, and in 1988, he practically did not visit his college for the whole year. One day, he expressed his feelings to Abir that he wanted to swallow a blade. His mental health was totally derailed. Then, his father decided to consult a psychiatrist. In his hometown, there was no qualified psychiatrist. All the reputed psychiatrists were available in Kolkata. In their local proximity, there was a lady doctor. She was an MBBS and had a diploma in Psychiatry. Sanjay's father wanted to consult her.

One evening, Sanjay was taken to her, and he was accompanied by his father. When the psychiatrist came to know that Sanjay was married, she wanted to meet Susan without fail. The next day, Sanjay went to her clinic along with Susan. She patiently listened to all the problems of Sanjay and after that advised Sanjay to wait outside, and she talked to Susan separately. After that, she prescribed antidepressants along with tranquillizers. The antidepressant was named Antidep and the tranquillizer was named Placidox–5. Antidep contained Imipramine Hydrochloride, and Placidox–5 contained Diazepam–5 along with nerve vitamin Pyridoxine (vitamin B–6). Sanjay started taking the medicines and felt much better. After consuming Placidox–5, he used to enjoy drug-induced sleep and drowsiness. At least, due to these medicines, he could control his irrelevant thoughts, and it was possible for him to concentrate for a few hours. The restlessness was controlled. Both Susan and his father observed a marked difference in the day-to-day behaviour of Sanjay.

Most of the time, Sanjay used to sit by his brimming bookshelves, and his bouts of insanity were controlled to a great extent. But, due to the treatment by a psychiatrist, Sanjay had a stamp of being a mental patient and all the family members tried their best to keep his treatment a secret. Because society is very dangerous. If society sees you in the clinic of a psychiatrist, within no time, people will give you the tag of a mad.

Everything was going smoothly but in April 1988, all the symptoms aggravated, and the prescribed medicines failed to give the expected results. Then Sanjay's father decided to consult the most famous psychiatrist in Kolkata, Dr Anadi Ghosal.

One morning, he took Sanjay to Dr Ghosal, who was the ex-Director of Lumbini Park Mental Hospital. When Dr Ghosal asked Sanjay about his problem, Sanjay said that he wanted to get a Nobel Prize in Chemistry. Dr Ghosal took it easy and prescribed four medicines to Sanjay. He told his father that Sanjay was suffering from fantasy. After coming out of the clinic, Sanjay and his father had some food and returned home.

Sanjay decided not to take any of the medicines prescribed by Dr Ghosal. It was the pre-internet era, and for that, it was very difficult to search for something. Sanjay continued the medicines given by the lady doctor. But, he could not leave his boozing habit, which was lethal for his health. Sanjay himself used to get the stench of alcohol on his breath but failed to control that nasty habit. Once or twice, he tried and stayed away from alcohol for two to three days, but after that, he started drinking with double energy. Susan's personal life was totally ruined, and gradually, she became a patient of depression due to induced depression from Sanjay.

Things were just rolling, but Sanjay's problem was not solved. It was August 1988. Sanjay's father decided to consult another psychiatrist named Dr Sudhir Banerjee. He was from Salt Lake in Kolkata. Sanjay went with his father. They were waiting in the chamber. There were many patients. There was a girl. She was continuously doing her hair. Another robust young man was sitting in a corner of the clinic. His eyes were bloodshot and he was continuously twirling a key chain. That was his mania. Another aged lady was also present there. She was continuously moaning. She had severe mental derailment due to the death of her only son in an accident. In due time, Sanjay's turn came.

Dr Banerjee talked to Sanjay for 10-15 minutes, prescribed a tablet called Amizep and told his father that Sanjay badly needed some engagement and engagement was the only medicine for him. Suddenly, Sanjay started chanting the complete periodic table of Chemistry. His father tried to stop him, but Dr Banerjee allowed him to continue and told his father, "Sir, look, this is the suppressed energy. It needs canalisation, and for that, proper engagement is a must. Medicine will work only ten per cent, whereas proper engagement — preferably any kind of teaching, let it be even tuition — will solve ninety per cent of the problems."

His father listened to the doctor. After returning home, Sanjay started the new medicine, and after consuming one Amizep, he slept practically for twenty-four hours and even after twenty-four hours, he had a hangover due to the composition of Amizep. It was a strong antidepressant. He was depressed, and he had the habit of brooding about his past. Susan tried her best to convince Sanjay that there was no point in lamenting over the past because it could not be changed. But, Sanjay's mind was not in a position to accept any sort of counselling.

The aftermath of Amizep was simply dangerous and Sanjay again discontinued the new medicines and started consuming Antidep and Placidox-5. Susan was suffering from emotional starvation, and there was not a single person with whom she could share her problem. Except for Sanjay, there was no one to talk to her. But many times, Sanjay used to misbehave, and he used to curtly refuse to talk and listen to Susan. She used to be deeply hurt, but Sanjay did not have the mentality to understand that. Susan used to sympathise with Sanjay, but there was no one to pacify Susan.

24

Caste System and Religion

Sanjay never believed in the caste system and religion. Otherwise, how could he marry a Christian lady being a Hindu Brahmin? God created men and men created caste; God created rivers and men created pipes; God created flowers and men created bonsai. Whatever is created by man is small and artificial. Sanjay used to abominate the caste system and religious clashes from the bottom of his heart. Religion is mostly used by politicians. If there is no fight between two religions, politicians create a situation for intra-religious fighting, and once the fight takes place and the flame goes up, politicians come to sprinkle water on the fire, out of which they gain political mileage.

For common people, caste and religion are matters for their pastimes. There are religions where we see self-mortification as part of it. But, there is no point in torturing oneself. Asceticism is another aspect of religion. It is related to severe self-discipline for religious reasons. What is discipline? It is basically doing things we do not like to do. There must be a limit to discipline. Too much discipline spoils the essence of life and living. Sanjay found people pouring oil or milk in the name of God, and there was a wastage of thousands of litres of milk and oil. In this world, in countries like Somalia, people starve to death, and fanatics waste thousands of litres of milk in the name of God. Is it justified?

Sanjay was half mad, but in some aspects of life, his vision was very clear. He believed in racial fusion through interreligious marriage, and he practically did that. A proper thought process required selective aristocratic breeding. It is not for all. There is something that comes from family only. The son of a poor person can master mathematics, but he cannot master the English language because the flair for language mainly comes from the family.

If a person fails to accept the generation gap, it can be compared to an ill-fitting shoe, and he can never be comfortable in life. Acceptance of the change and generation gap is a must. If you cannot accept them, you will be perished, not the present generation.

Truly speaking, there are only two classes of people — healthy and unhealthy. The most common reason for bad health is malnutrition. Society is responsible for this. There is enough in the country, but poverty is a result of corruption and bad politics. Politicians do not give you anything. On the contrary, they snatch your things and promise you to give them back. The basic requirements of people are food, clothes, shelter, electricity, roads and water. In a country like India, there are regular accidents and deaths due to bad roads, and politicians seldom address these issues. They are only seen during the vote with begging bowls, and once elections are over, they vanish like camphor. But, I would say that the main culprits are not the politicians, the main culprits are the citizens who sustain all kinds of torture and do not protest and don't go for voting. With each passing year after the independence, common people increased their sustaining power. Unless you are involved, you cannot realise the depth of any problem. So, what is needed to get rid of the caste system and religion-oriented superstitions?

The thing which is needed is true education, not paper degrees. In today's world, people need true education, which will sprout their dormant souls from inside. Most people have qualifications without any education. And for that, we need a cohesive bonding between the guardians, teachers and students. It may take thousand years to build the character of a nation, but once the character is built, you need not look back. The best example is Japan. The coming sunrise is in store for you, and that can be truly enjoyed provided you make yourself properly educated.

25

Husband's Stubborn Attitude and Not Joining Any Job Except Teaching

Sanjay was extremely stubborn, and he was not ready to join any other job except teaching. He was not pragmatic. It was ok that teaching was his first love, but till he got it, he could have joined some other job. Truly speaking, he was a thinker-cum-philosopher, and his mind was miles away from any kind of Civil Engineering sites. He was an ardent reader of English literature. He possessed a chequered career with a varied profile. But, due to his unemployment, his earning was as good as zero. He used to go for three to four private tuitions and earn approximately one thousand rupees per month.

His father was an armchair critic, and all the while, he used to criticise both his sons. The influence of poverty was seen in every sphere of Sanjay's life. Their life became meaningless. Sanjay's father had a joint account with Sanjay both at the bank and post office. It was not done for the benefit of Sanjay; it was done so that Sanjay could be sent to the bank or post office to withdraw small amounts of money.

Every alternate day, his father used to send him to the bank or post office just to withdraw thirty rupees. It was a permanent vexation. Even the bank and post office staff were irritated with Sanjay. But, what to do? His father was the high command, and Sanjay was there just to obey the orders of his thrifty father.

Once, he suggested his father withdraw at least three hundred rupees at a time. But, his father did not agree. He had an in-built belief that if a bigger amount was withdrawn, expenses would increase. What could be the thoughts of a petty clerk after retirement? From his point of view, he was correct.

One incident must be shared with the readers here. Once, after withdrawing thirty rupees, Sanjay had two cups of tea, one biscuit and one cigarette, and while returning home, due to the gruelling summer, he came by a cycle rickshaw. He had already spent seven rupees from the thirty rupees and gave twenty-three rupees to his father. His father wanted to know about the expense of seven rupees. When Sanjay honestly told him everything, he became furious and said, "What's the use of withdrawing thirty rupees if seven rupees are spent just on luxury?"

For him, consuming two cups of tea and one biscuit was considered a luxury. He was very rude, and he used to say everything very curtly. He did not have the art to use words in a euphemistic way. There is a style of expressing the hard words in a softer way, but that needs proper grooming, training and aristocratic breeding. Sanjay's father was devoid of all these.

What is education? According to the views of famous philosopher-cum-mentor, J Krishnamurti, "It is essentially the art of learning, not only from books but also from the whole movement of life." Sanjay believed in this philosophy. But, for surviving, philosophy itself is not enough. But, Sanjay did not accept this simple truth, and the biggest sufferer was none other than Susan.

In spite of several requests from Susan, Sanjay did not bother to pay heed and sat idle at home. His father used to insult him regularly. But, he became insult-proof. He became thick-skinned, and Susan had to absorb all the shock, trauma and insult.

26

Husband's Suicide Attempt and His Uncle's Visit

Sanjay was a critical patient of morbid melancholy, and the root cause of his depression was his incomplete academic career. He wanted to pursue his PhD in Civil Engineering (specialisation in Environmental Engineering) at a famous American university, but the poor condition of his family prevented him from exploring his academic career. Sanjay was famous for his jittery nature in critical moments, and this habit was inherited from his mother. Due to acute depression, diffidence became an integral part of his character. Sanjay had an antipathy for common people and his neighbours because all the while they used to vex him by asking about his status of employment. Sometimes, he used to be angry and people used to enjoy that. The status of Sanjay's life could be compared to the retrograde motion of a planet.

In spite of rock-bottom poverty, there was no dearth of dutifulness in Susan's attitude. Susan had a good habit of preparing something out of the leftover food. She never liked the wastage of food. She used to concoct a meal from leftovers.

The day was just like any other day. Sanjay, as usual, got up late. Susan entered the room with breakfast for Sanjay. But, she read a special message in his eyes, which made her worried. She had developed expertise in reading the mental climate of Sanjay through his eyes. It needs time and patience. She was his caregiver.

Sanjay was wearing a collyrium blue t-shirt and faded jeans. The whole behaviour of Sanjay could be compared to aerial shots of the city, everything was seen, but it was blurred. Proper clarity was absent. The day went by. Sanjay did not leave the bed for a single moment apart from getting up to freshen up. He had already made up his mind to commit suicide on the same night. He crushed one hundred Placidox-5 (Diazepam tablet) and put them into a glass and poured water in it. After mixing the powdered tablets, he kept the glass behind the books on his bookshelf. It was midnight. Susan was sleeping deeply after the bone-breaking work of the whole day, and Sanjay had a sleepless night. He had insomnia due to two reasons. One was his regular habit of consuming tranquillizers and another was his indolent attitude and zero physical exercise.

It was around 3:00 am. Stealthily, Sanjay got up, approached the bookshelf and took out the glass, which contained 500 mg of a thick paste of Diazepam. He thought for a while. The blue hallow of the night lamp was partially focused on Susan's face. Sanjay thought twice and thrice, but ultimately, he listened to his brain and swallowed the whole thick paste of Diazepam. The rest of the story is history.

In the morning, Susan tried to awaken Sanjay, but in spite of her repeated attempts, she failed. There was neither any suicide note nor any used strips of the tablets. But suddenly, Susan found the glass, and within the glass, a very little amount of the paste was remaining. Immediately, Susan informed the matter to Sanjay's father, and with the help of local boys, he was shifted to a local hospital. Still, he was alive. But, by that time, a considerable amount of damage was done.

Urine was dripping drop by drop, and it was completely red. Doctors took special care of Sanjay, and after an emergency treatment, he was shifted to an ICU. It was a traumatic experience. The scandal of attempted suicide spread in the locality just like a forest fire. After three days, Sanjay came to consciousness, but he was in deep slumber, and it was difficult for him to recognise anybody. The doctor told the family that both his kidneys were severely affected, and he could not be discharged.

For the family, it was a traumatising experience, and apart from that, the added irritation was the inquiry from the neighbours. Susan had to narrate the whole incident repeatedly just like playing the same CD again and again.

After eleven days, Sanjay was discharged from the hospital. Luckily, he escaped death, but he was physically and mentally totally broken. Susan took him from the hospital. It was a winter evening. They reached home followed by a series of worries. Susan was advised by the doctor to keep Sanjay under strict surveillance.

After Sanjay's return from the hospital, his father became very much nervous because he did not have any hope. So, he contacted his younger brother, and his brother was settled in Nagpur for the last four decades. He was a lower division clerk at Nagpur GPO, but he was famous as a trade union leader and was a very good manager-cum-leader and expert orator in Marathi, Hindi and English. His qualification was limited only to matric, but he was a visionary. Sanjay and Abir received him at Howrah Station, and he stayed with them for a week, and while leaving for Nagpur, he took a set of Sanjay's resume. He also told Sanjay to give him ten blank papers signed by him. In Maharashtra, there were many private engineering colleges, and he saw advertisements for the post of lecturer in various colleges in and around Nagpur. He would send applications to those colleges on behalf of Sanjay. He would write application letters on blank papers signed by Sanjay.

27

Killing Poverty and Barren Days of Durga Puja

Susan had the misfortune to be associated with rock-bottom poverty right from the day of her father's death. That one incident changed her whole life. But, at that time, only poverty was there, agony was absent. But after marriage, the poverty was coupled with agony. Susan's youth was engulfed by the flame of poverty and there was no one to help. With her mother, there was no connection. The maternal side was diplomatic, and they did not even give a single rupee to Susan. Sanjay's elder brother was extremely selfish, and Sanjay was nothing but an imbecile who could only torture an innocent girl in the name of love.

The biggest festival, Durga Puja was at the doorstep. All the families were gearing up for celebrations. Only the members of Sanjay's house were morose and deprived of all kinds of merriments. Sanjay was morbidly melancholic and his father was a cynic. Susan was trapped between these two people, and she had no place to go. She was hardly twenty years old. Forget about joy, she was submerged in the ocean of sorrow for no fault of hers. She suffered like a wounded street dog just because of an irresponsible husband for whom right from study to marriage everything was an obsession. Obsession cannot be removed by medicine. It is an abnormal thought process. The thought process of every individual is different, and it cannot be changed. Sanjay used to hate his father for his continuous vexation. Sanjay was known for his antagonism, which most of the time, his father used to avoid him. Sanjay used to judge the attitude of his father and simper.

Gradually, the biggest festival of Durga Puja started in October 1988. One night, there was light rain. The next day, Sanjay decided to visit Kolkata along with Susan to see some pandals and their decorations, but initially, he had planned to visit the tranquil Botanical Garden, which was a stone's throw away from his alma mater, BE College, Shibpur.

He executed his plan. They visited the Botanical Garden and occupied a rain-drenched bench. Sanjay enjoyed a few cigarettes. Susan looked into Sanjay's eyes. Still, Susan felt the strength of Sanjay's soul in his intelligent look. But, she was helpless. Sanjay's post-graduation was still incomplete. The complete thesis and four tough papers were remaining. Susan did not have any hope. She had only a bunch of interrogative marks in her possession.

The condition was so bad that even a porn star was more respected than Sanjay. Susan realised one thing after marriage. Unless one is able to convert his knowledge to money, he is of no use. Only marks are not sufficient. Marks must be coupled with an ample amount of money if you really want to be accepted by this sad, bad and mad world; otherwise, there is no one to listen to your wincing.

28

The Unmarried Brother-In-Law

The unmarried brother-in-law of Susan was a spike in the boot for both Susan and Sanjay. He was elder to Sanjay by seven years and was unmarried. When Susan was married, Sanjay was twenty-four and his elder brother was thirty-one. He was a Chemical Engineer, and he was one of the most eligible bachelors in those days. He was handsome, popular, well-qualified and was working in a public sector undertaking as an engineer. What more do you need to fulfil the eligibility of a good bachelor? But, he knew his market value, and for that, he used to play with the sentiments of the middle-class Bengalis. He used to visit Serampore fortnightly from Durgapur. He was posted in Durgapur, and the distance of Durgapur was approximately 150 kilometres from Serampore. His diary always used to be full of appointments to visit houses of nubile ladies of different families in that area. He knew very well that he would not marry anyone of them but used to keep people in limbo.

Once, a gentleman came for his daughter. He was a middle-class Bengali. Sanjay's brother visited his house, talked to the girl and kept them waiting for four long years. Can you imagine such a kind of harassment? In a day, he used to visit four houses to see girls. It became his nasty hobby to play with the sentiments and emotions of people. He was a narcissist. He was apparently modern, but he did not possess an unorthodox view. From inside, he was very orthodox. For him, a wife meant a cook without any salary, like father, like son.

Being the eldest child, he inherited most of the bad qualities of his father. Due to his good position and good looks, people could not judge his inner personality and was surrounded by a lot of sycophants. If you become successful in life, you will see a lot of sycophants. On the contrary, in spite of having all qualities, if you fail to succeed, even an ass will kick you. This is the true picture of life. His whole attitude was full of frivolities and the plausibility of getting married to any of those ladies was practically nil in those days. He had visited at least two hundred houses to see two hundred girls, but no one could impress him. The basic reason was his confused mind. He did not even know his own requirements.

If you make both the brothers sit together, you will realise the true meaning of juxtaposition. Sometimes, Sanjay used to chuckle at seeing the childish activities of his elder brother. The world is full of hypocrites and sycophants, and Sanjay's elder brother was one of those hypocrites.

Sanjay's brother used to be elated by his joyful mental state, and he was least bothered about Sanjay and his family. Truly speaking, whenever he used to come, Sanjay's father used to give special instructions to Susan for preparing the dishes, which his elder son liked. She had to cook vegetables, whole grains and fish curry, while having acute asthma, using homemade *chula*. But, in the end, his elder brother used to bunk dinner because he would already be full by visiting the houses of many girls. He never bothered about the labour of Susan, and Sanjay was treated just like a parasite.

Susan did not have paraphernalia for standard cooking. The house did not even have proper utensils. Whenever Sanjay's brother used to come, he would give money to Sanjay followed by an order to bring sweets and cookies of his choice. Their father never protested for treating Sanjay like a slave. For both, his father and elder brother, Sanjay was good for nothing.

Sanjay's brother used to overflow with joy and was well-known for his exuberance. He was very careful about his clothes, hairstyle, perfume and trimmed beard. His cheeks were fluffy, and he was obsessed with his looks. His presence itself used to be a source of torture for Sanjay and Susan. Sanjay had a way to escape. He used to spend maximum time at Abir's house. But, for Susan, there was no way out. Her workload used to be double, but just for the unemployed husband, she had to sustain everything.

29

Husband Got His Dream Job of Teaching, Painful Days in Khamgaon

Ultimately, Sanjay's dream came true. Sanjay's uncle sent applications to nine colleges on his behalf. After applying to nine colleges, he got four interview calls. Sanjay had to leave West Bengal after receiving a telegram from his uncle within no time. He just came with two bags to Nagpur, and that was his first long journey.

He left West Bengal on 31st May 1990. It was Susan's twenty-third birthday, and he reached Nagpur on 1st June 1990. There were two calls from two famous colleges in Nagpur. The third interview call was from an Engineering College of Amravati, and the last call was from a remote place named Khamgaon. In the first three interviews, Sanjay consecutively failed, but in the fourth interview at Khamgaon, he cleared the interview, impressed the experts and got his dream job of teaching. It was a unique experience for him which could not be described in words.

He was accompanied to Khamgaon by his uncle whom he fondly addressed as BN. But, his uncle did not accompany him for the interview at Khamgaon Engineering College. His uncle was a trade union leader. He remained in the main post office of Khamgaon along with his staffs, and Sanjay was accompanied by an old clerk named Mr Kapse from the post office. Mr Kapse was on the verge of retirement. It was post-summer time. The month was August and the year was 1990. Sanjay started from the city and reached the college at 9:00 am. But, the day passed, and his turn did not come. At noon, Mr Kapse suddenly left the venue, and after half an hour, he returned with some snacks for Sanjay. It was a famous *kachori* of that area. Sanjay was touched by the gesture of this old person.

All the candidates waited all day in the open Amphitheatre of the college, and Sanjay's turn came just before evening. For the first time, Sanjay's intelligentsia was recognised by a team of experts for his teaching ability and capability. Initially, he was asked questions from Surveying, and he could not impress the experts. One of the experts (a South Indian teacher working as the HoD of the Civil Department of the college) asked him to leave, but another gentleman allowed Sanjay to sit and asked him about the topic of his thesis for ME. Sanjay could impress him heavily. That gentleman was the principal of the college, and the principal himself recommended Sanjay's case to the management.

He was offered the post of lecturer at the Department of Civil Engineering along with two increments for his post-graduation, and apart from salary, he negotiated for family quarters on the campus. It was the happiest day of Sanjay's life. His expectation was around two thousand rupees but, he got more than that. His starting salary was approximately two thousand four hundred rupees. Till that day, Sanjay used to camouflage his grief, but that day he was happy beyond measure. He returned to the city along with Mr Kapse and his uncle too was delighted and told him, "Now you need not return to West Bengal with bare hand. I am really happy about your selection as a faculty."

In those days, mediocre candidates were selected as lecturers since the internet was not there. Sanjay was totally cut off from the rest of the country for four long years. Because in the local newspapers and employment news, advertisements for teaching jobs in different private engineering colleges of Maharashtra, Karnataka and Tamil Nadu never appeared. Teaching is nothing but symbiosis, which means a mutually beneficial relationship between different people or groups, but to get that, Sanjay had to wait for four long years (1986 to 1990).

Sanjay had been aggressive right from his school days and impeccable politeness was not his cup of tea. He was a scholar, but his scholasticism was coupled with pride, and for that, he was disliked by many friends and people. Society never accepts people with pride. For a cruel society, criticising others was nothing but an intellectual pastime of logic-chopping, and their basic work was criticising others.

After selection, Sanjay wanted to go to West Bengal for a couple of days, but his uncle advised him to join the job first. Sanjay listened to his uncle. In those days, he was wearing his joy on his sleeves. From the college to the city, the distance was around ten kilometres, and the road was not good. In the locality of the college, there was practically no market. Even for simple knick-knacks, one had to depend on the city. There were city buses at regular intervals right from the college campus. But, the journey was not comfortable. It was a bone-jarring ride. Sometimes, Sanjay had to go to the city even by auto rickshaw, and he would never forget those bumpy auto rickshaw rides.

Even after thirty years, Susan remembers those sun-faded bricks and crappy memories of Khamgaon Engineering College. Sanjay's job was nothing but impunity for Susan. She got rid of the claustrophobic atmosphere of the house of Sanjay's father in Serampore. Though Sanjay's salary was not adequate to suffice day-to-day expenses for the family, she felt the taste of independence.

Susan never liked the teaching profession, but she had to accept it for Sanjay. Sanjay was made for teaching. There are teachers and scholars with a quivering voice, but Sanjay did not belong to that category. He possessed a majestic personality and a very impressive voice. For him, to control a class was a task of a few seconds. After getting into the teaching profession, truly speaking, it became his hobby. Sanjay was not pursuing his profession. He was pursuing his hobby, and when hobby and profession synchronise, they become the ultimate success for a person. The same thing happened with Sanjay. His happiness was flowing out of very much deeper springs.

Still, Susan vividly remembers the hem of mountains on the outskirt of Khamgaon, and at night, the dots of lights of passing vehicles seen from the terrace of their quarters. Sanjay's line of thoughts was totally different from other people, and that was why Sanjay was different, and wherever he visited, he was marked by people immediately for his magnanimous personality.

One thing is true, life is valuable because of sentiments, emotions, laughter, tears and smiles. But, in Susan's life, most of the good parameters were missing. She had only pathos and tears.

30

The Old, Widowed Elder Sister of Her Father-In-Law

The only members in their Serampore house were her father-in-law and his old, widowed sister. She was fondly known as *Phoi Pisi*. She was unfortunate by birth. She became a widow at the age of twenty-six. When she was only eighteen, she was married, and the age gap with her husband was unbelievable. She was eighteen and her husband was sixty-three. There was an age gap of forty-five years. Her husband was a widower and had two children from his first wife. He was an orthodox Brahmin and not much educated. But, he had passed his matric with the first division in the pre-independence era. So, whatever he knew was substantial. Because in those days, the term quality control was not there, but quality used to be there, and nowadays, quality control is there, but the quality is absent.

Phoi Pisi was well known for her thrifty nature. No one found her quarrelling with anyone, but she was the mastermind to create plots for fights. She used to play dirty politics. Politics can be compared to wars, which are played from back. Her stature was tall, complexion was wheatish and body structure was bony. She had only one son, but he died at the age of thirty-three due to Lupus. Her daughter-in-law again married and planned to send her to a vagrant home. When Sanjay's father came to know about that, he took her to his home. *Phoi Pisi* was known for her puritan nature and also her cynicism. She was at least seventy, and it was the start of amnesia. She had a bony glow of half-moons under both her eyes.

There are two types of living. One is fear-oriented, and the second one is love-oriented. Obviously, *Phoi Pisi* had a fear-oriented living right from day one. In the initial years, she was afraid of her mother, then she was afraid of her husband, and after her husband's death, she moved to her son's place, and she was afraid of her son. After her son's death, she was afraid of her daughter-in-law, and at last, she returned to her brother, and she was afraid of her brother. In India, a widow is nothing but an unpaid domestic worker. The same was the case with *Phoi Pisi.* Her whole life, wherever she stayed, they sucked her blood, and she was forced to work as a domestic worker. No one spared her, be it her son or her brother.

She was surviving without any aim. Since she could not die, she was surviving. Gradually, with each passing month, she became ill, and in 1996, she passed away without disturbing anyone.

31

Daughter's Birth

It was December 1990 at Khamgaon Engineering College. One fine morning, Susan was feeling nauseous, and she vomited. After two or three hours, she vomited again. Sanjay was supposed to go to college. But, because of Susan's bad health, he postponed his programme. They used to stay within the campus in teachers' quarters. Sanjay had doubts about Susan's pregnancy. In the evening, they visited a local doctor in the town. He was a very simple person. After a thorough check-up, he confirmed pregnancy and took his fee of only twenty rupees. He did not suggest any kind of test or sonography. He just advised Susan to walk two kilometres every day for a smooth delivery.

They were accompanied by Sanjay's friend, Mr Banerjee, who was posted in the college as Assistant Workshop Superintendent. When Susan disclosed the news of her pregnancy, Mr Banerjee congratulated both Susan and Sanjay. At the doctor's clinic, some very poor patients were there. Still, Susan recalls a poor woman. She belonged to the labour class. Susan remembers her mirror-studded blouse and watery eyes.

Months passed very quickly, and there was no one to care for Susan in the village of Khamgaon, and the college was at a distance of ten kilometres from the town. From Susan's house, all relations were over. So, Sanjay decided to keep Susan in Serampore, at his father's house for delivery. But, even in that house, there was no lady apart from his father's old sister. In the month of June, Sanjay went to Serampore along with Susan, and after dropping her in Serampore, after fifteen days, he returned to Khamgaon.

The main feature of Susan was her million-dollar smile and girlish look. She never entirely lost that girlish look even as she grew into a woman.

It was the month of September. On 10th September 1991, Sanjay received an inland letter from his father. In those days, there was no phone in Sanjay's father's house, and on the college campus, none of the faculty had a personal phone. The only phone available was in the college office. After opening the inland letter, Sanjay received the good news of his baby daughter's arrival. The daughter was christened Andria. He shared this good news with his friends and subordinates. He brought two kilograms of good-quality *pedha* (a typical form of Indian sweet) and distributed them among his friends, office staff and subordinates. A new chapter of their life started.

32

Nasty Ward of the Government-Run Hospital

There is a saying, "Heaven and hell are not in separate places. Both are available on the earth itself." If you want to cross-check the veracity of this adage, simply visit any government-run hospital in the vast Indian sub-continent. Any government-run hospital in India can be compared to hell. Patients were lying on the floor, and everywhere there was a stench of urine. The whole atmosphere was non-hygienic. Dogs and cats were freely moving within the wards. The staffs were inadequate in number, and due to enormous work pressure, they were rude and ill-behaved. Senior doctors were absent, and there was an overflowing commode where the cistern was non-functional. Most of the work was tackled by junior interns who had no place to go since their degrees were mortgaged. For that, all of them were practically blackmailed and sucked by the system. The whole atmosphere was boisterous.

I had the sad experience of visiting more than one government-run hospital many times due to some reason or other. Most of the time, I had to visit to see a patient who was known to me. But, the same hospital changed its entire look when visited by a politician and his side kicks for inaugurating a new ward or building.

Once, I visited a government-run hospital to receive the dead body of my friend's elder brother who died untimely due to a gruesome road accident. The body was kept in the morgue. We went in a group, but since I did not like the atmosphere of a hospital and the post-mortem scene, I preferred to stay away from them. I was sitting under a big Banyan tree on the hospital campus and was flipping through a book. The patients were poor, but the doctors were quite well off. Apart from their regular salary, they used to have private practices, and most of them were unapproachable, hard-nosed professionals. I had seen many things in the government-run hospital, e.g., weather-beaten faces of the poorest of the poor cross-section of the country, arthritic fingers of a patient, droopy smiles with droopy eyes of patients in the psychiatry ward, acne-scarred young men and, last but not least, patients grimacing in pain.

Many times, people protested against the private practices of doctors in government-run hospitals. People did have a thumping majority for protesting against the inhuman doctors of the government-run hospitals who practically neglected their duties and engrossed themselves in private practices, but common people could not do anything because this group of ethic-less doctors were closely linked to politicians and a substantial chunk of their income used to go to the higher authorities for keeping their mouth shut. Although all doctors are not bad, if we go for the generalisation of a statement, then I would say that ninety per cent of the doctors in government hospitals are escapists, and they are preoccupied with their private practice.

Once, Andria caught a bad fever, and she was admitted to a government hospital. Susan was there the whole time and stayed up the whole night. Sanjay was also there, but he preferred to stay outside beneath a big Banyan tree. Sanjay observed the dark and silent corridor of the hospital, but there was no one to take care of it. The light must have been stolen or damaged. Indifference is there in the Indian blood. Unless your drawing room is affected, you are least bothered by society, and this selfish attitude of people has brought the country down from a very enriched level to the lowermost stratum. While waiting under the tree, Sanjay did not even know when he fell asleep. In the early morning, he got up and found the dappled sunlight flickering through the leaves of the age-old banyan tree.

Sanjay went into the hospital building. The sister concerned allowed him to go inside. Susan was tired beyond measure, but Andria's fever had subsided. After a couple of minutes, the resident doctor came for a visit. When Sanjay asked about Andria's condition, the doctor was slightly irritated, and Sanjay remembered the wiggling of his eyebrows to indicate his impatience. A ward boy had a habit of eavesdropping, and he was stealthily listening to the conversation between the doctor and Sanjay from a close distance.

33

Seeing the Metamorphosis of a Man from a Scholar to an Insane Person

Susan was a lady who witnessed the metamorphosis of a man from a scholar to an insane person. Gradually, Sanjay's condition became worst. Initially, he had only depression and anxiety disorder. But, due to the discontinuation of medicines and too much consumption of alcohol, all those psychiatric drugs failed to produce positive results. On the contrary, his condition became worst. He used to feel numbness in his limbs and many times, there used to be twitching of muscles in different parts of his body right from his eyelids to his bicep muscles. He did not have any control over twitching. They were involuntary movements of muscles. Sometimes, he used to suffer from excruciating pain due to severe headaches. He used to yell loudly in pain, but apart from Susan, there was no one to take care of him, not even his father.

Partially, lunatic Sanjay used to think of transmigration and reincarnation. His thought process was transfixed. Sometimes, he alone used to go to the bank of the river Ganga and used to sit by the side of the gleaming water in the evening. He became the victim of denunciation due to his abnormal attitude. People used to tease him, and he used to chastise Susan to canalise his frustration. It was difficult to believe that Sanjay had a love marriage. Love was there for a few months only, and the rest of Susan's life was full of apathy, hatred, abuse, shock and trauma. She had tremendous patience, and she silently sustained all the torture, and since she never protested, the degree of torture went on increasing with each passing year.

Once, Sanjay's distant relatives came for a few days, and while returning, his aunt forgot to take a *saree*. But, without verifying the fact, the lady directly charged Susan for embezzlement. It was really very insulting.

Afterwards, that *saree* was found and returned to her by courier. Although Sanjay used to torture Susan, there was a hidden stream of love, which was not seen and only Susan knew about it. Due to this insult to Susan, Sanjay became violent and abused his aunt ruthlessly over the phone from a local telephone booth. At least, he had the self-respect to defend his wife. That is surely praise-worthy.

But, Sanjay's mental condition became worse. The treatment of different psychiatrists was nothing but a stamp of approval for his abnormal mental health. Even in that condition, Sanjay maintained his reading habit as an avid reader.

One day, the sun was setting on the western horizon. Susan was sitting by Sanjay in their room. Both of them were totally silent. The russet sunset was the only witness of this couple who were tied by an invisible cord of love and affection. But, Susan was afraid of the innocuous look that had turned into a brutal look as Sanjay's insanity aggravated.

34

Moved to Pune and Stayed in the Kondohwa Area — Just Like a Rehabilitation Camp

Days were passing very smoothly. But, Sanjay's uncle did not want Sanjay to wilt in a barren place like Khamgaon. So, he motivated Sanjay to shift his coordinates from Khamgaon to some other place and teach at a Government Engineering College in Maharashtra. Sanjay was travelling from Khamgaon to Kolkata via Nagpur. His uncle met him at Nagpur station and gave him a cutting of the Times of India and told him to apply. There was an advertisement from MPSC (Maharashtra Public Service Commission) for the recruitment of lecturers in the Government Engineering Colleges of Maharashtra. Sanjay used to respect his uncle, and he was convinced. Sanjay applied and got selected, and he was posted in Pune. Already by that time, Sanjay had served Khamgaon Engineering College for nearly two and half years, and within that time, he had authored a book on an Engineering subject. To present the gratis copy of the book, Sanjay visited Pune with the executive of his publisher, and that was his first visit to Pune. He liked the grandeur of Pune and visited more than ten colleges in Pune.

He had to move his base from Khamgaon to Pune. Initially, he stayed in Kondohwa. It was a place mostly populated by Muslims, and the area was not developed in the early nineties. The distance between his house and office was quite big. Sanjay took the help of his laboratory assistant, Milind. After being relieved from Khamgaon, Sanjay came to Pune by train, and his family did not shift on the same day. Along with Sanjay, Milind started, but he came by truck through which all the goods were shifted. Both of them reached the next day, and after their arrival in Pune, Sanjay's family started from Khamgaon. At that time Andria was only one and a half years old. Susan came to Pune by train along with Andria and a minimal amount of goods. All the major loads were already shifted by truck. It was the month of June, and it was a blisteringly hot day.

Sanjay and Milind received Susan and Andria from the station, and then they started towards Kondohwa by a private taxi via Pune Camp. Pune Camp is a very posh area. Susan was happy to see the atmosphere. But, the truth was yet to unfold itself. After crossing the camp area, when they approached Kondohwa, the scenario started changing, and ultimately Susan landed in hell. Everywhere there were ups and downs. The total area was very shabby and dirty. There were a lot of roadside kiosks. The rented apartment where they landed was very small. There was a severe scarcity of water. The whole area resembled a rehabilitation camp. The topography of the area was very uneven. There were many poor children who were deprived of the comfort of their childhood. The water supply was very irregular and less. There used to be fights and abusive behaviour among neighbours. It was less like an apartment and more like a slum. Only for Sanjay, Susan had to sustain all these troubles.

They did not have a gas connection at home. Susan used to cook using a stove for which kerosene was required. Since their ration card was not transferred, they were not entitled to purchase kerosene through their ration card. Sanjay used to visit a place at the top of a nearby hillock to buy kerosene. The area was known for the black marketing of kerosene. It was an open secret there. For the flour mill, Sanjay had to walk nearly one kilometre on that steep road with Andria in his arms. Even in the flour mill, Sanjay used to read. He was always accompanied by a book of his choice. He was a voracious reader, and no atmosphere could prevent him from his first love — reading.

35

Switchover to a Slum in Pune

It was literally impossible to stay in Kondohwa. Every Saturday, Sanjay used to have morning college, and it used to be a half day. One Saturday afternoon, after returning from the college, he found Susan sitting with Andria in a flustered mood as there was no water supply, and there was no guarantee of water supply in the evening too.

Till then, the builder had not handed over the project to the society. The society was not formed, and there were many defaulting flat owners who did not pay the total amount to the builder. Just by submitting a promissory note, they took possession of the flat and entered their apartment, and after occupying it, they started playing tactics. For that reason, being angry, the builder stopped the water supply. Sanjay had no *locus standi* because he was a tenant, and the house owner was a non-teaching staff of his college. Sanjay became fed up and decided to leave that place at the earliest. Still, some time was needed. Since his job was new, he did not have any leaves on his credit. But, he started searching for houses in the adjacent area.

Within three weeks, he got another apartment in the local proximity. Even though that place was not good, it was slightly better than Kondohwa. It was also a slum area, but a slightly more sophisticated slum. At least, the water supply was there. Its rent was three hundred rupees more, but at least a person could stay there without any trauma.

There were a few old bungalows, and most of the bungalows belonged to the Christian community who were staying there for a long time. All the old bungalows had ramshackle wooden staircases, and proper illumination was not there. Three kilometres away from their society, the boundary of Pune Camp started. It was one of the poshest localities of Pune. All the batchmates of Sanjay used to stay in the best apartments in different pockets of India, only this bibliomaniac scholar was an odd man out. In the quest for truth and knowledge, he forced his family to stay in a slum. Sometimes, Susan used to have a sinking feeling. But, for the sake of Andria, she used to come out of it just by sheer mental strength.

Life itself is like a series of hundred-metre races. Nobody can afford to take even a single stretch lightly. Since Sanjay took his life easily, the result was staying in a slum despite being a scholar.

In this life, your comfort is inversely proportional to the number of wrong decisions taken by you. If you do not take any wrong decisions, you are bound to be comfortable. A correct decision is a hundred times more important and effective than hard work. There are thousands of students who are doing hard work, but they never get the desired result. Why? Because their working style is not methodical. The working style itself is wrong. If you try to open a lid of a container by rotating it in an opposite direction, will it open? Never. On the contrary, it will be tighter and tighter with each effort.

So, have a vision. Fix your goals. Make the minimum number of mistakes. Only then success will be yours. Sanjay's whole life was wrapped by a cover, whose name was failure.

36

Initial Days of Daughter and Her Primary School Life

Andria was taciturn right from her initial days, whereas her contemporary children were quite talkative. So, Susan naturally had some inbuilt fear regarding Andria's admission to any of the good schools. Sanjay was indifferent about Andria's education. Truly speaking, being a father, he did not take any of the responsibilities of the child. Susan decided not to approach any good schools because it was of no use. Because Susan knew very well that Andria would not respond to any of the questions during the admission procedure. For that, Susan decided to admit Andria to one of the nearby English medium schools, which did not have any stringency in the admission system. Even the presence of the child was not essential.

One day, Sanjay went and gave a three thousand rupees donation and a photocopy of Andria's birth certificate along with the duly filled form signed by him. At least, the admission in junior KG was over, and Susan was relieved from the tension of admission. Truly speaking, Sanjay was naïve about all the procedures of admission, whereas other parents did a lot of homework and research about ten to fifteen schools in the locality and stand in a queue to collect the forms for admission in the good schools right from the wee hours.

Susan was acrimonious about Andria's admission. At least, her anxiety was removed after admitting Andria to the nearby English medium school. To date, Susan remembers the phosphorescent colour of the dress, which Andria used to wear in those days. There was a bungalow near the school. On the first day, Sanjay went to drop Andria at the school, and after a couple of minutes, Susan too joined Sanjay.

On the first day, the school was only for two hours. So, Sanjay and Susan decided to wait on the school campus to pick up Andria after school hours. Both of them decided to just go around the school and see the atmosphere of the neighbourhood of the school. There were many shops and bungalows in and around the school. Till now, Susan vividly remembers the snarled dog of a bungalow, who was chained but was very ferocious.

For breakfast, they had puffed rice and tea. The month was January, and it was a cloudy but windy day. In school, there was a big playground, and in one corner of the ground, there was a basketball court, and the basketball hoop was very new because it was recently made. Susan had bamboo-leaf eyes, and for that, her beauty was known to everyone, even in the school among all the guardians, one could easily locate Susan for her paragon beauty.

After a few minutes, the bell rang, and for junior KG, the school was over. They were done for the day. At least in that school, one good thing was that there was practically zero competition. School should be a soil in which children can grow without fear, happily and intelligently. The school was exactly like that. The children were free from stress. Even when Sanjay and Susan looked at the students in the senior classes, it was observed that they were relaxed. In very good schools, there is cut-throat competition. In every school, there are backbenchers who cannot express themselves, and they become a victim of juvenile depression. Expression is life and repression is suicide. After being admitted to a good school, if the child becomes depressed then what is the use of it? I always say that a student from a bad school is much happier than a backbencher from a reputed school. It is better to reign in hell than to serve in heaven.

Susan wanted Andria to be an all-rounder, and for that, she wanted Andria to know everything right from cycling to swimming. For all these things, childhood is the best time to learn. With age, it becomes difficult to learn new things. Susan got Andria admitted to a nearby swimming club and purchased a brand-new skimpy swimsuit for her.

37

Secondary School Life of Andria

Andria's secondary school life was chequered. Right from the second standard, she never stood second in the class. Apart from academics, she was very good in extracurricular activities, except for sports. She was never involved in sports, and Susan did not want her daughter to be a jack of all trades. Her basic focus was academics. Apart from that, she was trained and groomed for extempore speeches, leadership, class monitorship, debate, etc. Susan wanted Andria to converse with her in English instead of Bengali, although Andria's mother tongue was Bengali. Susan understood one thing. For dominating the academic world, one needed to master two subjects, and those were English and Mathematics. Neither Andria went to any tuition classes nor did she have any home tutor. Susan used to take care of Andria's studies, and many times, Sanjay used to teach her core concepts of Mathematics.

Sanjay was a genius as far as academics were concerned, but he did not have any routine or discipline. It was a question of mood, and Susan was the only person who had the mastery to judge Sanjay's moods. When Sanjay used to be in a good mood, Susan used to send Andria to her father for special tips in Mathematics and Science. Andria's basic fundamentals were very clear. She never counted pages of books or hours of study. She used to be engrossed in her studies. She had her own study table and her chair had a richly embroidered silk cushion, which was gifted to Sanjay by one of his NIT batchmates when he visited Rajasthan a few years ago to attend an international conference.

Andria was preparing for the draconian exam of NTS, and due to her clear fundamentals, she cleared the exam. It was a matter of great pleasure for the entire family. Two great attributes of human nature are faith and strength. Without these two, no one can succeed in any venture, whatever it might be. Susan took care of these two attributes. She generated self-faith within Andria, which helped her germinate inner strength. Knowledge of the self is the most important thing. One must assess oneself. Unless you are able to assess yourself, how will you succeed? One must have self-analysis. There is a famous saying, "If you cannot be happy alone, you cannot be happy together." Similarly, once you fail to asses yourself, you cannot excel in any venture. But, Susan taught Andria how to do self-analysis, self-assessment and self-introspection.

The most fabulous memories of school life were the memories of all the annual picnics. The children used to be excited right from the day of the announcement of the picnic date. Both Sanjay and Susan used to drop Andria to school early in the morning of the picnic day because on that day, the school bus used to be cancelled. Even in the evening, guardians were supposed to pick up their children from school. In the ninth standard, Andria became the Assistant Head Girl of the secondary section, and after being promoted to the tenth standard, she became the Head Girl. She had good leadership qualities along with the traits of a good manager. It was a picnic of the tenth standard, and it was the last picnic of secondary school life. After returning from the picnic, Andria was narrating the experience and incidents of the whole day to her parents. She was telling them how she enjoyed the twinkling sunlight in the side view mirror of the picnic bus. The sun was fading in the western sky, but Andria enjoyed the crimson beams, which were being filtered through the leaves of the trees.

Nowadays, we totally forget the real meaning of education. We go to school and ask about all amenities, e.g., playground, basketball court, gym, swimming pool, cricket ground, skating floor and air-conditioned classrooms, but seldom do we ask about the quality of the faculty. Good faculty is an extinct community. With each passing year, good faculty is being vanished like camphor, and teaching is becoming the platform for those who prepare for competitive examinations, and they do not have any affection or love for teaching. They just use this platform as a junction wherefrom their actual career will start and obviously that career is money and power-oriented. Out of one thousand students, hardly one wants to be a teacher. How unfortunate it is! The same is the condition all over the world, and the main culprit is Power Point presentations. There is no substitute for blackboard teaching. Nowadays, professors use PPTs to teach even highly mathematical and complex subjects like the Fourier series, and they do not even share their PPTs.

The right kind of education must help the student to discover what they are most interested in. If they do not find their true vocation, all their life will be wasted. They will be a victim of frustration for doing something that they do not want to do. True education is a complete change of the inner being. The total development of a child can be brought about only when there is the right synchronisation among the teacher, student and parents.

Andria was fortunate to have that. Only for that reason, she could really enjoy her complete school life and become a girl with a vision. What is the basic difference between sight and vision? All of us have sight, but most of us lack vision. One who can foresee the future is a visionary. We must design our career in such a way so that we can foresee where we will be after 5, 10 and 20 years. Andria's vision was very clear. By the tenth standard, she had made up her mind to be a Mechanical Engineer, and she had written off the term medicine from her mind. Because she realised that she did not have the inner power to be a doctor because of her sensitive nature.

38

Result of Daughter's Tenth Standard Examination

The result of Andria's tenth standard was shocking. It was a bolt from the blue. Andria never stood second in the class since the second standard. But, in the tenth standard, her position was sixth in the class. The moment she came to know about her result, she was shocked and traumatised. For the whole day, she cried, and Sanjay was continuously trying to console her. Susan still vividly recollects Andria's screams. A few of her classmates were there to console her, but no consoling worked because she could not accept this result. For the whole family, it was a defeat. In protest, Sanjay roasted *Hanuman Chalisa* (a very holy book for Hindus, which contains forty mantras about Lord Hanuman) in the gas burner and smashed a coconut and kicked the coconut to the face of God.

Andria was not ready to visit her school to collect her result. Ultimately, Susan had to visit her school. The girl who had never been in the top five was the topper. Andria's English was extraordinary, and she secured only seventy-one out of a hundred. On the contrary, the rustic students secured more than eighty-five. Andria could not accept the marks she secured in English. Even the backbenchers of her class had secured more than seventy-five. Still, Susan remembers tears pouring down Andria's cheeks. Sanjay also felt a lump in his throat and tears filming his eyes. His vision became blurred due to the film of tears.

Truly speaking, the rustic examiner could not even fathom Andria's knowledge. Even Susan's voice was choked. She was trying her best to keep her tears back, but ultimately she too could not control herself. Tears rolled down her cheeks.

Andria's English answer sheet must have been assessed by a teacher having a background in vernacular medium. This is the subjectivity problem in the Indian education system. You cannot expect true results unless you go for objective-type questions and answers, which are nothing but MCQs (multiple-choice questions).

Her result and its impact were a thought-provoking matter for the entire family. She had a propensity toward pure science. After three days, gradually, her mental climate settled down, and she started with the preparation for her admission to a junior college, which was the world-famous Fergusson College of Pune. After a lot of introspection, all of them decided to admit Andria to Fergusson College. The day she was supposed to submit the form was a rainy day. It was raining very heavily. Sanjay accompanied Andria to the form collecting centre. Fergusson College of Pune is considered a blue-blooded institution.

After submitting the form for admission, they felt relaxed, and there was enough time before classes started. So, for a change, Susan decided to go on a small trip to Mahabaleshwar for a day along with Sanjay and Andria.

The beauty of Mahabaleshwar is beyond description. It is impossible to express it in words. It can only be felt. They enjoyed the beauty of lush green and soggy grass fields. Sanjay had a problem with unorganised memory due to his disease and disorders. Susan was always there to take care of Sanjay's mental health. Andria had her mobile phone with her, and all the time, she used to be preoccupied with it; it became an obsession.

On holidays, too, Andria used to practise Algebra, and Sanjay used to teach her the core concepts of Mathematics. Andria had a bad habit of nibbling the end of her pen. Through repeated warnings, Sanjay became successful, and Andria got rid of that bad habit.

One evening, they decided to visit a good hotel, and after occupying seats, all of them were provided with a menu card. Andria was always there to select food. She fiddled with the menu card. Susan wanted to stay away from conventional seafood, and she ordered a *ghee masala dosa.* It was served within no time. It was very crisp. She dunked her first piece of *dosa* in *sambhar* and gulped it. From her facial expression, Sanjay could fathom her satisfaction. By the time the order was served, Andria was busy with her soft drink, and Sanjay was occupied with chilled beer. Due to the fear of cold, Andria preferred to have a coke at room temperature. Initially, she was sitting with lukewarm coke, and after a couple of minutes, sipped it very slowly. By that time, food was served, and they enjoyed a sumptuous lunch.

39

Result of Daughter's Twelfth Standard Examination

Andria's twelfth standard result was not up to the mark, and for that, Andria herself was responsible. Because throughout junior college, Andria had an affair with one of her classmates, and the boy was handsome. This teenage obsession cannot be controlled. Andria used to be busy 24X7 with her mobile phone, and there was a continuous exchange of SMS and e-mail with the boy. Both of them used to attend the same tuition class. Using the excuse of the tuition class, Andria used to leave early and return late. Before and after the tuition class, she used to spend time with her boyfriend. Once Susan asked Sanjay to control Andria. Sanjay called the boy and insulted him mercilessly in front of Andria, but that did not work. The influence of mind over mind is the biggest influence in the world. The boy practically occupied Andria's brain. She used to put effort into her studies, but there was a lack of concentration, and because of that, she cut a sorry figure both in Higher Secondary and all the entrance examinations of Engineering. In the Common Entrance Test (CET) of Maharashtra, she secured only one hundred and twenty-three marks out of two hundred, whereas she had the capability to score at least one hundred eighty. Truly speaking, only through her mental diversion, she became an underperformer.

In those days, Andria deviated from her studies and became obsessed with her attire, looks and hairstyle. A horde used to observe her, but they did not say anything. Once, one of Sanjay's neighbours complained to him about Andria's movement and said that he found Andria with her boyfriend in the nearby rock garden. Sanjay was a staunch supporter of Andria. Instead of entertaining his neighbour, he flatly replied, "It is none of your business to comment about my daughter. I will see everything. You just leave and oil your own machine."

Sanjay always wanted Andria to have a happy frame of mind. He was more like a friend and lesser like a father. The academic climate of Andria was not good for her split mind. A greater part of her mind was occupied by her boyfriend. There was no viable option to come out of that affair. A green jackfruit can be softened by blows but you cannot make it sweet. That was the major problem. Many times, due to excessive mental pressure and the stress of the ensuing examination, Andria used to suffer from splitting headaches and fear psychosis. Ultimately, Susan consulted a famous psychiatrist who prescribed two medicines. One of them was an antidepressant, and the second one was a mild tranquillizer. Andria looked slightly dazed after the consumption of the medicine.

Gradually, the year was over, and the Higher Secondary examinations were at the doorstep. She fared average in the Higher Secondary examination. After the traumatic tragedy of the tenth standard, Andria did not have any aim or expectations, and this time, in English, she secured eighty-four marks out of a hundred. She was casual, and still, her result in the Higher Secondary was better than her result in the tenth standard.

40

Frustration and Depression of Her Husband in His Profession

A depressed person always gives an excuse for his depression, but it is totally wrong. If you remove that cause, he will still be depressed and will give some other excuses. It is a fact and Sanjay is a burning example of that. For years, he was depressed about not getting a teaching job. But, after getting the teaching job, within six months, he became depressed because of the atmosphere of the college.

He was not comfortable with his HOD and the hierarchy. Truly speaking, a person like Sanjay cannot tolerate a boss or superior. He had the habit of comparing, and that bad habit was the root cause of ninety per cent of his problems. He did not have taciturnity. On the contrary, he was foul-mouthed and horribly argumentative. There was no metamorphosis in his basic character. He was too stubborn, proud and egotistic. He was a dipsomaniac, and if anyone would have vivisected his soul, except ego, nothing could have been seen. Truly speaking, any common man would describe Sanjay as mad.

Have you ever seen a professor of Engineering who was engrossed in his etymological hobby? He had a tremendous interest in the English language and literature, and for that, he used to concentrate on the origin and historical development of English words and their meanings. As far as the administration was concerned, Sanjay was totally mundane, and in any of the departmental meetings, he used to be in a sombre mood. But, he used to follow all the statements of all the members in the departmental meeting and was famous for his truculent nature. For that, most of the departmental faculties developed an allergy to him, and he was mostly side-tracked by all in his department. People used to discuss his nature surreptitiously. Due to depression, Sanjay used to remain absent from duties for days together, and he was known to the higher authorities for his absenteeism. All his leaves were consumed, so he used to apply for leave without pay.

After a year of pursuing the profession of teaching, Sanjay realised that in India, the teaching career could be compared to a slippery foot. Here people got a promotion and higher posts not because of merit and intelligence but because of paper degrees and Government policies. Once, Sanjay made a very good statement. He said, "To date, only some teachers remain who do not go for a PhD degree. Most of the teachers who completed PhD became permanently impotent academically. In the name of research, they polish boots for three to four years, and they do not even know the true meaning of research. Real research means knowing more and more about less and less. But, here the so-called PhDs are just degree holders. Ninety-nine per cent of PhD research have no market value, and they are of no use to society."

Sanjay wanted a roller-coaster teaching career, but on Indian soil, that was not possible. He had enjoyed flashing success many times in his studenthood, but in service life, there was no chance to enjoy any kind of flashing success. He used to be haggard and possessed a bohemian lifestyle. He didn't even take a bath regularly. He had grizzled hair, but he never opted to dye his hair. Due to anti-depressive drugs, Sanjay had put on extra weight, and as far as the term 'exercise' was concerned, he was miles away from it. After consuming tranquillizers, he used to be morose and his eyelids used to be heavy. In the evening, drinking was a regular affair. Susan could see death hovering over him but could not tell him anything because of his short temper. After consuming liquor, Sanjay used to enjoy the journey of the liquor down his throat.

Once Susan protested against his excessive consumption of alcohol. Being angry, Sanjay broke five bottles of alcohol, and the glass had broken into little bits. Susan had to clean it all because the tiny glass bits were scattered throughout the room, and most of them, occupied the corners of the room. Susan was fed up with her stormy relationship with Sanjay. But, there was no way to escape. I would say Susan was one of the most unfortunate spouses on this earth. And for that, her luck was responsible. There are thousands of ladies who are happy with their husbands who belong to Group–D employees or at the most lower division clerks. But, there is no point in having a scholar husband coupled with insanity.

41

Bipolar Disorder of Her Husband

Sanjay had a lot of psychiatric problems, but in 2011, when the problems became surmountable, Susan decided to consult one of the best psychiatrists in Pune. He thoroughly examined Sanjay and talked to him for forty-five minutes. After that, the psychiatrist talked to Susan separately for nearly twenty minutes. The doctor came to a conclusion and diagnosed Sanjay with anxiety disorder, depression, mood swings, bipolar disorder and absurd thoughts.

It was true that Sanjay was a victim of bipolar disorder. Sometimes, he used to be in a very good mood and then people used to use him. Students used to get favour and good recommendations, the staff used to get money, and even people like rickshaw pullers used to receive favours from Sanjay. On the other hand, when Sanjay used to face the opposite side of bipolar disorder, he used to be deeply morose and depressed. The speciality of bipolar disorder is that, sometimes, the patient is highly elated, but after a couple of days, they are morbidly melancholic. It is just like a giant wheel. It goes to the top, but cannot retain its position and again comes down. Sanjay's mood always used to dwindle between two extreme situations. There were times when he had given four hundred rupees as a tip to a hotel waiter. On the contrary, there were times when he physically assaulted his wife and daughter. He used to suffer from infatuation. When Sanjay was a college student, he could not maintain a long-lasting friendship with his batchmates. He always had fissiparous tendencies. Being hyper, he used to adopt brandishing, and both Susan and Andria used to be frightened. Due to heavy stress and fear, Susan and Andria used to have anorexic conditions.

Susan used to judge Sanjay's mood right from the morning. She was an expert in reading old fire in Sanjay's eyes, and when he used to be violent, his eyes would light up. Once, Sanjay became very angry and tried assaulting his daughter, but Susan tried her best to prevent him from doing that. Sanjay then twiddled Susan's nipples. It was highly embarrassing and shameful for both Susan and Andria, but semi-lunatic Sanjay had lost his common sense.

He had a bogus habit of chewing *paan*, and he was famous for his crooked smile with *paan*-decayed canines. When he used to be in a good mood, his arrival was felt by the sound of twirling of his key chains. It is the toughest job to stay with a psychiatric patient because, indirectly, those who stay with such a patient suffer.

One may say what about professional psychiatrists? Here is the answer. Psychiatrists are never affected because for them it is a profession, and they never become emotionally attached to any of their patients. There are millions of cases of bipolar disorder, but hardly ten per cent of them are treated. The rest of the ninety per cent remain untreated. Who will take care of them? The patient is totally unaware of their mental climate, and the family members are always in denial mode.

42

Anxiety Disorders of Her Husband

Sanjay's anxiety disorder came to the surface by the end of 2011. It was November 2011, and Sanjay was supposed to go for a tooth implant process under a very famous maxillofacial surgeon. Right from childhood, due to lack of care, Sanjay suffered from teeth problems, and by the age of fifty, he practically lost all his teeth, and it was difficult for him to adjust the false removable dentures, so he wanted to go for a full mouth implant. He needed at least ten implants, and he was suffering from a suppressed fear of how he would face the public and his students with a toothless mouth. The surgeon assured him that he would do some arrangements by providing Sanjay with some false caps.

Still, Sanjay's inner mind was preoccupied, and he used to think of his teeth all the time. The result was heavy nausea without vomiting. The bout of nausea used to be so severe that his eyes used to be protruded and his face used to be red. Immediately, he needed something to chew like a biscuit or cookie. Susan was fed up with Sanjay. Sanjay's day used to start with heavy nausea. No medicine was working. A psychiatrist diagnosed it as heavy acidity. He prescribed a PAN-D capsule, but it was of no use. Finally, after changing two psychiatrists, in the mid of 2012, Sanjay was brought to one of the best psychiatrists in Pune, Dr D M Patankar.

Dr Patankar talked to Sanjay for a long time and then talked to Susan and Andria separately. He prescribed Sanjay some other medicines for his anxiety disorder and wanted twelve weeks to allow the medicines to work. In the first eight weeks, no result was obtained. Susan was restless. But, after the eleventh week, a cumulative effect of the medicines started showing the result. The bouts of nausea decreased to a great extent, and along with psychiatric treatment, Sanjay went for his teeth implant programmes, too. He inherited this anxiety disorder from his mother who was also a patient of neurasthenia (weak nerves) and acute mental depression. Sanjay was oblivious by birth. He never read newspapers and did not have an interest in any of the incidents taking place in and around him.

Only Susan realised how Sanjay's radiant personality of college days underwent a radical transformation. Sanjay who used to celebrate life at every stage and age became totally dependent on high doses of psychiatric medicines.

Though Sanjay possessed strong animosity with his elder brother, during those spans of illness, he wanted to patch up all his relations, which were strained. He lost all hopes of survival. So, before death, he wanted all the relations to be normal. He came out of his veil of anger and ego and wanted to normalise all his relations with all his relatives and friends with whom he possessed a bad relation due to his fault or their faults. The anxiety disorder killed the wild sex of Sanjay. He used to suffer from morbid preoccupations, and Susan's only effort was to bring Sanjay back to normalcy.

Sanjay was capricious by birth. At different times different ideas flashed in his mind. One day in the evening, Sanjay decided to go and sit by the side of the river Ganga, which was hardly five hundred metres from their rented house. He was accompanied by Susan. Sanjay purchased a few egg devils and mutton cutlets from the famous shop of Luci Babu, and then, along with Susan, went to the banks of the Ganga and occupied a seat which was made for visitors. The evening was yet to envelop the whole atmosphere. The crepuscular darkness was accompanied by some boats, which were languidly sailing in the Ganga. After consuming all the snacks, Sanjay wanted to have some brewed tea, but it was not available there. So, he decided to move towards the main market of Serampore. There were two small restaurants, which were famous for tea, coffee and non-veg snacks.

43

Noticing the HIV Report of Her Husband

The year was 2011, and Sanjay was continuously sick for months. He had a fever and swollen lymph nodes under the left armpit. Susan consulted their house physician, but he could not help him. It was the month of March, and he had severe herpes at the back on the left side and suffered like a neglected street dog. Then, he changed the doctor, and the new doctor wanted to know about his sexual life. Sanjay openly confessed his habit of visiting red-light areas. The doctor asked about the date of his last visit to a prostitute. It was somewhere in the mid of December 2010. After listening to everything, the doctor immediately suggested an HIV test, and Sanjay went for it.

On the day of collecting the report, he was a bit apprehensive. In the evening, he visited the laboratory and got the report. It was just like a bolt from the blue. He was diagnosed with HIV infection. The new ordeal started. Susan was not aware of these things, and this new development. For Sanjay, it was practically impossible to face Susan. The report was a cause of great dismay to Sanjay. Sanjay could guess the vicissitudes.

He returned home and sat in a morose mood. After seeing him, Susan thought, like many other days, his mood must be off. Andria went to her friend's place. Susan came to the drawing room with tea for both of them. Along with tea, Susan had prepared homemade *paneer* (cottage cheese) *pakoda*. Even after seeing the mouth-watering *pakodas,* there was no reaction from him, which was very unnatural. Susan could sense something was wrong. Sanjay was looking at her in an apologetic way. She could see the glint in his eyes, and he was about to break down. Susan could not realise the reason behind this sullenness. For Sanjay, there was no other option than to tell her the fact because the term ludicrous was not applicable to Susan. Sanjay's voice was quivering, and he had a very deep guilty feeling, but he was in a state of incontrovertibility.

Sanjay did not even touch the plate of *pakoda,* and Susan, too, forgot to eat. Sanjay took out the report from his office bag and handed it over to Susan. Initially, it was indecipherable, but when Susan carefully read it, she lost the ground below her feet. She was shocked beyond imagination. Her cabbage-round face became red, and she was shell-shocked. For a couple of minutes, she was completely transfixed. Unfortunately, Susan was unaware of this side of Sanjay. After twenty-five years of marriage, she was yet to discover this new quality of her husband. At the same time, she was angry and sad. Already, she was perennially distracted, and now another negative parameter was added. Over the floor of the drawing-room, there was a mosaic of light and shadow. The friends who influenced Sanjay for developing this bad habit of visiting the red-light area were no longer present by his side. Fraternisation is a word which looks very sweet in a dictionary, but in real life when you are in deep water, most of your friends leave you. Sanjay wanted to say something to Susan. Susan could see the capped teeth of Sanjay and told him to keep mum. She did not want to listen to any excuse. Within a fraction of a second, she lost all respect for the person for whom she left her house for a lifetime. Susan's relationship with her mother was totally blocked, and the person whom she believed in so much cheated on her. What a great fortune of the daughter of a professor who was no more!

Susan left the drawing room and there was rattling within her mind. She became restless and exasperated. It was a great defeat for her. Even after being so beautiful, she could not prevent her husband from going to others. She was hurt deeply. She realised that due to HIV, Sanjay would have a squeamish nature, and it would be difficult for him to fight even a small infection. Susan thought that if the local Bengali community ever came to know about his HIV infection, both Sanjay and his whole family would permanently be ostracised by the Bengali community. For this heinous act of Sanjay, there was a demeaning attitude within Susan's mind.

Only one shadow remained to darken her mind, and that was nothing but the future of the family.

There is a famous Bengali adage, '*Jekhane abhaga jai, sagar sukaye jai*' (wherever an unlucky person goes even the ocean dries up). Sanjay was that *abhaga* (unlucky person) for Susan.

44

She Is Also Detected with HIV

The episode was not over only with the detection of Sanjay's HIV. In those days, Susan was going through her menopause. For that, whenever they had sex, it was unprotected. So, fear fermented in the mind of both. Susan was already prepared to face the consequences of her worthless and insane scholar-husband. She would have preferred a normal-behaved clerk than this insane professor. Sanjay's all activities were very bizarre. Still, the whole matter seemed to be incredulous to Susan, but it was the fact, and therefore, she had to accept it.

Being angry, Susan left for Kolkata and checked-in at a moderate hotel. Andria was with Sanjay in Pune. Susan, too, went to a reputed lab and gave her blood sample. While returning, she embarked on a tram after many years. Right from childhood, Susan was fond of the tinkling bells of trams, but that day she was not in the mood to enjoy them. For trams, one good thing is that they have a dedicated track. Susan got a seat at the rear end of the tram, and from there, through the window, she was looking at the snarling traffic and jostling crowd of the city of joy — Kolkata. Susan still remembers the creaky stairs of the old building where the laboratory for collecting the blood sample was located.

She returned to the hotel by evening. A surge of anger choked her voice, and after some time, she found that she was sobbing silently. She looked at the mirror hung on the wall. The kohl used by her was smudged below her eyes. She was fond of makeup. Even in that worst mental condition, she had basic make-up before giving a public appearance. She was looking at her face in the mirror and was thinking of the last twenty-five years of her married life. She did not get anything except Andria. On the contrary, she was converted into an unpaid domestic worker right from day one. Due to depression and stress, her eyes were crinkled.

The report had to be collected. On the day of collecting the report, Susan started early. A beggar was sitting at one corner of the building in which the lab was located. The beggar had two plastic bottles, a ragged tennis ball and a packet of biscuits with him. The beggar, too, was insane. In her mind, Susan compared Sanjay with the beggar. There was not much difference, except for qualification. On the contrary, the beggar had a plus point that he did not have a family.

Susan collected the report, opened it and, seeing the second line, she lost the ground from under her feet. Sanjay could not give her a comfortable living, could not give her a single vacation, could not give her one week of joyful life, but very successfully presented her with HIV. That is why, truth is stranger than fiction.

45

Series of Treatments and Survival without Any Hope

Before going for treatment for HIV, Susan decided to have a clear idea about HIV, and after frantic research, she prepared a brief article, which is given below.

There are two types of HIV. One is HIV-1, and the second one is HIV-2. The full form of HIV is "Human Immunodeficiency Virus". 95% of patients are affected with Type 1. HIV-1 virus destroys CD 4 cells, which results in damage to the immune system. These cells are responsible for fighting infections in our bodies. So, the person who is infected with HIV-1 is left with a poor immune system that may lead to full-blown AIDS (Acquired Immune Deficiency Syndrome) in future. There are a few symptoms of an HIV-infected person. A few of them are sore throat, headache, swollen lymph nodes, aching muscles, fever and red rashes on the skin, mainly below the neck. One or more symptoms may be present.

There are many sources of HIV, e.g., unprotected sex with an HIV-affected person, blood transfusion and tattooing. When the body fluid of an HIV-infected person comes in contact with the mucous membranes of an uninfected person, then there is a high chance of HIV infection. But, if the carrier of HIV is under regular treatment, in that case, the infection to the partner may not take place. But, once HIV is detected, there is no chance of zeroing it.

There are cases where both partners have HIV. Still, they must not have unprotected sex. Because all HIV patients do not carry the same strain. For two HIV patients, the strain of the virus may be different. Due to unprotected sex, a patient may switch over from a single strain to multiple strains, and in that case, the treatment becomes difficult, and the whole regimen becomes complicated. There are various kinds of strains of HIV. Two different people with HIV may carry two different strains. If a person carries multiple strains, then the chance of spreading HIV increases. The viral load increases and the other parts of the body may become the victim of HIV.

In the early 1990s, the treatment of HIV was really difficult, but in the last three decades there has been a significant amount of research on HIV and AIDS, and nowadays, the treatment has become more streamlined.

There are various conditions, which need to be inspected before treating a patient with HIV. Depending on the health condition of the patient, the doctor prescribes one to four tablets daily. And, in many cases, more than one medicine is combined into a single tablet or capsule. The most significant part is a quick diagnosis and immediate start of the treatment.

The treatment for HIV is 'antiretroviral treatment'. There must not be a delay in treatment, and the patient must take the medicines at the same time regularly. Skipping any dose of medicine is not at all recommended. Skipping the dose will lead to the enhancement of the viral load and lowering of immunity. Systematic treatment will help the patient and prevent the spreading of the virus to other parts of the body and the attack of full-blown AIDS. Systematic treatment and sincerity of the patient enhance their immunity and the chance of spreading an infection reduces.

There are NABL, ISO and CAP-certified laboratories, which give very accurate reports, and the sample is collected by a skilled phlebotomist. There is some window period for testing HIV. If one has unprotected sex with an HIV-infected person, then one is not immediately tested positive. It needs some time for the infection to be reflected, and that time is called the 'window period.'

There is a PCR RNA test. This test looks for viral RNA and is independent of antibodies. If one decides to go for this test, one needs to repeat the HIV Duo combo (p-24 antigen/antibodies screening) after 28 days of suspected exposure. The window period for p-24 antigen is very small.

Nowadays, the most sophisticated HIV tests are able to detect HIV after four weeks of the patient's exposure to HIV. An antigen/antibody test conducted by a laboratory on blood from a vein can usually detect HIV infection after 18 to 45 days of exposure to an HIV-affected partner. HIV result has to be confirmed with a Western Blot test. An antibody-antigen blood test checks for levels of both HIV antibodies along with p-24 antigen. The p-24 antigen test can detect p-24 protein on average after 10 to 14 days after exposure to HIV. One significant drawback of this test is that levels of the p-24 protein peak at around three to four weeks after exposure to HIV and are usually not detectable after five to six weeks.

Fourth-generation tests are accurate 14 days after exposure because this is when the p-24 antigen becomes high enough to be measured; effectively reducing the window period by an average of 14 days. That means the window period reduces from 28 to 14 days. A negative result at 28 days is good news, but it does not indicate that the patient is free from HIV. Once a person is infected with HIV, for the rest of his life, they will be infected with HIV. Only by treatment, the viral load will be reduced, and the main aim of the treatment will be to keep the patient far from full-blown AIDS.

Fourth-generation tests look for HIV antibodies, and it is something called p-24 antigens. The p-24 antigens are part of HIV itself. In the first few weeks after infection, a patient does have a lot of p-24 antigens in his blood sample. Fourth-generation tests are reliable enough to detect HIV from one month after another has been infected. Mainly, the treatment lowers the progress of the virus in the patient's body. HIV is a special type of virus, and it is called a retrovirus, and that's why the treatment of HIV is known as Antiretroviral Therapy (ART). ART reduces the viral load in the body fluid of the patient, and it also reduces the chance of transmitting HIV to others. Generally, three to four drugs are used. They may be used separately or in combination. It all depends upon the patient's physical condition, the level of viral load and other medications, which the patient has.

There is the availability of a combination of more than one drug in a single pill. If a patient does not respond to the treatment, then the line of treatment is changed because, for different patients, different combinations of drugs are prescribed based on several conditions. Only the treatment must be started at the earliest.

There are a few side effects of ART, and generally, they are nausea, vomiting, diarrhoea, dry mouth, headache, difficulty in sleeping, dizziness, rash, pain and fatigue. Every patient with HIV is supposed to take medicines as per the advice of their physician to keep the viral load minimum and the CD 4 cell count high. If a patient takes the treatment sincerely, it helps them from many angles.

i) *The viral load in their body becomes minimum*

ii) *Chance of infecting others reduces*

iii) *Chance of full-blown AIDS is practically zeroed*

iv) *The immune system becomes stronger, and the patient can fight other diseases.*

Due to effective medication and the sincerity of the patient, even the viral load can be undetectable, and the chance of infecting others becomes quite minimum. But, sometimes, the virus changes its form, which means it mutates and stops responding to a particular class of medicine. In that case, the combination of drugs needs to be changed. This phenomenon is known as drug resistance. This drug resistance is a big challenge to the treatment of HIV. HIV attacks the immune system and destroys 'T' cells, which are nothing but white blood cells that fight several kinds of infections.

After the virus attacks 'T' cells, it replicates them. Then, the cells burst open. They release innumerable viral cells, and those cells go on to attack other cells in the body. This particular phenomenon destroys the immune system completely and the patient cannot even fight the slightest infection, and it prevents the body from functioning well. The drug prescribed by the doctor depends on several factors, e.g., the person's viral load, the 'T' cell count of the patient, the severity of the case, different strains of HIV (single or multiple), the extent of the spreading of HIV and other health issues of the patient. If the patient suffers from other diseases, then the doctor has to see what medicines the patient is taking and if there is any reaction between the medicines already in use along with ART. Simply, there must not be any reaction between ART and the other drugs taken by the patient. When more than one drug is combined in a single pill, that is called a Single-Tablet Regimen (STR). One advantage of taking more than one antiretroviral drug is that it prevents resistance to the drug.

A patient may be given two to four individual antiretroviral drugs or they may be prescribed a single combination drug in, what is sometimes known as an integrase inhibitor. Integrase is a viral enzyme that HIV uses to infect 'T' cells by putting HIV DNA into the human DNA. HIV requires a host 'T' cell to make copies of itself. Fusion inhibitors block the virus from entering a host 'T' cell. This prevents the virus from replicating itself. All entry inhibitors work by blocking the virus from entering healthy 'T' cells. STR is generally used to treat people who've never taken HIV medications before.

One needs to focus on seven factors to know how to live with HIV. They are ART, its side effects, healthcare visits, outlook and life expectancy, diet and exercise, relationships, support and takeaway. The medication taken for HIV is often known as a treatment regimen. For ART, the medical history of the patient is mandatory. Initially, a patient is supposed to visit his doctor quarterly so that the doctor can monitor the progress of the treatment. Sometimes, even more frequent visits are required at the start of the treatment. With time, viral load decreases, and the doctor gets a fair idea about the line of treatment. The treatment reaches a particular level where it is fixed, and there becomes a good tuning among the doctor, patient and the line of treatment. After that, one annual visit is more than enough. But, consistency in the treatment is much essential.

The patients who started ART after 2008 are much luckier than those who started the treatment in the early nineties. Because there is significant research in this field, and with each passing month, new development is there. Nowadays, the average life expectancy of an HIV-infected patient is very close to the life expectancy of a person who is HIV-negative. If one sticks to ART sincerely, one will survive long and certainly not die of AIDS. Maintaining a healthy diet and regular exercise boost the immune system of the patient. Plenty of fruits are recommended, and the patient must consume a minimum amount of oil and fat. At least two and a half hours of exercise (e.g. walking, swimming and cycling) is recommended per week.

Last but not least, in this era of social media, there are many NGOs working with HIV-infected patients, and there are plenty of groups on social media. A patient should join these groups and interact with the members of the group. There is nothing to be ashamed of. If a patient feels uncomfortable with a particular group, they need the help of a physician so that they can get a local counselling service. One inseparable part of HIV is depression. If required, the patient must consult a psychiatrist to get rid of depression and anxiety.

Actually, after knowing about Sanjay's and her HIV reports, Susan became irritated beyond limits. Her whole life became shoddy. She was intensely exasperated. Since it was related to HIV, she had to hide it from society. If it would have been a heart attack or some other serious disease, there would have been a powerful current of sympathy, but in this case, it was not possible. Because HIV is nothing but a social taboo. Everything happened due to Sanjay's obsessive and self-destructive passion. He was least bothered. He had a bohemian lifestyle and never bothered with any responsibility whether it was Andria's education or Susan's health. He was a typically selfish and depressed person. He used to enjoy drug-induced sleep after consuming 20 mg of Diazepam. Susan became extremely depressed after this outbreak of HIV.

One morning, after sending Andria to college, she left for Pune and went to the zoo at Katraj. She sat below a tree, which had a spiny trunk. Children from a local school also visited the zoo on the same day. They brought pyramids of cherries and mounds of grapes. Susan was fond of cherries and grapes, but certainly, she could not have them from those children.

Most of the time, she was sitting below the tree and was thinking of ART and the lifetime treatment. Already, she was overloaded, and this HIV incident became an added headache for the rest of her life. There was no question of suicide. Andria was to be looked after for which she had to survive. She was looking at the young and relatively low-paid teachers who accompanied the children. They were busy with sundry gossip, and Susan was feeling those moments in a state of semi-trance.

Time fled away. The evening started grasping the whole atmosphere. The crowd in the zoo started thinning, and the closing hour of the zoo was nearby. Susan was talking to herself. She realised that strength would not come from physical capacity but from an indomitable will. So, this willpower helped her to stand on her feet. It was around 6:00 pm. The twilight was scattered everywhere.

Susan slowly started walking to the main gate of the zoo. She was supposed to reach the bus stop near Bharati Vidyapeeth to get a Yerawada-bound bus. Suddenly, she saw a person selling gas balloons. She approached him and purchased half a dozen balloons and immediately released them. People in and around her were awestruck. But, she was calm and composed. In this life, she was jailed, but after releasing the balloons, she felt the taste of independence and the taste of being free from the bondage of family responsibilities. The bunch of balloons started occupying higher and higher coordinates in the blue sky, and Susan started walking slowly to the bus stop.

46

Atmosphere of a Government-Run Hospital

Poverty shows you many things, and one of the worst things you can see in your bad days is a government-run hospital in India. It is nothing but hell. Even hell is better than a government hospital in India. For a series of treatments, both Sanjay and Susan had to depend on the government-run hospital. There is stupendous poverty, and all those poor people depend on the government hospital of the town.

Due to a high variation in mood, Sanjay used to be exasperated whenever he visited the hospital for his treatment, and it was a routine affair. After periodic intervals, both Sanjay and Susan had to visit the hospital for HIV treatment. Medicines used to create an insipid taste in their mouth. But, they did not have any choice. Medicine had to be taken for the sake of survival. Most of the doctors were escapists, and they used to give less than fifty per cent of their duty time to patients. Most of the work was tackled by the junior resident doctors. Sanjay used to hate this sordidness of the senior doctors. Due to the heavy rush, they had to be in the queue right from the wee hours before sunrise. From distant villages, people with HIV used to visit the town hospital because, in those villages, there was no facility for the treatment of HIV-infected patients. Susan used to count the silhouette of those poor and uneducated people who were victims of HIV because of their uncontrolled and unsafe sex with multiple partners. There were many young housewives who became victims of HIV just like Susan for no fault of their own, and those poor ladies used to shudder in OPD (outpatient department) due to the fear of injection.

The hospital was big but ill-maintained. People used to come there with aching frustration, and there was not even ample place to sit. So, patients used to occupy *paan*-stained staircases. There were many beggars in and around the hospital. Susan still remembers a beggar who was known as a crawling beggar by the people since he was not able to walk. All the echoing corridors were full of garbage, and there was no periodic cleaning. The total atmosphere was very unhygienic. Susan still recalls the woebegone expressions of the doctors in the OPD.

There was a lady doctor, and she was quite senior. Susan asked her a question, and instead of answering, she just stared at Susan. Her eyes were bigger than any normal eyes. Susan could not forget that Bharatanatyam-style glare of that lady doctor.

The patients were like wilting leaves. They were born to die prematurely due to the lack of treatment and unavailability of medicines in time. The corridors were inadequately illuminated. Even the lights were not changed from time to time. There was a hospital superintendent. He was the senior-most doctor, but he knew everything apart from medical science. He was more interested in purchasing than treating, and he was an invincible figure. For common patients, he was not even approachable.

All the walls were splotched maroon with *paan* spittle. Dead bodies used to lie unattended below the staircase. Susan had seen a young girl whose father passed away due to pneumonia, and she could remember the tears of that teenage girl, which welled up in her hazel eyes. She was gasping and hitching between sobs.

In the OPD, clerks used to prepare case papers of patients on computers, but only one computer was in operation. So, many patients and only one computer! Everywhere there was a similar mess. The clerk's fingers used to move furiously over the keyboard, and he was ill-tempered due to the huge quantum of work. An adequate number of staff members was not there. Posts which were vacant were not filled in time. In any government-run hospital, you will always find a certain cross-section of staff and doctors on leave because they know that nothing will happen. This was nothing but a misuse of the security of the service in government sectors.

Once Sanjay and Susan visited together. After seven hours, when they came out of the hospital, Sanjay looked very bleak due to fatigue and lack of food since morning. Sweat beads popped on his forehead. For his bohemian and perverted life style, both of them had to see these days, otherwise, the question of visiting the department, which deals with HIV and AIDS would not have been there. This world is sad, bad and mad. If you make a mistake, there is no excuse for the same. You need to pay the befitting price for your mistake. Free people do not know the value of freedom because anything received free of cost is the least cared for. So, Sanjay did not realise the consequences of his bohemian and voluptuous life style.

When Susan and Sanjay were stepping out of the Department of AIDS and HIV, they found a beggar who was tearing a bread loaf like a famished man, and a wild dog was looking at it. Susan could never forget this scene, which was even worse than hell. Susan's whole life can be compared to an under-salted dish. She did not have an opportunity to enjoy even a single day off in her life. Generally, parents face problems with children. But here, from Andria's side, she never faced any problem. Sanjay alone was enough to ruin her life.

47

Two Kinds of HIV Patients

There are two kinds of HIV patients. The first group is the main culprit. They get infected by their partners for their voluptuous attitude and unsafe sex. Even prostitutes are aware of AIDS, but these blunt people are not ready to listen to the advice. There is a big group of people who enjoy unprotected and unsafe sex with multiple partners, and obviously, Sanjay was one of them. Sanjay inculcated this nuisance habit of visiting red-light areas right from his NIT days, and the ultimate result was being infected by HIV.

But, the second group is the most unfortunate, in which they get infected for no fault of theirs. They just believe their better half and that is their crime. Obviously, Susan was one of them. Even in her wildest dream, Susan could never imagine the extent to which Sanjay could go. There are lakhs of innocent ladies in this world who are infected by HIV just because of their life partners. Even there are lakhs of children who are infected by HIV by birth.

People say education and awareness are required. Was Sanjay uneducated? If a post-graduate from a prestigious institute makes this kind of mistake then where would uneducated truck drivers go? Sex is a need of human beings which is accepted and one can't disagree, but at the same time, one is supposed to take proper care to be on the safer side. Sexually transmitted diseases like syphilis can also be cured, but for HIV infection, there is no hope. They are always in a fingers-crossed condition, and at any moment, the HIV infection can be converted into full-blown AIDS, provided there is irregularity and inconsistency in the treatment. It may take two years or twenty years. So, it is brutal waiting, and the patient is always under an underlying threat. For the second group of patients, in spite of having a monogamous relationship, they are infected with HIV only because of their voluptuous husbands.

48

Treatment by the Doctors and Their Behaviour

The treatment by the doctors was routine, but their behaviour with patients was not at all good. They were a heartless community. They seldom bothered about the patients who sought their help for their HIV state of health. For most of the doctors, it was their routine job, and they were least bothered because they had no attachment to the patients.

The era has changed. Nowadays, doctors do not have attachments with the patients, and teachers do not have any emotional view point for their students. Both groups are running after money. Teaching and medicine are the two most sacred professions. But, in today's scenario, both are controlled by those who do not even deserve to be doctors and teachers. These two professions are highly dependent on emotional values. Without emotions, no one can flourish in these two professions. But, in this country, neither the professionals bother about patients and students nor the government bothers about them. The government is cruel. If you are a good doctor or a teacher without any political backup, you will be transferred to an odd place. On the contrary, doctors and teachers with good political connections are always posted in prime cities of the state. This is India where merit and talent are considered at the last.

Frivolity is an integral part of the whole medical profession nowadays. I found the superintendent of a government-run hospital sitting on bolsters comfortably and working at the slowest possible speed. The actual lunch hour is from 1:00 to 1:30 pm. However, these kinds of doctors are rarely seen after lunch hour. I personally found doctors of government-run hospitals pursuing private practice during their duty hours. But, who will rectify this egocentric community? It is easy to tackle hundreds of idiots, but it is extremely difficult to tackle ten qualified and intelligent people. In the medical profession, many things are done in a clandestine way. Common people cannot even reach there. Due to the profession, doctors do have the liberty to pursue cases in a clandestine way. Even ministers cannot intervene in this profession.

Once, Sanjay visited the hospital in the afternoon. He noticed the eerie atmosphere of the hospital. Whenever he visited the hospital, due to the foul smell, he used to suffer from anorexia for two to three days. He still remembers the plastered smile of the doctor who used to treat him along with other patients. In the evening, when he stepped out of the hospital, he witnessed the westward crawl of the sun. He was terminally ill, but his peripheral vision was not blocked. He sensed the total atmosphere of the hospital.

49

Overall Ambience of the Hospital Where the HIV People Go for the Treatment

The overall ambience of the hospital where HIV-infected people went for treatment was simply horrible. The treatment was shoddy. The plight situation was seen everywhere. Namby-pamby sentiments of the supporting staff were of no use. There were ward boys who did not discharge duties well and played with their key rings and mobile phones by sitting in one corner of the room. Jiggling their key ring was their hobby. Various kinds of insects were seen. One would often find uncared patients grimacing in excruciating pain, but they were not attended to for the lack of medical professionals.

Everywhere dirt and used syringes of injections were seen, and the sight of ravens was a common visual, which could be compared to a scavenger. Your flight of imagination would totally be ceased if you were put in this kind of atmosphere. You could see the level of illiteracy and grinding poverty from close quarters. People waited for their turn by sitting on tattered rags, and in the summer season, they were drenched with sweat because there was not adequate shade for people to wait in.

In one corner, you would find used crepe bandages and used bloody sanitary napkins, and they were eaten by giant and ferocious stray dogs. Many times, Susan had qualms, but there was no one who could clear her doubts. The doctors were not even ready to speak. For them, these patients were just like criminals. At the end of the day, all the energy used to ooze out and Sanjay used to suffer from peevishness.

Truly speaking, in a subcontinent and developing country like India, the complete medical sector is dominated by private hospitals. So, when a person is detected with HIV, that itself becomes the beginning of the end.

Whenever Sanjay used to visit OPD, he would eyeball the crowd and every time he would find that except for him, all were non-qualified labour class or driver class.

The doctors used to prescribe some medicine and always all the medicine would not be available in the hospital medical store. So, he had to purchase it from the nearby drug store. The printer of the drug store used to churn out bills once purchasing was over.

Once, Sanjay returned from the hospital. Susan was not in the house, and Andria went to school. That day, Sanjay was on leave for his appointment with the doctor. As a habitual bibliomaniac, he was flipping through some books in his library. Suddenly within one book, he found a rose. The petals were dry and detached, and he vividly remembered the initial days of their relationship. The same rose was presented by him to Susan. He was submerged in his past and remembered many things.

50

Suppressed and Permanent Fear of AIDS

All HIV-infected patients suffer from a suppressed and permanent fear of full-blown AIDS. In spite of taking the required medicine, no one can guarantee that full-blown AIDS won't be there. They suffer from fossilised depression. And, most HIV-infected patients are treated with antidepressants too. The taste of the medicine leads to acridness. There are several side effects. All HIV-infected patients come under the sphere of influence of the fear of AIDS. They lose their mental balance, and for most of them, death used to hover over their head. They did not have a mindset to enjoy the beauty and serenity of a topaz blue sky. Because due to fear of AIDS, their whole mind used to be preoccupied. And, you know the fear of suffering is worse than the suffering itself.

Susan was mentally very strong, but she was also affected by the same virus. Sanjay used to go and have routine treatment, but Susan used to interact with other patients and their family members. She used to get a lot of input. Mainly poor people used to visit the government hospital.

Even though there was a rich cross-section having HIV infection, they would never give a public appearance in a government-run hospital. For them, visiting a government-run hospital was below their dignity. The medical sector and set up in India is extremely poor. Whereas, in Great Britain, most things are free. They can do it for two reasons. Their medical set up is not controlled by politicians, and there is practically zero corruption. Apart from that their population is much less.

On the contrary, in India, in most of the government sectors, you will find more than one piece of equipment, which is never used and not even commissioned. The party is supposed to get ninety per cent of the payment after the delivery of goods and ten per cent payment is released after successful commissioning. The parties are so clever that in that, ninety per cent, they make a considerable profit, and they do not even turn up for the commissioning and balance payment. The authority gives them one after another letter as reminders. The party ignores those letters. After a few years, the concerned person is transferred, the reminder is closed forever, and the equipment is not even unpacked. It is kept as it is. I saw it with my own eyes in a very reputable college in India. After ten years, the brand-new equipment is written off. Why does it happen? It happens only due to the indifference of the higher authority and unnecessary political intervention of the local politicians and MLAs.

The same is the case with hospitals. Government hospitals receive the maximum amount of grants, but they are misused. No one takes care of manuals. There are machines of millions of rupees, but small spare parts, having a cost of a few thousand rupees, are not supplied. Only for the want of that small spare part, the whole equipment stays unused for years together. Initially, a few follow-ups are taken, and after that, the machine or the equipment is kept idle in an unused condition. In this way, equipment of crores of rupees is rusted because of lack of follow-up and indifference of the higher authority. Till the purchase procedure is completed, the higher authority is much interested and involved, but once the purchasing is done and payment is released, the higher authority shows practically zero interest. The readers are requested to read between the lines.

51

Blood Test Report of Her Daughter

Once, Andria suffered from a high fever, and it did not subside for ten days in spite of different combinations of antibiotics. Susan became nervous, and she thought she must go for Andria's blood test to know whether she was also infected or not. Though the chance of Andria getting infected by HIV was very slim because Andria was born in 1991, and Sanjay was detected with HIV in 2011. She went for an RNA PCR test. Due to Andria's agony, Susan's mental climate was very disturbed.

After the test, Susan came out with Andria. It was summer noon; the whole city was burning, and the temperature was more than 43 degrees Celsius. Andria's temperature subsided, but still, she was not free from the grip of the fever. Susan was ravenously hungry. She went to a local restaurant and had a *masala dosa* and fruit juice. Andria did not have anything except fruit juice.

After a few days, Susan got Andria's report, and the result was negative. A negative report was expected. The pathology clinic was famous for its pitch-perfect report. They returned home by early afternoon. Sanjay was yet to come. Due to her fever, Andria was divorced from her regular study schedule. She was missing her college lectures due to this prolonged fever. But, Andria was not lazy like her father. For her, right from her initial childhood, Susan was a role model. After coming home, Andria started arranging her books and notebooks in the niche of her study room. When Andria was arranging her books and notebooks, Susan was ruminating and she was totally lost in thoughts. Probably she was holding the post-mortem of the past.

In their decorated drawing room, the ceiling fan was slicing the air, but Susan reduced the speed upon observing the feverish glitter in Andria's eyes. After a few minutes, Sanjay returned from college, and luckily, he was in a good mood after many days. He immediately put on the television and started flipping through various Bengali channels. He was mainly interested in Bengali news. But, after half an hour, the power went off.

Susan had all the household chores to do. She pulled her hair back to tie them with a rubber band. She started preparing some evening snacks. Still, she retained her beauty in spite of all odds. Sanjay cut through the furniture of the drawing room and came to the kitchen and stood by her. It was almost impossible for Sanjay to keep his eyes off her.

52

Her Daughter Was Her Only Inspiration

If one compared Susan's life with a desert, then Andria could be compared with an oasis. After Sanjay's downfall, Susan diverted her complete attention towards Andria and tried to nurture and groom her in the best possible way. First, she taught Andria how to stoop in front of seniors and elders as a mark of respect because she realised that, in life, humbleness was more important than scholasticism. Susan was well known for her orthodoxy and Puritanism.

She was mainly concentrating on Andria's career, and there was a sea of speculation. From that sea, she had to choose the correct profession. By observing Andria's nature, Susan ruled out the medical profession right in the beginning, and in high school, she could not develop an interest in the subject of Physics, especially the chapter on Electricity. Then Susan decided to make the choice narrower. She excluded all circuit branches, e.g., electrical, instrumentation, computer, IT and E&TC.

After a series of meetings, both the mother and daughter came to the conclusion that after the twelfth standard, Andria would opt for mechanical engineering. It was a tough life. Sanjay's salary was minimal. Most of the time, they used to depend on credit cards and other sources of loans. For Andria's career, the whole family deprived themselves of small pleasures — no movies, no popcorn, no new *chappal* or dress and no restaurants. Once in a blue moon, Susan used to purchase *samosas* (an Indian snack item) from a local shop, and after eating all *samosas,* one of them would pick up a broom to clean the *samosa* crumbs.

Andria did not have any private tutor, and she never went to any tuition for any of the subjects. Right from nursery to the tenth standard, she was taught by her mother only. Truly speaking, Andria's career can be compared to a garden, and Susan can be compared to the gardener. When we see a garden, we do not even ask who the gardener is, but we always forget that without a devoted gardener, none of the gardens of this world can be beautiful. The role of a gardener is just like sugar in tea. It is taken for granted. If you do not add it, then you realise the value of sugar. Andria was the only inspiration for Susan, and Susan was totally obsessed with the proper development and design of Andria's career. As a mother, she did that, and it was a challenge for her.

53

Some Good and Bad Friends of Her Husband

The selection of true friends is a very big art, and Sanjay did not have mastery over this art. He was qualified, but due to his emotional and sentimental nature, he failed to recognise good and bad people. Right from his college days, he was in bad company, and such a company is like a catalyst. People say if you become strong, no one can influence you, but in this world, hardly one per cent of people are that strong. Any common person is carried away and gets influenced by friends very easily. Right from smoking and boozing to visiting prostitutes, everything was introduced to Sanjay by his friends. But, those friends were professional and cunning. They knew where to put a full stop, but Sanjay could not control himself. Whether it was smoking, boozing or visiting prostitutes, in each sector, he went to the extreme level. Generally, Sanjay was not a gregarious person. Susan possessed a judgmental view of Sanjay's friend circle, and she was unhappy with most of them. They were highly qualified, but within most of them, a debauch was hidden. Because a lady can scan the character of a man just by looking at him.

One of his very good friends was Abir. He used to stay on the other side of the railway track at Serampore. His house was located at the rear end of a deserted alley. Even Sanjay did not know how many yesterdays of his life were buried in Abir's house.

Sanjay had a habit of talking too much with his friends over the phone after the arrival of mobile phones, and at that time, it was too costly. Sanjay used to put one's line on hold and call another person. He had a good network of friends. But, all of them were not good. Whenever a person becomes much emotional, sentimental and sensitive, he is carried away more easily. The influence of a mind over another mind is the biggest influence in human relationships. Exactly, this influence of bad friends sent Sanjay to dogs.

For the overall degradation of Sanjay's character, his few friends were very much responsible. They were cunning. In proper time, they set back gear and saved themselves, but they did not care for Sanjay. They were not addicted, but Sanjay became addicted to alcohol and prostitution, which ruined his mental and physical health. In the mental plane, he was already a chronic patient of morbid melancholy, and due to the consumption of a huge amount of alcohol, those psychiatric medicines failed to produce desired results, and in the physical plane, due to unprotected and unsafe sex with multiple partners, he became a victim of HIV. What more damage do you expect? He was ruined from all points of view, and the saddest part was that he was ruined by his choice, but he ruined Susan's life and even Andria's life partially.

54

Changing the Focus from Husband Towards Daughter

When Susan realised that Sanjay was a gone case, she diverted her complete attention to the development and design of Andria's academic-cum-professional career. Sanjay had one good habit. Although he never took any pain for Andria's career, at the same time, he never intervened in Susan's working style for Andria's career. He was totally indifferent, selfish and depressed. Sanjay had cataclysmic power like camphor, but due to the series of wrong decisions and wrong acts, his suppressed talent remained unexplored. Susan shepherded Andria's career in the perfect direction as Susan was a very effective manager.

Sanjay did not have the capacity to befriend others, but Andria got this art, and she was very popular among her friend circle. Susan had given Andria only a pointed message, and the message was nothing but exploring a career totally and not marrying before being financially stable. Andria's presence itself was a stress buster for Susan. Sanjay used to build stress and Andria used to neutralise that.

In spite of all odds, Susan and Andria both were working very hard. All the obstacles in their road could be compared to stumbling blocks. A stone on the path can either be a stopping stone, hindering the path; or it can be a stepping stone, helping you go higher on the path. The stone is the same, but how you use it is the question. It is just like 6 and 9.

Susan was overworking, and there was no room in her heart for anyone else except Sanjay and Andria. Despite all the tortures of Sanjay, in the deepest core of her mind, there was a fountain of love for him. But, her main attention was shifted to Andria just like a sunflower turning toward the Sun.

Susan taught Andria that if she wanted to live richly, she had to live here and now; not a single moment was to be lost. Susan was very disciplined, and by the influence of her mother, Andria, too, became disciplined. Both of them used to get up at 7:00 am at the bleep of the alarm clock.

Susan taught Andria one more thing and that was to start any big project very slowly. Because she knew that any big thing that was started slowly, gradually gained momentum. A river begins in the high mountain as a very small stream, lonely and far away, but it gathers momentum and turns into a huge river with the passage of time. So, one must begin with a little.

The same was the case with Andria. She used to start all her projects and assignments very slowly, but there used to be a hundred per cent consistency. It is easy to walk five kilometres a day, but it is difficult to walk five hundred metres daily for the whole year. For the first act, you want a temporary urge for only one day, but for regular walking, you need constant self-motivation throughout the year. Susan was a mother who taught Andria the true meaning of self-discipline.

55

Duty of a Mother

Susan was a lady with old doctrines, but at the same time, she was logical enough to accept the generation gap. Regarding Andria, Susan was very assiduous. Susan knew the art of prioritising the work to be done.

Susan was an expert cook, and she used to train Andria in cooking to become independent. Susan used to say that every person must know two things, the first one is cooking, and the second one is driving. Without knowing these two things, one is bound to depend on others, and one has to compromise one's own comfort, health and privacy. Susan was considered a connoisseur by others for her great sense of taste as far as food was concerned. Susan always used to be careful about the repository, and from time to time, she used to take review the things stored in the inventory of her kitchen.

Many times, due to overwork and health issues Susan used to suffer from pounding headaches. She used to apply some balm and then watch the television on mute. The television used to be muted to keep the serenity, which was needed for Andria's study. Susan never forced Andria to study, and she never gave any task for any subject. She just wanted her daughter to accept her textbooks as storybooks, and the basic teaching of Susan was converting one's work into one's play. If that is done, then your work becomes your hobby, and you never feel that you are working or you are overburdened. Every student possesses a huge amount of suppressed potential, but they need a proper mentor who knows how to tap the springs of suppressed strength. Susan was that mentor in Andria's life who knew how to awaken the hidden spark within her daughter. Susan used to recharge Andria's battery and awaken her from her deep slumber. It was a continuous process. Motivation cannot be a process of only one day. If a person is motivated for months together, a time comes when he becomes self-motivated.

Susan taught Andria many things, and two of them were honesty and sportsman spirit. As per Susan's statement, it is always better to be defeated by honesty than to win by unfair means. Susan was much attached to Andria, so she could read her mind and needs. For the sixth sense, one does not require a brain; one needs only common sense.

Susan always had given maximum stress on concept building. For example, for swimming the depth of water does not matter. It can be 10 feet or 10000 feet. It does not matter because you are always swimming at the surface. Knowing swimming is the prime important thing. Susan never expressed her love for Andria publicly as she never believed in showing off. On the periphery, there was an attachment, and at the centre, love was there. The first requirement of real love is to allow absolute and unconditional freedom to the other. Susan had given it to her daughter.

Susan used to think of her whole life, which could be compared to swimming against the current. Due to the hectic work of the whole day, she never had any kind of rest. Only in the time of dusk, she would be free for two hours. She used to sit on the window sill of her bedroom and see the setting sun moving through the sky, ready to die punctually before the crepuscular darkness enveloped the atmosphere.

56

Demolition of the Bedroom Furniture after Consuming Alcohol and Smashing the Piano Due to Rage by Sanjay

Sanjay was widely defamed for his aberration. The whole family suffered beyond measure because of Sanjay's bipolar disorder. Though he used to take regular medicine under the observation of the best psychiatrist in Pune, due to regular consumption of alcohol, those medicines failed to give the desired results. Anger was in his genealogy. Truly speaking, anger is a symptom of a person who failed in life. How many times have you seen a successful person being angry? The root cause of anger is frustration, sadness and depression, and the root cause of these three attributes is none other than failure.

Both Susan and Andria used to be very scared when Sanjay used to be angry. The outside world did not bother about him, and he, too, knew that if he canalised his anger on the outside world, they would smash him. He picked up the old typewriter to throw at Susan. Once, he threw it, but Susan very quickly moved to the corner of the room, and she was saved by whiskers. Otherwise, she would have been injured beyond measure. Her skull could have been damaged and death was just an inch away from her. Once, Sanjay threw a stone at Susan, and immediately, she cringed and narrowly escaped. The easiest and soft targets were his wife and daughter. They were physically weak, and for that, it was very easy to torture them.

Both Susan and Andria used to be scared by his brandished condition. Their day-to-day life was totally tormented by Sanjay's torture. Both Susan and Andria used to sulk over the pathos and grief of their life. In her thirty-four years of married life, more than a hundred times, she was brutally assaulted by Sanjay. Still, she did not leave his company or complained to anyone. Due to his mental disorder, all the time, Susan used to excuse him. After a day or two, Sanjay used to realise his guilt, and every time, he begged for forgiveness, but that apology was of no use. It is Susan's sheer luck that, to date, she did not lose any of her body parts.

When Sanjay used to be aggressive, he used to lose total control over his mind, and he remained unstoppable. Once, after consuming a huge amount of alcohol, he started breaking the furniture, and at last, he broke the beautiful piano of Andria, which was gifted by himself on her last birthday. When he used to be angry, his only motto was to annihilate everything. He used to tear papers, throw books and smash tube lights. And, for the two ladies, it became impossible to prevent him from destroying household goods and furniture. The neighbours used to enjoy the drama.

Too much of anything is bad. In the same way, too much of a bibliophile nature of Sanjay was the root of all losses. He was a bibliophilic-cum-bibliomaniac right from his school days, and that became one of the prime reasons for his distance from society. Books are there to be read, but books are like an ocean. You must decide how far you want to go from the coastline. You cannot make the mid-sea your target.

Most of the time, when Sanjay used to assault Susan, she used to crouch to avoid the intensity of the assaults, but ultimately, she used to suffer torture beyond the tolerable limit. Andria was seldom attacked by Sanjay, but once she wanted to prevent her father from beating Susan, and she was mercilessly beaten up by her mentally ill father.

There was a very nice photograph of ballet dancers, which was purchased by Susan from one of the art galleries in Kolkata. Once, being angry, Sanjay smashed the photo frame, took out the photo and burnt it. His main aim was to give maximum pain to Susan, whereas Susan was the only person in the world who used to take maximum care of Sanjay 24X7. This is the speciality of any psychiatric patient across the globe. They love their caregivers most, and at the time of their mental derailment, the caregivers are tortured the most. Susan rarely lost her cool because she knew, for the sake of Andria's career, she had to be silent. She only wrote in her diary her experience in desperation, but there was no one to read it.

57

Husband Was Shifted to Mental Asylum

With each passing month, Sanjay's mental condition deteriorated beyond the limit, and it was becoming impossible to keep him at home. He used to light a candle and audaciously pour hot blobs of wax on his forehand. He used to murmur, and at the same time, he was the questioner and the answerer, too. He used to titter at periodic intervals. He was known for his sullen temperament. He was completely derailed from mainstream life.

As per the suggestion of his psychiatrist, he was shifted to the mental asylum. Though it became a black spot for the whole family, there was no other option for Susan. She realised that shifting her husband to mental asylum was a matter of great mortification for the whole family. The vehemence and rage of Sanjay crossed the limit, and Andria's career was severely affected by the odd and lunatic behaviour of her father. The atmosphere of the whole house was not worth living in. Only Susan and Andria knew how they passed every day under the trauma and assault of a mad family member who was supposed to be the sheet anchor of the family. Instead of being the sheet anchor, he became the biggest burden and liability for the whole family.

Susan's dreams became lopsided, but she did not distance herself from her willpower. Sanjay was not ready to go to the mental asylum. It was a Herculean task to take him to the asylum. The special squad came, and they practically chained him with rope and dragged him to the van. While controlling Sanjay, one of the staff members was unable to do his job properly. There were four people. Another person nudged him for drawing his attention. One of the staff members of the squad rolled the windows up to maintain privacy. Within no time, the news proliferated in society.

After his departure, both mother and daughter felt a sudden vacuum in the house. Andria was sobbing, and Susan was just steady with her commitments. After three days, Susan visited the asylum and went to meet Sanjay. The facade of the asylum was pale yellow. It was an age-old two-storied building. When Susan went near Sanjay's cell, she found him sitting in a morose condition at one corner of the cell, wearing a sky-blue-coloured uniform. When he saw Susan, he approached her, and from behind the iron bars, he spat on her and said, "You bastard. You planned and conspired with the doctor to send me into this hell."

Susan did not reply because there was no point in arguing with him. Sanjay was not in a position to accept any logic. He was never a gregarious person, and in the asylum, he was totally cut off from all other inmates.

If anyone sees the atmosphere of a mental asylum, they will totally lose faith in God and spirituality. Because, after seeing this hell, it becomes really difficult to believe in God and spirituality. Irritating cacophony was there throughout the atmosphere. Sanjay was in a totally delirious state of mind. He did not talk to Susan. Susan stood silently, and after the visiting hours, she left the place and came out of the hospital. At that time, Sanjay treated Susan as his biggest enemy, whereas Susan was the only person in the world who sustained Sanjay for decades through all conditions. Even for no fault of hers, only because of Sanjay, she was infected with HIV. This time due to the stringent advice of the psychiatrist, and for Andria's career, she had to take this bold step. Otherwise, one person was ruining three lives. While leaving the asylum also, Susan was remembering Sanjay's grumpy mood. Sanjay was the victim of pensive sadness. He was never a home-keeping person. Always, he was the victim of tepid insanity.

It was a winter evening. There was a chill in the air. In a hurry, Susan forgot to take a sweater and a scarf. When she came out of the asylum, she found some relatives of some patients sitting below the soft light of the lonely corridor, and there was a blue glow from the tube light in one corner of the long and barren corridor. Susan was internally very sad and broken. Even in her wildest dream, she never thought that a day would come when Sanjay would have to shift to a mental asylum. There were tears in her eyes, but she controlled herself. She was thinking about how beautiful it would have been if she could have taken a year off from her busy life. But, the condition was such that she did not have the scope to take even an hour off from her hectic schedule. A big car was starting, and due to the cold, the engine failed to start; there was just a horrible whining of the engine.

Due to the severe cold, her teeth were chattering. Somehow, she clenched her teeth and was in search of a local tea shop so that she could get a warm feeling. There was muffled stillness in the whole atmosphere. After a slight search, Susan could locate a tea vendor on the right side of the gate. A middle-aged man was preparing tea in a big container. He had wire-rimmed bifocals. Susan ordered black tea and occupied a plastic chair, which was there for customers. She did not have any hope for Sanjay. She could realise that it was the beginning of the end. Never had she seen an icy look on Sanjay's face, but in the asylum, she witnessed that. That icy look of Sanjay aggravated her agony for him. The whole atmosphere of the asylum was horrible. There was a patient who was repeatedly banging his head against the wall and was bleeding profusely. Other inmates were laughing, and there was a lack of staff, so there was no one to control him. Another patient was wincing with pain and bubbles of spittle were drooling from his mouth, and he was lying on the floor in a half-naked condition. Those were traumatising scenes, and the trauma remained vividly etched in her memory.

Even in Sanjay's case, a progressive decline was visible. Susan thought, even the relatives of the patient, who is on a ventilator, are happier than the relatives of an insane person. Due to continuous work, stress and agony, beautiful look of Susan was also affected. Gentle half-moons had gathered under her eyes. For Sanjay, fear used to ferment in her mind.

Dusk was falling. By that time, she had left the tea shop. She was walking slowly on the road. She found tears welling up in her eyes and running down her rigid cheeks automatically. After a couple of minutes, she called an auto rickshaw and started for home. Andria was alone in the house for the last couple of hours, and it was a winter evening. When Susan reached home, it was nearly 9:00 pm. Her neighbours were curious, but since Susan maintained a distance from society members, no one dared to ask anything about Sanjay. In spite of so many odds, Susan never used to appear in public without make-up. After reaching home, the first work she did was to remove her makeup. That day, she slept early.

The next morning, when she got up, she felt a heavy silence in the house. Andria was still sleeping, and the absence of Sanjay was felt in every nook and corner of the house. Right from the morning, the weather was dull. Ink-black clouds were hovering over the horizon. After some time, it started raining, but since it was winter, the rain did not stand for a long time. The rain came down quickly.

58

Returning from Mental Asylum

Only a mental patient knows the pathos and experience of a mental asylum. There are thousands of cases across the world where a mental patient is declared fit, but the family members abandon them and do not even come to support them. From that point of view, Sanjay was lucky enough because both Susan and Andria were by his side in his support. From the very beginning, Susan beseechingly requested the dean of the mental asylum to relieve Sanjay at the earliest. Susan's forgiving nature cannot be described in words. The person because of whom she became infected with HIV, even for that person, her door was open, and even for a single second, she did not try to distance herself from Sanjay. Most families consider sending their relatives to a mental asylum as a vanquished state, but there is no question of defeat. It is the need of the patient for the time being.

The day Sanjay was discharged from the mental asylum was a red-letter day in his life. Both Susan and Andria went to welcome him home. The atmosphere of the mental asylum was serene. There was no hue and cry of the patients. Sanjay nonchalantly walked out of the asylum. He came out of the asylum, and first, he hugged Andria. He was in a very good mood. Due to freedom from bondage, Sanjay's appearance was splendid. After so many years, Susan had an opportunity to see Sanjay in his pink of health, though he was a carrier of HIV and had mental disorders. In a joyous mood, Sanjay picked up a small stone from the road and hurled it at the top of the adjacent tree; it was nothing but the manifestation of liberty. Andria, too, was happy beyond measure for the discharge of her Bapu (fondly, Andria used to address Sanjay as Bapu). Both Andria and Sanjay possessed an affable relationship.

Sanjay's elder brother had a floundering business after taking VRS, but he never bothered to inquire about his younger brother. In India, there is a small number of head start programmes like the advanced countries like the USA. If there would have been good head start programmes, poor and intelligent girls like Andria could have benefitted to a great extent in their school days.

Sanjay had claustrophobic feelings in the asylum. After coming out of the asylum, he breathed fresh oxygen to his heart's content. In the asylum, he learned to appreciate the little things in life. There, he really missed his family, which is nothing but Susan and Andria. They are like a triangle. Without one of them, the triangle is incomplete.

Susan took a taxi, and they left for a good restaurant. The air conditioner of the taxi was malfunctioning, so it was hot. The month was April, and the atmosphere was humid. Few spells of rain were awaited. There was a film of perspiration on her forehead. Within a couple of minutes, they reached a good restaurant, and both Susan and Sanjay told Andria to order. Andria knew about Sanjay's choice. So, first, she ordered a bottle of chilled beer along with *masala papad*, without chilli powder, and *tandoori* chicken. Sanjay was happy beyond measure. Then Andria ordered a veg starter, which was Susan's favourite. It was nothing but *paneer* (cottage cheese) *tikka masala.* After a long time, all of them were in a joyous mood, and it was a long-awaited dream for each of the family members. Sanjay finished his drink and casually tossed the lid of the beer bottle into one corner of the room. Though Susan did not like this behaviour, she did not say anything. From her body language, Andria could guess that. No matter how much treatment and counselling is there, a psychiatric patient is bound to behave abnormally, and the same abnormality was visible within Sanjay.

Since it was a joyous day, Andria wanted to wear a traditional *saree.* Susan helped her with that because Andria did not know how to wear a *saree.* Nowadays, all girls who are familiar with Punjabi and western wear do not know how to wear a *saree.* So, Susan helped her, and in many places, the *saree* was pinned so that it did not slip. In spite of that, while eating, one corner of Andria's *saree* slipped away. She caught hold of the pin and clenched it in the middle of her teeth. Susan immediately helped her, but while pinning the *saree*, the pin pricked Andria's skin, and she winced in pain. Sanjay, too, became nervous after hearing Andria's scream. But everything became normal within minutes. Susan had the managerial skills to control any odd situation within minutes.

Then they ordered the main course. Truly speaking, all were full from starters only. Still, they ordered wheat *roti* and *daal fry* along with *masala* chicken. After lunch, when they were about to move, Sanjay asked Andria, "*Gnyeru*, won't we have double scoop butterscotch? How can the lunch be completed without ice cream?"

Andria was touched by this fatherly adore, warmth, care and affection. For both of them, they ordered ice cream, and Susan preferred to have coffee.

In Sanskrit, there is a famous adage called, '*Madhurena Samapayet*', which means that lunch or dinner must be completed with a sweet dish. How true it is! After the completion of lunch, they started for home. For Sanjay, it was a special day because, after a couple of months, he would enjoy the care and comfort of home. Sanjay was fond of succulent fruits. So, to give him a surprise, Susan prepared watermelon juice. When they returned home, Susan served him chilled watermelon juice. Sanjay enjoyed the first glass, and as usual, wanted Susan to fill the second one.

59

Her Self-Motivation — the Only Driving Force

All the family members of Sanjay were famous for their ostentation; they never wanted their poverty to be surfaced. Because showcasing poverty does not bring any sympathy. On the contrary, it brings disrespect and pity from common people. No one helps, but they do shower their criticism. So, for all the family members, ostentation was an inseparable part of life.

Andria never used low-quality dresses and foot wears. The same was the case with Susan, and Sanjay, too, always used branded apparel and wristwatches. Even by taking a loan through credit cards, they maintained their lifestyle. There was no compromise with the standard of living, and there was a distinct difference between the looks of Andria and her classmates. She had many classmates who were rich, but due to the thrifty lifestyle of their parents, they did not have that aristocratic look, and they missed the grandeur. Andria's lifestyle could be called an antithesis as far as her classmates were concerned.

Both Sanjay and Susan possessed repugnance for the ordinary standard of living. They were known for their philoprogenitiveness. Really, they cared for their child and ninety per cent credit goes to Susan. She practically groomed Andria from day one. Right from ironing her dresses to polishing her shoes, everything was her job. and she used to do it happily. Andria never went to school in a shabby condition. Her uniform was always properly ironed and her shoes were properly polished. There are many guardians who have a fierce lack of ambition, and they become indifferent to their children. Those children grow like weeds, and without proper soil, nurturing and watering, you can't have a rose. If you want good results, you are supposed to put in sincere efforts.

Susan had indiscrete enthusiasm for Andria's career. In her life after marriage, she had to discontinue her graduation for eight years and become a victim of comments and criticism from her saturnine father-in-law, and after eight long years, she completed her graduation in Arts with a specialisation in history from IGNOU (Indira Gandhi National Open University), and after that, she completed her master's degree from the University of Pune, but for the sake of Andria's career and Sanjay's health, she did not go for a job and sacrificed her professional career. Otherwise, she could have easily reached the position of the principal of a good school. But, these sacrifices are rarely seen, felt and recognised by society. For recognition by society, one needs to create data, because data cannot be denied. There was a tremendous bonding between Susan and Andria. There was a light of deeper understanding in their eyes, which seemed to grow beyond spoken words.

Whatever happened, Susan's love and thoughts would always be there with Andria. Mother's blessings and good wishes were like an invisible shadow, which protected Andria at every moment of her life. Susan was highly self-motivated. Her self-motivation was the only driving force for the whole family. Susan taught and motivated Andria to learn everything right from cooking to driving. She always supported her daughter but never pampered her. She was a visionary. In those days, she realised that only scholasticism was not enough. Unless scholasticism is blended with smartness, it is of no use. Only for that reason, Susan concentrated on each sector of Andria's life and tried her best to groom her in the best possible way. She never gave any scope to others to chuckle at her. Ordinary people are preoccupied with sundry gossip and criticising others. They do not know proper mannerisms. A person who knows proper mannerisms will never involve in public gossiping.

Once, Andria wanted to have an omelette. Susan chopped an onion and tossed it in the pan and then instructed Andria to complete the rest of the task. Andria was surprised and asked Susan, "Why don't you complete the task?" In reply what Susan told is still etched in Andria's memory. Susan replied, "If I really want you to take the driving test, then in the middle of the road, I must hand over the steering to you." What a classic thought of a mother who is a role model of motherhood and women's empowerment.

60

She Never Bowed Down Even in Extreme Conditions

Right since the day Susan left her house, her life became barren. Before marriage, she did not have peace from her wretched mother, but the scenario was worst after the marriage. On one side was a mental patient in the name of the husband who had no earnings, and on the other side was the wretched father-in-law. She was thrown from a frying pan to fire and was sandwiched between Sanjay and her father-in-law. In those days, Sanjay was much influenced by his father. Even his father provoked Sanjay in such a way that Susan was brutally assaulted by Sanjay, and her father-in-law enjoyed those moments being a mute spectator.

Susan was not a lady to bow down. Even in extreme conditions, after being brutally beaten by Sanjay, she was profusely bleeding but did not surrender. She could have easily sent both Sanjay and his father behind bars by visiting the police station and lodging an FIR. But, she never made things public. The public and the neighbours were much interested to interact with Susan to get juicy gossip. But, grave Susan always distanced herself from the people and never ever vented her feelings. For her, self-respect was the first and foremost priority. Many times, she retaliated and was mercilessly assaulted, and due to his strength, Sanjay always overpowered her, but she did not bow down. She always stuck to her views and decisions.

Gradually, with each passing year, she became exasperated. People used to judge the peace of Susan's mind ostensibly. But, many times, they could not read the actual situation of the family. While assaulting Susan, Sanjay used to look at her black eyes, which attracted him like a magnet years ago, but in the same eyes, Sanjay could see the spark of revolt and a suppressed woman's empowerment. Susan did not have much faith in God. Generally, people remember God in days of distress, but Susan was the last person to genuflect in front of God for her own benefit. She hated that cross-section of people who traded with God.

After being beaten, Susan used to be left alone, and Sanjay used to leave the house. There was no one at home to even ask her if she would like to have some food or not. Her father-in-law was confined in his room, and he did not have any interest in Susan's welfare. For him, Susan was nothing but an unpaid domestic worker. Susan used to look out of the window panes and used to watch the swollen rain droplets trickling down the glass panes, and unknowingly, she would fall asleep after a couple of minutes in a hungry and depressed condition.

61

Every Evening She Used to Think about What She Did for the Whole Day

Susan was a visionary. At the end of each day in the evening, Susan used to think about all the work done by her on that day. She used to maintain a to-do list. It was an unending list. If four tasks were done, eight new tasks were added to that list. But, due to this to-do list, she never forgot to complete any important work, and there was harmony in her working style.

When Susan was in Serampore, at the end of the day, she used to visit the famous library of Serampore and sit by the side of the gleaming water of the Ganga. She used to see boats languidly ferrying on the Ganga. Sometimes, she used to visit other places in and around Serampore. Once, Susan visited the famous temple of Dakshineshwar, located by the side of Vivekananda Bridge. Vivekananda Bridge can be compared to the marvels of Civil Engineering. Susan's faculties of observation were very powerful, and she used to grasp any new concept very quickly. There was a particular place, which was known for its tangles of trees. Susan used to be much disturbed when Sanjay's bout of insanity used to aggravate. She felt profoundly sorry for Sanjay, but she had nothing to do. Many times, being depressed she used to visit the famous church in the place named Bandel. It was around twenty-five kilometres away from Serampore.

Her father-in-law was very strict, and there was a standing order that Susan had to reach home before sunset. When the western horizon used to be tinged with red, Susan used to start for home, which was nothing but an open jail for her. There was a routined life. After reaching home, she had to get back to her cooking, and first, she had to prepare evening tea for her father-in-law. Many times, her inner mind wanted to pour a few drops of poison into that tea, but her wish was limited and restricted to its thought only.

Then she used to prepare *rotis* (handmade bread) for the family members. They were three. Susan, Sanjay and Sanjay's father, but Sanjay alone used to consume 10-12 *rotis*. Susan used to push dough with the heel of her hand. It was an irritating and boring job to cook every day, that too, both times. Secondly, there was not even a gas connection. There was no refrigerator and no domestic worker. She had to cook both times using a conventional *chula*. Sometimes, being exhausted, she used to rest her chin on her elbow and just think for an indefinite time.

62

Two Generations

Generations are changing. My age is fifty-nine plus. Our generation, which was born before 1965 witnessed a colossal change. Right from the time of Trunk Calls to the present time of Whatsapp calling. Even the generation has changed, and along with that, everything else has changed to a great extent. The dress style has changed, food habits have changed, methods of learning have changed and the banking system has changed too. Computers and the internet changed everything. In earlier days, for paying an electric bill, people used to stand in a queue for hours. Nowadays, it is just a matter of a click or touch on a laptop or mobile phone.

Today's generation is blessed. They have got everything that can be purchased with money. They have good quality smartphones, tablets and laptops, and apart from that, they enjoy innumerable facilities. But, at one point, they lag. They do not get quality time from their parents. Nowadays, most families are nuclear families and the number of members varies between three to four depending on the number of children. But, I have personally seen all the members of a family busy with Whatsapp. Even at the dining table, they do not talk to each other. While eating, too, they go for browsing, and it is a national obsession. In malls, I personally witnessed people talking over cell phones even while urinating. Their hands were more concerned about holding the phones than their penises.

In a book, an author had written that for having a girlfriend, four things are necessary, and they are: jeans, cell phone, pizza and bike. I do agree with him, but where is a guarantee that the girlfriend will stay permanently? I have personally witnessed a girl changing her boyfriend, and the reason was that the first boyfriend was an MS from an ordinary university in the USA and was working in a small company, and the second boy was an MS from Stanford and served in Google. If this becomes the criterion for choosing and dumping a boyfriend, then I would compare this kind of girl to a domestic prostitute. Even a prostitute has a heart, and she too has soft corners for someone. But, this type of girl, for whom the relationship is just like a deal is the cancer of the present generation. Today's generation is intelligent, but its intelligence is coupled with cunningness. This cunningness will annihilate everything. So, for avoiding this, parents have to be serious and cautious. There is a huge difference between our generation and the present generation. We have to accept the generation gap.

There is only one truth in the world, and that is a single word 'CHANGE'. So, we have to accept the change, but along with that, we must see the negative points of today's generation. After pointing out negative points, we must counsel our children so that they can be shown a proper track.

If you are a parent, you must design the career of your child, and while designing it, you must see which is their favourite subject. You must see whether they want to pursue their career in that subject or not. Nowadays, parents do not give time to their children and seldom are they aware of the choices of their children. Without knowing about them, how can they advise children? All parents must read the mindset of their child. It is mandatory. Parents who have less time for their children do not have the right to advise their children. A father is supposed to guide his son, but unfortunately, if the father does not know about his son, how can he guide him? Every child has his own propensity towards some line and the guardian must unearth it by giving proper time to the child. Interaction with the child is a must. Unless parents interact with their children, they will never know about their choices. The best thing a parent can give to their child is time. A parent must observe the child throughout childhood. The greatest pleasure lies in tracking the unfolding of the petals of a blooming flower.

63

Breakup of Daughter's Affair

Andria's affair continued for seven and a half years. Her boyfriend, too, cut a sorry figure in Higher Secondary and all competitive examinations for entry into any of the Engineering courses in any of the good colleges. But, that boy had a special quality. Right from his school days, he decided not to go for a job. He wanted to be an entrepreneur. Along with his study, he parallelly developed expertise in software and hardware.

When he was in the eleventh standard, he started his own business of website development and providing other kinds of solutions to clients. The boy got into Production Engineering, but the college admission was just for the namesake. Throughout the day, he used to be busy with his business. He did not have a dubious mentality. He was very clear as far as his aim and vision were concerned. He never wanted a dichotomy between his academic career and professional career. He had zero interest in academics, and he was totally money-minded.

Andria's view was totally the opposite. Andria had her complete bend towards academics, and she was not at all after money. This difference in mentality started becoming a stumbling block in the path of their smooth relationship. Secondly, the boy used to belittle Andria, and many times, taunted her by saying, "Out of academics, how much would you earn? Look at me. After five years, I can hire ten engineers like you."

Andria used to feel insulted but kept everything in her mind. Sanjay always told Andria not to repress anything, but it was her habit to repress everything from her parents. Habit is second nature. In those days, Andria used to feel cocooned in her home, and she wanted to stay away from her parents.

Gradually, a gulf was started in their relationship and it became an ever-widening gulf, which could not be bridged. Both Andria and the boy distanced themselves from each other. At that time, Andria was in her final year of engineering. One day, Sanjay found Andria with glistened eyes. Her eyes were filled with tears. When he inquired, he came to know that their affair was no more. Internally, Sanjay became happy because, due to the influence of that boy, Andria's career would have been damaged beyond measure. Only due to this affair, Andria's axis of thought was diverted and she lost her complete concentration and attention. The result was her doing badly in exams. As long as they were of the same opinion, there had been a psychological unity, but once their views became opposite, they distanced themselves from each other. Secondly, the boy had a male ego and male chauvinism. Because he was brought up in an atmosphere where a male child was always pampered. For this, the decayed society is mainly responsible. Ladies are the biggest enemies of ladies. If a lady herself wants a male child, then nothing can be told. Sanjay had the capacity to read the eyes of Andria, and he always gave more importance to eye talk than words.

64

Admitting Daughter to an Engineering Course

After the twelfth standard, Andria decided to go for engineering, and she did not have any interest in the circuit branches, e.g., Electrical, E&TC, Instrumentation and Computer. On the contrary, she wanted to be a Mechanical Engineer. All of them did a lot of homework for Andria, and it was unanimously decided that they would compromise with the college but not with the branch. Because a stream is the most important thing. If by mistake a candidate accepts the wrong stream, their career will never flourish. Sanjay was the burning example. One must not lose interest in one's subject. Once a person loses interest in their subject, they automatically become mentally dead and are grasped by frustration and depression.

Since Andria's CET score was relatively low, they had to be very serious and careful in giving the choice of colleges while filling up the application form. Because, if a candidate gets the choice in the first round, he or she has to accept it. Otherwise, they will be thrown out of the total admission procedure. Only for that reason, the three family members did rigorous homework before submitting the form. There were many choices. They gave the choice of only Mechanical Engineering. Initially, they gave the choice for the most reputed colleges and in the fifth place they had chosen AISSMS College of Engineering, Pune. The homework was so well done that Andria got a chance in Mechanical Engineering at AISSMS College of Engineering in the first round.

After her admission, they went to purchase books, notebooks, instruments, drawing instruments, mini drafters, etc. Till her admission to Engineering, Andria was not familiar with the paraphernalia of the domain of engineering. Gradually, she became accustomed to the new atmosphere of the engineering course. Susan always wanted Andria to be a go-getter.

It was a private college and students had average merit. Most of them belonged to the mediocre category of students.

After her admission to the course of engineering, Andria was in an exultation mode for a few days, and it was expected. Being a post-graduate in Engineering, Sanjay was familiar with the complete gamut of an Engineering degree course. Common people say, "Drawing is the language of engineers," but Sanjay used to say, "Mathematics is the language of engineers."

In earlier days, the complete admission process for private engineering colleges was donation-based. There was no transparency, and people were there with venality. They used to act as agents between the management and confused guardians who were seeking admission for their children. At the eleventh hour, many candidates used to flip-flop while selecting branches, and the time given to them used to be inadequate. Many of them used to select the wrong branch of engineering to study and suffer later. You may get anything, but it is your thought process, which has to decide whether you are fit for that or not. For example, if a student who is weak in Mathematics takes Electrical Engineering as his core branch of study, he is bound to suffer.

Clarity of vision is essential both for guardians as well as children. Proper synthesis of thoughts is essential. Susan still remembers the day of Andria's admission to the course of Mechanical Engineering. Due to some urgent official work, Sanjay could not accompany them. Initially, the weather was cloudy. It was the month of June 2009. Tufts of clouds were visible in the western sky. Both Susan and Andria reached the admission centre at AISSMS College of Engineering in time. With the passage of time, the weather became sultry and humid. At the front counter, a clerk was receiving the forms. He had a crew-cut hairstyle and a good personality. Due to humidity, Susan drew her loose hair into a knot. There were a few guardians who came from villages, and they did not have an iota of knowledge about Engineering education. They only knew that if their child completed an Engineering degree, at least they would get a job for basic survival. A person there was a farmer, who had mortgaged his land for the sake of his son's education. The story of a poor man's life was engraved on his face. Susan used to observe everything very minutely and scrupulously.

Outside the admission centre, a few trucks were parked for the ongoing construction of the college building. A truck's engine was revving up, and due to that sound, the whole atmosphere was disturbed. In city life, ongoing construction activity is an inseparable part and that becomes the source of sound pollution, and it dampens the tranquillity of the atmosphere.

Andria's turn was yet to come. Susan was flipping through a magazine. Around 3:00 pm, Andria's turn came. Demand drafts were ready along with the necessary documents. The admission process was over, and by 5:00 pm, they were back home.

After reaching home, Andria wanted to have some tea, but Susan was tired beyond measure. She told Andria, "Milk is kept in the refrigerator. Prepare two cups of tea for both of us."

Then, Andria prepared it, and both of them enjoyed the flavour of the Darjeeling tea.

65

Struggle of the Duo During the Complete Span of Andria's Engineering Course

Andria's Engineering course was for four years, from 2009 to 2013. For the complete span, both Susan and Andria were equally disturbed by the problems, which were created due to Sanjay's mental health. Many times, he became violent during these four years. For any student, the most crucial time is the preparation leave before a semester examination. Sanjay used to pollute the serene atmosphere of the house even during Andria's preparation leaves. Andria used to go to the local railway station to study. Even the atmosphere of the local railway station was better than the atmosphere of the home. Though the railway station was not a congenial place for studying, at least Sanjay's disturbance and violence were absent there. By sending Andria outside the home, Susan alone used to suffer all tantrums of Sanjay.

Once, Susan was replenishing a drum of water. Suddenly, Sanjay came and kicked the drum. The drum was made of plastic. Immediately, due to the impact of the kick, the drum ruptured, and the complete floor was flooded with water. Sanjay used to keep most of his books on the floor due to inadequate space in their 1-BHK flat. The water took its own course and most of the books became soggy due to water absorption within no time. Both Sanjay and Susan could not shift those books quickly. Due to this, Sanjay became furious and beat Susan mercilessly for no fault of hers. He hit Susan in her left eye. After one hour, the eye was swollen and there was a blood clot below the eye.

In the local proximity, everyone was aware of this routine torture, but no one took the lead to come forward and protest. The morning became barren. Sanjay did not even allow Susan to cook. Andria was out of the home. Both Sanjay and Susan starved the whole day, and Susan was thinking of this inhuman torture, but she was helpless. She lost on both sides. Her mother abandoned her and Sanjay's father, too, did not like her because of their love marriage. That wicked father-in-law had the intention to take a huge dowry in his son's marriage, but he never thought that his scholar son was an abnormal and insane person. The most pathetic punishment for a sane person is to stay with an insane person, and Susan became the victim of that worst punishment. People get only one life, the same was the case with Susan, but her complete life was spoiled by a wrong choice.

In the evening, Andria returned home after her examination and, from the mummified silence of the house, she could sense the turbulence. When she looked at her mother, she was literally shocked by seeing the extent of swelling in Susan's left eye. Immediately, Andria took her to a doctor. The doctor asked the reason for the injury, and Susan lied. The doctor smilingly said, "Madam, I am a doctor, you can't befool me. But, as long as people like you are there, the male community will keep on torturing ladies." Susan kept mum. The doctor prescribed some medicines and an eye drop and commented, "Luckily, you escaped by whiskers, and because of the fraction of an inch, your eyeball is not injured."

The next day was Andria's examination, and the paper was the toughest, Mathematics III. She had a clear idea about rudimentary Algebra and basic Calculus. For that, she was not afraid of the examination. Andria compartmentalised the whole syllabus and practised each unit for attempting all six questions. Mathematics could never be a stumbling block in the path of Andria's career. For most Engineering students, clearing Mathematics III can be compared to a nail-biting finish.

Andria used to reduce all public contacts in her preparation leave. As the end-semester exams edged closer, Andria reduced mixing with her friends. Once, one of her close friends called her a day before an exam, and she replied, "I'll catch up later. I have a test tomorrow." As far as examinations were concerned Andria was thoroughly professional, and due to day-to-day struggle, her level of maturity was much higher than that of her contemporary friends and classmates.

66

Hospitalisation of Susan

Unfortunately, with the medicines given by the doctor, the swelling of Susan's eye did not reduce at all. On the contrary, the left cheek was completely swollen overnight. The next morning, all of them became nervous. Even Sanjay became very nervous and started realising his guilt. Sanjay decided to take Susan to the hospital. Susan was well aware of the nature of Sanjay. She knew that in spite of all the torture, in the deepest core of his mind, Sanjay possessed a fountain of love for her. Andria went for the examination, and both Susan and Sanjay went to the hospital.

Susan was clearly not a simpering female who could be pushed around. In spite of the regular hustle-bustle of the hospital, a hostile silence was reigning in the complete atmosphere of the hospital. It was afternoon, and the chink of the late afternoon light was coming through the panes of the long windows. Due to eye pain and swelling, Susan could not sleep properly. She became a victim of sleep deprivation. The physical torture by Sanjay could be compared to an attack by a frenzied mob. At that moment, nothing could be done. For a frenzied mob, the only solution is a bullet, but it is not always possible to give an order for firing due to political pressure. The same was the case with Susan. She, too, thought of murdering Sanjay many times during his sleep, but only for the sake of Andria's career and her suppressed love, she changed her decision and continued to sustain torture and physical assaults for years together.

The atmosphere of the hospital was ill-maintained. Everywhere there was knee-high grass, and in the backyard of the hospital, there were weeds. The blades of grass were yellow due to wilting. There was no watering or maintenance of the lawn, which was filled with grass.

They were waiting. During that time, there was a sporadic outbreak of conjunctivitis. So, there were many patients, and most of them thought that Susan also had conjunctivitis.

After nearly one and a half hours, Susan's turn came. Both of them went inside the doctor's cabin, and before Susan expressed herself, Sanjay confessed that it was his action for which Susan suffered. The doctor was a lady. She just frowned but did not say anything. She asked Sanjay to sit outside the cabin. The doctor had a slain body, but she was beautiful. She told Susan that there was nothing to be worried about, but she needed hospitalisation for three days to get rid of the infection. The wound made by Sanjay had become infected. She was advised to get some blood tests, and they had to be done at a particular pathological lab.

Already the agent and his sidekicks were very much present in the hospital to grab new patients. There was a nexus between the pathological lab and hospital authority. For each recommendation, the hospital used to receive some particular commission from the owner of pathological labs.

If Susan's eye infection was not taken care of, the problem could have been insurmountable. Susan was asked to deposit ten thousand rupees in cash at the counter and get herself admitted, and Sanjay had to fill out a form and sign it. Susan was admitted, but she was not ready for that. So, after admitting her, Sanjay had to rush home for bringing the knick-knacks for her (e.g., toothbrush, comb, a few undergarments, and other required things).

For dinner, what they gave could be called a mound of rice, which was totally disliked by Susan. But, there was no other option. There are two places where your options do not have any values. One is hospital and the other is jail. At night, it was Susan's routine to enjoy triple-strength coffee, but in the hospital that pampering was absent. But, due to her habit, she started feeling an aching headache and informed the doctor. She wanted a cup of coffee, but it was a hospital, not a restaurant. Instead of giving her coffee, the doctor prescribed her a painkiller. Then Susan took other medicines, and she was lucky that she could avoid an operation. If she would have been late, then an operation would have been the only remedy.

In the evening, Sanjay and Andria came. Andria brought cream biscuits for Susan. It was her favourite one. Due to heavy swelling of the left cheek, it was difficult for Susan to chew food on the left side. She slowly ate a few biscuits with the right side of her mouth. Once she finished, Andria went close to Susan and mumbled something. Then Andria parked herself in the hospital bed, and around 8:00 pm both Andria and Sanjay left. There was no other visitor because Susan was famous as a private person. She never liked socialisation and even Sanjay's mental health prevented Susan from socialising.

After dinner, Susan took medicines, but just below the left eye, severe pain was there. Even the vision of the left eye was partially obstructed due to heavy swelling. She started moaning and groaning. The sister observed that and gave her an injection, which was nothing but a sedative. Gradually, she fell asleep.

The next morning when she got up, she found that both swelling and pain had reduced to a great extent. She observed a gentle half-moon below the left eye, and it lit up her mind. Due to the reduced pain and swelling, she was relieved and relaxed. Then she waited for Andria and Sanjay to come. Through the window, a small garden of the hospital was visible. Susan looked at the sunflower, which was freshly bloomed. In the deep core of her mind, Susan compared the freshly bloomed sunflower with Andria.

After an hour, Andria and Sanjay came, and Susan got discharged. After reaching home, Susan found that there was a poster on the wall, and on it, Andria had written, "Dear Mom, Welcome Home." Right from childhood, only Andria was an expert in embellishment, and the poster was nothing but the manifestation of that embellishment.

67

Abstaining Her Daughter from Students' Politics

Susan was very careful about one thing. She never wanted Andria to involve herself in student politics. Andria had all the required qualities for joining student politics. She was an expert orator in English, Hindi and Marathi, and she had the capability to mesmerise her audience and control the mass. Though her mother tongue was Bengali, she was weak in Bengali because she was brought up outside West Bengal right from the first year of her life, and Susan, too, did not get the required time to teach Bengali to Andria.

Susan was much worried about the political parties. Because political parties locate talented orators from schools and colleges. Though the students of West Bengal and Delhi are more prone to student politics, Susan took due care of it. For example, the names of Jadavpur University and JNU (Jawaharlal Nehru University) can be mentioned as the den of politics.

In any country or state where students are involved in politics, political parties present over there mainly use the energy of their youth, and the energy is extracted just like sugarcane juice. After repeated extraction, when no energy is left, these young cadres are thrown, and a new generation of cadres is born by that time.

The plausibility of Andria's involvement in politics was very less because that trend came from family. Neither Sanjay nor Susan was interested in college politics. So, there was no family history. Still, as a mother, Susan was doubly careful about Andria's career. Because many good and promising careers were shattered just because of students' politics.

The political climate of Maharashtra is far better than the political climate of West Bengal and Delhi. Here students are involved in politics to a much lesser extent. Their mental horizon touches different corners of the sky.

Susan had an ardent wish to place Andria on the global map, and that is why, she was careful about all the parameters, which affect the career of a student. Andria can be compared to a flame, and Susan protected that flame with both her hands so that it won't extinguish by external forces.

68

Admitting Daughter to a Driving School

Susan realised one thing at the very beginning, and that was nothing but the importance of smartness. She realised that academics alone would not be enough. It is just one of the spokes of the wheel. For the complete balancing of the wheel, there must be equilibrium and harmony among all the spokes. So, she wanted Andria to be self-sufficient from all angles. For that, when Andria crossed twenty-one, Susan decided to admit her to a local driving school because that was the perfect age for learning to drive. If you do not know driving, your whole life you would be dependent on public transport and your condition will be just like the flopping of a frog in shallow water.

It was the month of May. It was summer, and Andria's sixth-semester exams were just over. In the afternoon, Susan took Andria to a local driving school. It was in their colony only. The owner of the driving school was a middle-aged cynic person. He was occupying a rickety table in the mid of a small room and there was a very old computer on the table. Susan talked to him, and he said that the fees for the driving lesson would be two thousand two hundred rupees, and the lesson would be provided for twenty-two days. He requested Andria chose the slot for the lesson. Andria opted for the evening slot. There was an age-old Maruti-800 parked outside the room, which witnessed the driving lesson of hundreds of people. Susan paid the complete fee along with the documents and a photograph of Andria. Then Andria was asked to appear for a formal written test for the issuance of the temporary driving license for beginners, and with a brittle smile, the owner told Andria, "Madam, the most important thing in this driving lesson is your concentration. Without that, no one can be a good driver. And in driving, there is no excuse even for a small mistake."

After admitting Andria to the driving School, Susan deleted another item from her to-do list. This decision of Susan can be compared with a seismic shift in the progress of Andria's career because only people who do not know driving can realise the importance of driving, and in foreign countries like the USA, you must not step in without the knowledge of driving. If you know driving then it won't take much time to adjust to the left-handed driving system, but if you do not have the initial training, you will be in difficult waters. Because in the USA, the fee for driving lessons is quite high, and it is really difficult to master driving from zero level by adjusting to the busy schedule of western life. Susan possessed a wide vision, and she was steadfast as far as the duty of a mother was concerned.

The next day, driving lessons started. It was a big adventure for Andria, and it was really difficult for her to balance between a clutch and a brake for the initial week. After coming from the driving school regularly, she used to narrate her experience. There was one more girl with Andria named Snehal. She belonged to a rich family and used to stay in an up-market neighbourhood. The owner of the driving school was a good teacher. For the first two days, he advised Andria not to touch the accelerator, and only with the help of the clutch, Andria practised. Gradually, her confidence started building. The owner-cum-teacher shepherded both Andria and Snehal in a perfect way. There was a rush for morning slots. But, in the evening slot only Andria and Snehal were there.

One day, while driving, there were some instructions from the teacher, and during that time, Snehal was doing her hair, and Andria was steering. The cynic owner scolded Snehal for the breach of concentration and flatly told her, "This is a driving session, not the time for hair styling."

He was rude, but he was hundred per cent correct. But, he used to give instructions too fast, and sometimes, it was difficult for both Andria and Snehal to catch his words. But, due to his irritating nature, none of them dared to request him to slow down his speed.

Andria told about it to Susan. By this time, one week of training was over, and Andria was comfortable with the basics of driving. She was not familiar with driving in traffic, and it is quite natural. So, Susan called the owner of the driving school and requested him to slow down while giving instructions. The cynic person was humorous, too. He said, "Madam, let your daughter express herself. Why are you pleading for her? The steering will be in your hand or her hand while driving? Let her take her own decision. Being the mother, interfere only where it is really required." Susan did not mind.

Gradually, all twenty-two days of training were over, and Andria did it in one stretch. Then it was time for the final test for having a permanent driving license. Andria left home in the morning with the owner of the driving school. She returned by 3:00 pm with a beaming smile. From her appearance only, Susan could read that she must have given the test very successfully. Susan's guess was correct. She satisfactorily appeared for the test, and the inspector was impressed by her driving. Within a few days, her permanent driving license was delivered by a registered post, and another chapter of her life was over.

Now what she needed was continuous practice, but they did not have a car. But, Susan started thinking of purchasing a good-conditioned second-hand Maruti-800 for Andria's practice. Ultimately, she became successful in buying one.

69

After Engineering, Daughter's Placement in an MNC

Generally, I observe students and anxious guardians thinking of placement even before admission. It is too much. Whenever you go on a flight, you must have observed that there is a big group of people who unzip their seat belts and stand immediately after the plane lands and then they clog the aisle between the seats for nothing. It takes a minimum of five to ten minutes to open the door, and it takes time to fit the aerobridge or staircase, but still, these groups of people immediately untie their seat belts and fill the aisle. The same is the case in movies. The moment a movie gets over, people start rushing towards the exit, and the narrow passage after the exit gate becomes saturated with people. Why not enjoy the promotional song or item song after the movie gets over? The same is the case with placement. The community wants the child to laugh even before the formation of teeth. How ridiculous it is!

Both Susan and Sanjay were never preoccupied with the placement of Andria. Too much thinking about placement ceases the creative energy of the child, and this paralysis of creative energy is not at all good for the career of a student. This thinking of placement became a national obsession-cum-preoccupation.

Even thirty-seven years ago, when we graduated, this stress of placement was not there. Only for that reason, our generation could enjoy the four-years engineering course. We had tousled intimacy with our friends, and we had time to see the dappled shadows of tall trees and time to listen to the silence of huddled trees. The thinking pattern has totally changed. In the era of 1980-1990, people used to think in one direction, but in the era of 2020-2030, people started thinking in multiple directions. Nowadays, the thinking pattern is more money-oriented and everywhere we can smell the presence of commercialisation. There is an unbridgeable gulf between the thinking pattern of those days and nowadays, and it is an ever-widening gulf, which can never be filled.

The day Andria's last exam was over, the whole family went shopping. Andria liked a high heel footwear in a shop named Shoe-Express. Before this, Andria had never used high heels. But somewhere one has to start. Andria took the shoe for trial, and Sanjay told her to follow him slowly after putting on the heels. There was a teetering feeling after putting on the heels. She was losing balance initially. There was a feeling of swaying back and forth.

They returned home around 9:00 pm. Andria received a call from the Training and Placement officer of her college for an interview on the very next day. It was a tyre-manufacturing company and a Japanese MNC. Andria was supposed to be present with all mark sheets for all seven semesters. The result of the eighth semester was yet to be published. She got all the mark sheets; however, she was not getting the mark sheet for the fifth semester. After a frantic search, she got it, and within one night, she had to be ready for the interview at an MNC. Susan was a bit worried, but both Sanjay and Andria were absolutely calm and composed. Susan was slightly tensed because all her life and strength were given to the career of Andria.

The next morning, Andria reached the venue and had a warm handshake with the receptionist of the MNC in their main office in Pune. After that, she was called for an interview. The whole interview was video recorded. Andria was very calm and composed because she knew the art of balancing between the external world of science and the internal world of introspection. She got the job, and the company wanted her to join immediately. Her last exam was on 31st May 2013, the interview took place on 1st June 2013, and she was given an offer letter and asked to join immediately. Since it was a job, she too did not delay and joined on 3rd June 2013. Truly speaking, after the last exam she did not even get rest for three days.

After a month, Andria got her first salary. She presented a beautiful wristwatch to Sanjay, and for Susan, she purchased very good-looking earrings from the Bund Garden branch of Tanishq. It was a stone's throw distance from their house. For herself, she did not purchase anything. It was a red-letter day for the whole family. Sanjay was touched by Andria's affection; his voice was choked. Sanjay decided to throw a party for all the family members and decided to proceed towards Shisha Café in KP (Koregaon Park).

But, Susan advised Andria not to fritter her money away on some temporary thrill like a crazily priced designer bag or very costly footwear. Susan's thought process was always very practical. Sanjay was driven by emotions, and Andria, too, imbibed the same habit to a great extent from her father, but Susan was driven by logic. Susan was the sheet anchor of the family. Susan can be compared with the main sailor of a ship who controls the whole team. At the same time, Susan advised Andria to live life to the fullest extent.

70

Should One Only See the World or Should One Enjoy It?

There are two kinds of people in this world. The first group of people always thinks that luxury is not for them; it is for the rich cross-section of society. They accept their poverty and are ready to be poor for the rest of their lives. Even my father belonged to the same group. It was 1997. I was looking at a dazzling white new car and praised the beauty of the car. My father was with me. He told me, "Never think of purchasing a car. It is not for us." What a poor mentality! Trying to be happy means you have accepted that you are unhappy. In a similar way, if a person thinks that he is not worth purchasing a car that means he has accepted his poverty and never wants to come out of it.

So, there are clearly two cross-sections of people. There is one who enjoys a lot and from day one till one's death. They enjoy all the amenities of the world and leave the world in a satiated state of mind. The second group belongs to the frustrated class with an inbuilt inferiority complex who always thinks that luxury is not their cup of tea. For their whole life, they see others enjoying themselves and suffer from an inferiority complex and jealousy. The basic reason for this kind of mindset is nothing but low self-esteem.

Susan never wanted Andria to be like the second category. Susan always wanted to explore all the possibilities of life. Truly speaking, Susan was dynamic, and for that, she did not even like the indolent teaching profession of Sanjay, but in front of Sanjay's stubborn attitude, her choice lost its value. Susan knew Sanjay very well, and for that, she never wanted to interfere in his personal affairs. But, as far as Andria's career was concerned, total care was taken by Susan. She thought if anyone wanted to be a faculty, then they must explore the possibility of being a faculty in a foreign land like the

USA where teachers are really respected and the teaching profession is not a profession of compromised attitude. Sanjay had never taken any interest in Andria's career, but at the same time, he never became a stumbling block in the path.

There was an unbridgeable gulf between the thought process of Susan and Sanjay, and Andria was sandwiched between them. Sanjay's total thought process was emotionally driven, whereas Susan's thought process was driven by valid logic. Being the single child of her parents, Andria was influenced more by Sanjay and was emotionally driven to a great extent, but from time to time, Susan's counselling showed her the correct path. Susan only taught Andria how to win by inches, not by miles. Susan always gave maximum impetus and importance to consistency and uniformity of work. If you don't practise for one month, the audience will realise; if you do not practise for a week, the family members will realise; and if you do not practise only for one day, you will realise. A person can escape, but they cannot escape from their own conscience. So, Susan was very particular about Andria's life routine. New winds of thought used to come into Susan's mind, and Susan implemented and experimented with all the good things in Andria's life. Susan never believed in metaphorical examples. Susan taught Andria not to have an inferiority complex at any point in life.

Once, Susan and Andria were in Bombay, and they went to the Gateway of India. From the Gateway, Andria was looking at the Taj Hotel. Susan could read her mind. She asked her, "Do you want to visit the Taj?" Andria was surprised and said, "But..." Susan realised what Andria wanted to say. She told her, "Don't worry, dear. We may not be able to afford a buffet, but we can easily afford two cups of coffee. Come, let's go to Taj." This is called motherhood, which must be respected by all. The main role of a mother is to make her child bold and brave, not timid and cowardly. In the same way, Susan went on training Andria, and a day came when Andria realised that for her the best slice of the world would be the University of Texas A&M (TAMU).

71

Making a Passport for Her Daughter

Just like admitting to the driving school, Susan realised that, for being a global citizen, one needed to leave one's country, and for that, one needed a passport. These all are very simple teachings of life, but most of the guardians are impractical and lack vision. There are thousands of people who missed the scope to visit a foreign land just because of the absence of passports and at the eleventh hour it was not possible to make a passport ready. One must keep one's powder dry so that in the hour of need, it can be used. Most people go for making a passport when they plan to visit some foreign land, but why delay? One must keep it ready well in advance. You must not work too hard, but you need to work harder than your contemporaries, and that makes the difference. On day one, you won't realise it, but after years you will see the difference.

Whatever is done with honesty and effort needs time, and time is required to get the desired results. But once one gets the result, it becomes permanent. Susan always taught Andria to do both hard work and smart work. Unless hard work is coupled with smart work, it is of no use. There are lakhs of people who do hard work, but very few of them become successful in the true sense. Why? Because of lack of vision and smart work. Always do slightly extra than others. Your working style must be dynamic and exuberant. When you work with your team, people must feel that they are attending a course of dynamic meditation.

Let us come to the point. Susan decided to go for Andria's passport, and at that time, Andria was in her final year. The year was 2012, and it was the month of August. Andria got an appointment from the Passport Office. It was located in the Mondhua region of Pune city. They were residing in Yerawada. Yerawada was not very far from Mondhua. The scheduled time of the appointment was 11:30 am, and that day, the Passport Office was supposed to take Andria's biometric data.

Susan accompanied Andria. The weather was very bad. It was a rainy season, but some low-pressure region was very close to Pune. The weather was very squally. There were whistling wind and driving rain followed by flashes of lightning. Andria was pitch-perfect in her dress code. Susan had a forest green *salwar kameez,* though initially, she wanted to go for a pistachio green *kurti.* Both were looking great. When they were leaving the house, Sanjay was sleeping as he had decided to take a day off from college. For the time being, the rain had stopped, but the air threatened a second spell of rain. Susan hired a cab. They started for the Passport Office, and by that time, the rain started again, and after some time, the rain had dwindled to a drizzle. After reaching the Passport Office, both of them disembarked gently from the car. Susan was not allowed to enter the office. She had to wait outside, but before Andria left with her documents, Susan ran both her hands across her forehead. That could be compared to the best form of blessings of a mother.

Andria entered the Passport Office, and Susan was waiting in a shop, which was mainly dealing with the photocopying of documents. By looking at Susan's elegance, the shop owner provided her with a chair. She really looked charming with wispy eyebrows and soot black eyes.

Susan had an inbuilt aristocracy. That aristocracy was reflected in her looks. After a few minutes, Susan's cell phone beeped. On the other side, Sanjay was there. He just wanted to know whether both of them had safely reached the Passport Office or not. About Andria's career, Susan was very hopeful. Hope grew in her heart like snow collecting on a damp wall, one flake at a time.

72

Motivating Her Daughter to Resign from the MNC

It was 2015, and by that time, Andria had already served the MNC for more than two and a half years. By extrapolating Andria's career graph, Susan could easily guess the stagnancy and see her future. Susan realised that if Andria would stick to the MNC, even after ten years, she would do very little progress, and by that time all the opportunities would be blocked. Because once you rot in a company for ten years in a particular department, you are of no use for any other job. Andria was in the purchasing department of a tyre company. Being a qualified Mechanical Engineer, she was looking after the routine purchase matters of the company.

The first and foremost question, which comes to mind is, "Is it the job of a full-fledged qualified engineer to look after purchase procedures?" It can be done by any graduate with some training. It does not require any engineering skills. At the most, they need training for two weeks. Truly speaking, Andria was rotting there. Even the atmosphere of the company was not good. There was a staff who surreptitiously used to steal the personal belongings of other staff, and the same staff had stolen Andria's pen drive, and in that pen drive, a lot of important data was stored. The only thing was that no one could catch that person red-handed. Andria was gradually becoming frustrated, and by that time, she had already crossed the age of twenty-four. So, gradually all hope was oozing out.

So, Susan decided that Andria would discontinue her job and would go for MS in the USA. It was a mammoth project, and for that, money was an essential requirement. Sanjay was earning the normal salary of an Associate Professor, and that might have been enough for the family, but for sending the daughter to the States, Sanjay was not mentally ready. But,

Susan could realise that if Andria wanted to explore her potential, she would have to leave India. She suggested Andria resigned from her job, but Andria, too, was slightly sceptical and was not in a position to leave the job immediately. At that time, Andria was earning approximately seventy thousand rupees, and she gradually became a big support to Sanjay. But, to prepare for GRE and TOEFL, time was needed and proper guidance was required. Susan wanted Andria to resign and join one of the famous academies of Pune, which provided all training and guidelines for the GRE and TOEFL. Apart from that, they helped in selecting universities after the declaration of the GRE score and used to conduct mock interviews for visa procedures too.

On one of the Saturdays, Susan and Andria visited the academy. Andria used to have five days working a week and every Saturday and Sunday were holidays. The MNC used to suck the blood of their employees, and every day, after duty hours, the staff was asked to work for extra two hours, squeezing ten hours of free labour from their employees per week. So, the holiday of Saturday was nothing but compensation for those ten hours of free labour.

After inquiring at the academy, they came to know that there was a provision for weekend batches for office goers. It was a big solace for Andria. At least, she got an opportunity to continue her job along with the preparation of GRE and TOEFL. Regarding TOEFL, Andria was confident, but to have a good score on GRE was a challenge. Because, she had to prepare for GRE, along with the work pressure of the office, whereas other aspirants were free, and they were preparing for GRE 24X7.

Immediately, Susan decided to admit Andria to the weekend batch. They gave an advance of twelve thousand rupees and booked the seat. Then the struggle started, and Andria started working very hard for GRE. After a gruelling work schedule of office from Monday to Friday, even on the weekends, she did not have rest. On each Saturday, there used to be an evening class, and on Sunday, she used to attend morning classes. Since they already possessed a second-hand Maruti-800, Andria didn't have to depend on public transport.

Due to this decision of Susan, a new horizon was opened for Andria, and she became hopeful and optimistic for a bright future. At least, Andria realised that either tomorrow or the day after tomorrow, she would get rid of the stagnated water of the tyre company. The changes crept in gradually, and Susan was always there by the side of Andria as her staunch supporter. It was possible only due to Susan's vision and movement of thoughts. Many times on weekends, Susan used to accompany Andria to the class. Andria used to drop her at a nearby mall, and after three hours of class, she used to join her. They would go for lunch to a restaurant, and Sanjay used to be in his college. Susan could read the glint in Andria's eyes and judge her confidence level.

One day, they went to a purely vegetarian restaurant, and Andria initially ordered corn soup. Susan did not like the insipid taste of corn soup. After that, they enjoyed good starters and the main course. Susan always used to motivate Andria, and she never wanted any kind of stultification in Andria's academic journey. Susan gave maximum importance to the evocative attitude so that Andria could be motivated by the examples. Susan neither possessed a bourgeoisie attitude nor a Marxist view. She only believed in hard work coupled with smart work. She wanted Andria to be the creator of her own destiny. Susan always tried her level best to cloth all her decisions with reasons.

After that, they came out of the hotel. Andria went to the parking lot to take out the car and Susan was standing beneath a big tree, and all the area in and around her was full of dry autumn leaves. Susan observed one thing. If an animal dies it becomes stale and people cannot tolerate the smell due to the decomposition of the organic matter, but a dry leaf of a plant is also dead, but it is not stale. On the contrary, there is a hidden beauty within the dry leaf. Andria took the car in reverse gear, and all those dry leaves were crushed under the tyre. Susan gently got into the car and parked herself beside Andria. Both of them started for Yerawada. Sanjay must have been waiting for both of them.

73

Sending her Daughter to the USA for Higher Education

Andria appeared for GRE and TOEFL in the month of November 2015 and successfully cleared both exams. Two weeks before GRE, Andria was literally crammed for sixteen hours per day. In GRE, her score was 324, and in TOEFL, she had an excellent score of 110. Regarding GRE, she was a little bit apprehensive, but about TOEFL, she was damn confident.

During the span of exams, Susan was out of Pune for some change. She went to West Bengal for a few days. But, Sanjay was always there by her side and cooperated a lot with Andria. Sanjay was ready to accompany Andria to the exam centre, but Andria told it was not required.

A day before the exam, Andria and Sanjay went to see the examination venue in Kondohwa, and Sanjay wanted to show Andria the place where they used to stay long back. It was a slum area. Andria took her car inside the slum. In twenty-two years, a lot of change took place, the slum became denser, but Sanjay could locate the building. They entered the building and were ascending the staircase. The staircase was completely dark even during day time. They reached the landing. From outside, Sanjay showed Andria the apartment where they stayed. Andria was surprised by seeing the nasty atmosphere of the place. It was a Muslim-dominated area.

After having GRE and TOEFL scores, Andria had her counselling from the academy wherefrom she took the training. Based on her GRE score and the choice of subject, the experts of the academy suggested 8-10 universities, which were good for Andria. Andria applied to seven universities. Texas A&M (TAMU), University of Houston, Clemson University, Vermont

University, University of North Carolina, Florida State University, and last but not least, Virginia Tech University.

After applying, there was waiting for the confirmation of admission. Sanjay helped her with her transcripts from the University of Pune. Two professors and a senior manager of the tyre company where Andria used to work recommended her. For admission to a good university, a candidate needs a few things. They are good GRE & TOEFL scores, three good recommendations, one good Statement of Purpose (SOP), and last but not the least, a consistently good academic track record. In all the sectors, Andria was good. Only in her graduation, her score was not very good. She had first class in all the semesters, but she never secured more than 70% in any of the semesters, whereas students from autonomous institutes like COEP (College of Engineering, Pune), IITs, NITs, VIT (Vellore Institute of Technology) and SRM had very good scores throughout the eight semesters of B.Tech, and most of them had an average SGPA (Semester Grade Point Average) of more than 8.5. This difference in SGPA matters a lot. Andria knew her weak points; the rest was left to luck.

It was a barren afternoon in February. Andria got a confirmation mail about her admission to the University of Vermont. It is a very reputable and old university, and Vermont is famous for its cold atmosphere as it is in the extreme north of America. But, the tuition fee in Vermont was quite high. Andria was waiting for the response from other universities. After a couple of days, she got admission to Clemson University. Clemson is a very reputable university.

Andria was mentally ready for Clemson, but she was actually waiting for the response from Texas A&M. It was the first week of March. Andria was in the office. There she got the good news through mail regarding her confirmation of admission to Texas A&M. Even after that, she received one or two confirmations, and the rest of the universities did not respond.

After the confirmation of admission from Texas A&M, Andria was happy beyond measure. Texas A&M is globally reputed and very famous for the branch to which Andria wanted admission. She wanted her MS to be in Environmental Engineering. Though, basically, her graduation was in Mechanical Engineering, in MS, Andria switched over to Civil Engineering because Environmental Engineering comes under Civil Engineering.

Then she applied and completed all the formalities and received the I-20 from Texas A&M. After that, the final process of departure started. It was a big task. The semester was about to start by the last week of August, so Andria had to fix her journey date. She booked a one-way ticket to the USA on Qatar Airlines, and her date of departure was 16th August 2016. Now, the main thing left was a visa interview. She applied for the visa interview and got an appointment in the month of July.

It was June first week. She was very busy planning her journey and new life. So, now she decided to leave the job. Otherwise, it was impossible to concentrate. In the month of June, she resigned from the MNC but did not disclose the actual reason for resigning. Then there were innumerable tasks to be done. One was the required vaccination suggested by the University before landing in the USA. The second one was shopping for the bag and baggage. Gradually, she completed all the work, and the final date of departure was around the corner. Andria was happy about her admission to MS, and at the same time, she was upset about leaving her parents permanently. She realised that this departure would be permanent. She had a feeling of exhilaration.

The expenditure was very heavy. In her three years of service, by the influence of Susan, she saved some amount and that became useful during these days. The expenses used to surpass the estimate. Texas is a very big state and the college station of Texas A&M was nothing but a megalopolis. The ambience of Texas A&M was simply astounding.

Susan was always there, by her daughter's side, and her presence could be compared to a breakwater. Susan was happy beyond measure about the turning of Andria's career path. She really wanted Andria to be a global citizen, and her dream was coming true with much effort by all of them. In this venture, Sanjay too cooperated. Truly speaking, not having disturbance from Sanjay itself was great cooperation.

Everything was over except the visa interview, and that was the most important part of the whole process. Generally, student visas are approved, but there are many examples of denial, too. One colleague of Sanjay failed in the interview for the student visa four times in 1986. He, too, got admitted to a reputable university, but because of failing in the visa interview, for the rest of his life, he was confined in India, and he became a faculty with Sanjay in the same department.

It was the third week of July. All of them went to Bombay for Andria's visa interview. On day one, the initial biometrics was done, and the main interview was on the second day. It was a rainy day. On the second day, Andria's appointment was scheduled at 9:30 am in the American Consulate building of BKC (Bandra-Kurla Complex) area. They reached at 8:30 am to keep an one-hour margin. The whole family stayed in a nearby hotel in the BKC area, which was a walking distance from the US Consulate. Intentionally, Susan chose that venue so that despite all odds they could reach the visa office in time. In due time, Andria was allowed to enter. She had to hand over her mobile to her parents. Both Susan and Sanjay were waiting with their fingers crossed on the footpath opposite the visa office near the hotel Trident.

After nearly three hours, they found Andria coming out with another boy with a smile on her face. On seeing the smile, Sanjay jumped in enjoyment. Andria cleared her visa interview successfully. All the hurdles were over. Now the countdown started. There were hardly three weeks in hand. They bade goodbye to the visa office and started for their hotel in a relaxed mood. Andria's passport was taken by the visa officer, which would be delivered to Pune after stamping.

Before the departure, there was an orientation programme conducted by the academy wherefrom Andria had her training. That year, only from Pune, nearly one thousand and five hundred students were leaving for the USA for their MS. It was a record number in the history of the academy. Andria was felicitated for her admission to one of the world's topmost universities Texas A&M. In that orientation programme, Andria came to know about others who, too, got admission to Texas A&M. They formed a Whatsapp group, and their parents were also introduced to each other. A fresh bond of friendship started from that moment only.

Due to excitement and joy, Andria was emotional and her eyes glistened due to the feeling of excitement, happiness and elation. The weather was good. It was the month of August, and still, the sky was clear. Susan was looking at the serenity of the azure cloudless sky, and Sanjay was engrossed in deep thought, and he, too, was very much attached to Andria.

Sanjay could only do a little help to his daughter because American education was wildly expensive. Rich people were occupied with namby-pamby sentiments, but poor people thought of money and thought about how to arrange it. Still, expenses were left. By showing the service of Sanjay, they took an education loan for an amount of twenty-three lakhs, though the whole amount was not disbursed in a single go. Initially, they took twelve lakhs for the fee of the first semester and the expenses required for the initial set-up in the USA.

After the function, they went to a hotel for some snacks. Susan was looking dead tired. Her hazel eyes became pale with fatigue. She used coral-tinted lipstick, and the central attraction was her raindrop pendant.

The time for Andria's departure was at hand. Their hearts were heavy, and their eyes were dim with tears. In the famous book entitled *Prophet* authored by Khalil Gibran the author stated, "Love knows not its own depth until the hour of separation." Sanjay read the book more than one time, and that day, he could realise the meaning of the line in its truest sense.

After reaching the hotel, Andria and Susan slept, and Sanjay was listening to music. They did not start for Pune that day. They had booked the hotel for three days, and they were supposed to check out the next day around noon.

At night, they enjoyed a good dinner, and in an elated mood, Sanjay consumed two large bottles of beer, but Susan realised this consumption of beer would lead to a mood swing in Sanjay within the coming twenty-four hours. Exactly that happened.

The next morning, at the breakfast table, Sanjay became angry for no reason for the late supply of chicken sausage. It was finished. The team of managers was arranging for it, but Sanjay was not ready to wait even for a minute. He created a scene by insulting the manager in charge, who was looking after the complete menu and management of the breakfast. The manager was not aware of Sanjay's psychiatric disorder. He became very nervous at the scolding of Sanjay. Somehow, Susan and Andria pacified Sanjay, but Sanjay was derailed, and he left the breakfast table and returned to the room. As usual, like many times, Sanjay spoiled one more morning of Susan and Andria.

Andria slowly asked Susan, "Mummy, how would you stay with *Bapu* after my departure? I am really very anxious." Susan just consoled her. They too could not enjoy their breakfast. Just after having a cup of coffee, they returned to the room and found Sanjay in a very angry mood. The whole atmosphere was silent. Both Susan and Andria did not dare to utter a single word. Because they were well aware of Sanjay's temper. Suddenly, Sanjay said, "I would complain about the bastard manager to the hotel authority." Susan and Andria kept mum. Because any kind of advice or protest would make him more violent. So, the best way was to sustain all his deeds and activities. Somehow, within an hour, the situation became mostly normal.

Gradually, the day of departure came closer and closer. Her flight was on 16th August at 2:40 am. So, she was supposed to check in before midnight on 15th August. For that, all of them left Pune on the 14th of August. This time they took a hotel near the airport. Andria had two very big bags and one small bag. Apart from that, she had her handbag with her to keep the documents and other important things.

Since it was the Independence Day of India, the complete area of the Chhatrapati Shivaji Maharaj International Airport was decorated with tri-colour. The lighting was very soothing all over the area. Andria was standing, and both Susan and Sanjay were also standing by her side. Andria was strong. Even though Susan was strong, Sanjay was losing emotional balance. Already, he had consumed 20 mg of Diazepam (Four Valium–5 tablets) to keep his cool.

Andria was about to enter the airport. Hardly a few minutes were left. Andria came to Sanjay and told him, "*Bapu*, please take care of yourself and Mummy. I will be far, but I will always be by your side like an invisible shadow. Never be sad. We are nothing but a triangle. No one can separate even an arm of this triangle." Sanjay was touched. He planted a kiss on Andria's forehead. Now, Andria was a bit emotional. Tiny tears appeared in her eyes. Then Susan, too, kissed Andria, and Andria told her, "Mummy do not worry. If I don't get any RA/TA (Research Assistance or Teaching Assistance) then by working in some cafeteria, I will supplement my income. I am the last person to increase any sort of pressure on both of you." Susan was touched by the maturity of her daughter. She just kept mum, and her silence spoke of her grief for Andria's departure. Susan knew that Andria was going for a greater cause and no society could go ahead unless the women of that society became educated in the true sense.

Andria was wearing jeans and a green shirt. Before her final departure, Susan advised her not to go for hyper-socialisation and avoid the party animals in the USA. She went to the gate, and there was a small queue. Andria was a very down-to-earth human being. In her dictionary, the word 'vainglorious' was absent. Both Susan and Sanjay were looking at her continuously. Then she entered, and the bottom half of her sky-blue jeans melted away with each passing step. Sanjay was trying his best to have the last glimpse of Andria. Ultimately, Susan could convert the impossible into possible. Susan had already seen the photographs of the pompous campus of Texas A&M.

After that, they sat for a while on a wall adjacent to the departure terminal. A few flights were taking off one after another. Screams of jets were there. After half an hour, they came to the multi-level car parking of the airport and went to the seventh floor. From there, they booked an Uber cab and started for the hotel, which was very close to the airport, but certainly, it was not within walking distance. Sanjay was sitting by the driver, and Susan was occupying the rear seat. Suddenly, in the rear-view mirror, Sanjay found a sobbing Susan but did not react. But, internally, he realised that even soldiers cry. It was the tears of victory.

74

EMI of the Education Loan

The terms mostly hated by Sanjay were 'loan' and 'EMI'. It is a trap, but being a common man with a sizeable income, you cannot go ahead without loans. In previous days, things were cheap. Even a lower division clerk could construct his own house, but after the open market system and globalisation, the whole scenario has changed. Now, the situation is such that without a loan you can't go ahead. In the 1980s, the fee for an engineering course was less than one thousand rupees per year, and nowadays, it is in lakhs. The whole scenario has changed. Now, the concept is that you take a loan, have an education, have your placement, and after that, from the earned salary repay your loan. It's a loop.

Sanjay always had an abomination for loans, but he had no other option for Andria's education. Already, he had three personal loans, housing loan, and apart from that, Andria's education loan was an added headache. But, one good thing was that the system of CREDILA was very user-friendly. Initially, for three years, they deduct only interest, and after that, they start deducting the capital. For the initial disbursement of the amount per month, the EMI for the interest was approximately fifteen thousand rupees. Every month on the eleventh, the amount used to be debited from Sanjay's account. After a couple of months, some more amount was disbursed, and the EMI of the loan was slightly increased.

Though the amount was not very high, still it was an added expenditure for Sanjay. Due to the comparatively less tuition fees of Texas A&M, the education expenses of Andria were much less as compared to the other students of other universities in the USA. Secondly, right from the second semester, Andria got a job in a cafeteria on campus. She used to earn eight dollars per hour, and her weekly load was twenty hours. So, per week, she used to earn, one hundred and sixty dollars. That was great support for the family. At least, Andria was self-sufficient for her day-to-day expenses. Though Andria was granted an education loan of twenty-three lakhs rupees, in three steps, the total loan amount was disbursed, and in total, she had to take approximately twenty-one lakhs seventy thousand rupees.

In the cafeteria, she had to arrange chairs, and after the whole day, she had to keep the chairs one above the other. It was tedious physical work to handle approximately two hundred chairs. The biggest quality of Andria was that she never shared her pain (both mental and physical) with her parents. She knew that her parents were already in trouble, so she did not want to intensify the mental agony of her parents. Truly speaking, Andria was a gifted child. Rarely any parent gets such a loving and caring child.

She worked very hard and completed her MS within the minimum possible time, and in the end, the EMI was approximately eighteen thousand rupees only. After graduating, Andria got a job, and that was a matter of great solace for the whole family. After getting the job, Andria wanted to repay the capital amount of the education loan from the very first month. But, Susan suggested Andria enjoy her salary for the initial six months, and after that, she could start. Andria listened to her mother's suggestion and started repaying the capital amount at the rate of one lakh rupees per month from June 2018.

75

Didn't Want Her Daughter to Be Married before Being Financially Independent and Properly Qualified

Susan never wanted Andria to get married before being properly qualified and before having financial independence. The problem that Susan faced, she did not want her daughter to face. Still, in India, uneducated ladies are nothing but unpaid domestic workers. They are the wives of different people just for the namesake. Truly speaking, in the name of marriage, people get an unpaid domestic worker for a lifetime, and this male chauvinist society tortures their wives for a lifetime.

Susan wanted Andria to acclimatise to the atmosphere of American job culture and never wanted Andria to get married before she attained the age of twenty-eight. Susan was married at the age of nineteen, and her total life was a waste. She could not change her life, but she had got a valuable lesson from her own life. There is a famous saying, "Your last mistake is your best teacher." Susan followed the same adage. In her personal life, there were lots of mistakes, but Susan never wanted Andria to commit the same mistakes in her life. Susan was the person who was there to point out potholes in the career path of Andria. All the time, Susan gave correct advice to Andria from her lifetime experience.

If you want to learn a subject and have mastery over it, then either you need to go through a number of books on the subject and prepare notes, which is a very time-consuming process. Another way is to go through the teaching of a person who is an exponent in that subject. The second option is always preferred because you get the essence of the subject from the concerned expert within a small time. They give you the extract of the subject. That is the advantage of proper guidance. Susan was that shepherd in Andria's life who shepherded her correctly all the time. Andria also adopted the same view. She did not want to marry without being properly settled from an academic point of view as well as a professional point of view.

76

Taken an Internal Oath to Create a Perfect Career for Her Daughter

Susan was very obsessed with Andria's career, and she took an internal oath to make Andria successful both on the academic and professional front. An academic career and a professional career are totally different things. There are thousands of people having very strong academic careers, but in the field of job or service, they cannot excel. There are lakhs of M.Sc holders who ended their lives just as clerks or cashiers. On the contrary, there are examples where it is seen that a person with a very average or below average academic record reached a very senior position in a government or private organisation.

For this reason, Susan always wanted a balance between Andria's academic and professional career. There are many examples where it is observed that a person with a very strong academic background is totally trapped in a system, and the condition of that person can be compared to a booby trap. In spite of their will, they cannot get rid of the system. Without launching Andria, Susan was not able to achieve a foot-stomping mood. The influence of mind over mind is the most influential factor in human history. The same was the case with Andria. She was highly influenced by her mother.

In one book, the author wrote, "For success four things are required. They are intelligence, imagination, self-confidence and failure." I totally agree with him. For true success, failure is required, and then only you can relish the real taste of success. A person who doesn't have an idea about darkness can't enjoy the light. The same is the case here. If you taste failure once, you have no fear. You can take risks more easily.

Susan had unconditional love for Andria, and she was the real architect of Andria's career. Actually, Andria was very lucky. One in a million gets such a loving, caring and intelligent mother. In most cases, we come to know about fathers of successful persons, but rarely do we see examples of mothers. But, Susan was a mother with zero pampering. She was actually a life coach for Andria. Since Andria had a life coach in her house, she never bothered about teaching and counselling from outside. Susan was always there to support Andria in all activities whether it is the craftwork of senior KG or the mathematics of the tenth standard. Through the efforts of both the mother and daughter, the would-be career was just blooming and everyone had to wait for the complete blooming. Whether it is a flower or a career, it takes its own time to bloom.

77

Giving the Best to Her Daughter at the Cost of Her Life

Susan was determined to give the best of her to Andria even at the cost of her life. She taught Andria to be accustomed to all kinds of atmospheres and environments. Andria was comfortable in all conditions. Right from their 1-BHK apartment to five-star hotels, everywhere, she was comfortable. Susan gave special impetus to the grooming of Andria. Regarding Andria's attire, Susan was very selective, and Andria was never shabbily dressed. Even when she was in school, never did she go with a uniform which was not properly ironed. Susan used to make Andria familiar with good perfume, and from her mother, Andria knew about perfumes with woody and floral fragrances. To this day, Andria remembers how Susan used to squirt perfume on Andria's dress during any occasion or function.

Susan was devoid of a humdrum domestic life; appalling poverty was their regular affair. They had to go through an unceasing struggle. In spite of those odds, Susan always tried to provide the best slice of life to Andria. They were not poor, but due to the high standard of living their savings were practically zero. The other faculties who used to work with Sanjay used to live like beggars. They had a very poor lifestyle, and from their looks only, anyone could figure out that they were all starved people from all points of view. Forget about luxury, they never used to even go for ice cream during summer. Their only motto was to save money at the cost of their life.

But, Susan's philosophy was different. For the sake of tomorrow, she was not ready to sacrifice her today. When they used to visit the posh restaurants or hotels of Pune, the owner of the restaurant or hotel used to come and sit with them for chatting. It was a routine phenomenon. They were under the misconception that Sanjay was a very rich person. Because the look of Sanjay and Susan was very aristocratic and Andria was also a charming girl. Aristocracy was engraved in their look, and that is why, people used to be attracted by the whole family, and all of them enjoyed a cult status wherever they visited.

Susan was a good cook, and Andria too adopted the culinary skill and expertise from her mother only. When Andria did not have the expected result in the tenth standard, then Susan thought of a befitting revenge. After the result of the tenth standard, Andria had to face many adverse and pungent comments from many of the parents of her classmates. Actually, all were jealous of Andria, and her relatively poor result opened an avenue for them for criticising and insulting her. Susan injected the thirst for revenge into Andria's mind, and Andria did that afterwards. In future, when she reached Texas A&M, she found none of her classmates was in and around her because none of them could even reach the threshold of Texas A&M. In this life, for belittling others, you need not fight. If you just scale the rungs of the ladder of your career, they would be automatically small.

For Susan, Andria could be compared to a spot of green on a wilting leaf. Susan's energy could be compared to the power of an engine, which sputters in the first gear and is ready to accept further changes of gears. Andria was a sensitive, intelligent and delicate girl. The desert weeds live, but a rose needs proper caring, proper soil and proper nurturing. Otherwise, it would wilt. In this world, whatever is delicate needs special care, otherwise it won't survive. So, every plant needs a soft and kind touch from a gardener. For Andria, Susan was the gardener. The gardener must know where the seed must be planted. If he puts the seed on a stone, it will never sprout. It will remain a seed only. Even after ten years, it will be a seed only. Many people in this world can be compared to that seed because they did not get proper soil in time, and only for that reason, they could not germinate properly. These are the unfortunate children of God, neither had they got the proper soil nor did they get a gardener who could nurture them. So, from that point of view, Andria was really blessed. A lady like

Susan could bloom a rose even in a desert. It is the skill of a life coach who shapes a child.

There are many guardians who are highly qualified, but they fail to guide their children. Because they do not have any idea about proper parenting. They are qualified but not educated. Qualification comes from outside but education comes from inside. The first and foremost thing for a parent is to be friendly with their child. As long as fear is there, the child will not be close to his parents. The atmosphere of a house and school both must be love-oriented, not fear-oriented. A true genius is born out of love and affection, not stress and fear. Susan knew the art of being close to her child. Not only that, she mastered all the qualities that a parent needs for proper parenting. Andria and her chequered career are nothing but the result of twenty-five years of hard work and vision of Susan.

78

Boycotting the Programmes of the Bengali Association

Both Susan and Sanjay were known widely for their unsocial nature. Truly speaking, Susan was quite social, and for her, socialisation was not a problem, but for the mental health of Sanjay, Susan maintained a constant distance from socialisation, and especially, Susan maintained a safe distance from the local Bengali society. Their only attachment to society was while visiting Durga Puja for one or two days and contributing the yearly subscription for the Puja.

From day one, Susan decided to keep a safe distance from the Bengali Community of Pune. It is better not to mix than quarrel after mixing. Sanjay, too, supported her decision, and due to Sanjay's nature, he was unsocial by birth. Once, the Bengali community approached Sanjay for lifetime membership of the local Bengali club, and the fee was two thousand five hundred rupees. Sanjay gave it and got rid of it.

There were some cultural vultures in the Bengali community who were known as cremation experts. Once, Sanjay saw with his own eyes the cremation of a young Bengali boy. The members of the Bengali association decided to pour twenty litres of diesel on the funeral pyre to accelerate the speed of cremation. It was a manual cremation. After seeing this, he lost his complete respect for his own community permanently.

There used to be annual cultural programmes arranged and organised by the Bengali society of Pune. Susan used to go there. But, her overall experience with the Bengali community was vicarious.

79

Not Giving Divorce to Her Husband

Susan's biggest quality was that she was never influenced by others. Firstly, after leaving her house, her relationship with her mother, sister and brother was cemented. With her maternal side, she had just maintained a formal relationship. The most praiseworthy point of Susan was that she never criticised Sanjay in front of anyone. Because she knew this kind of criticism would just bring some pseudo sympathy and nothing more than that could be achieved. Susan was a private person.

She had very few friends, which could be counted within minutes, but they were her permanent friends. A good and reliable friend is equivalent to one thousand relatives. Some of her friends advised her to file a divorce case against Sanjay and get rid of him. There was logic in their statements, but deep inside, Susan possessed a fountain of love for Sanjay, and the intensity was the same as her feelings that had been there in the very initial stage of their affair. When her other friends were enjoying an aromatherapy massage and mouth-watering dishes in flashy restaurants in their summer holidays, Susan used to be busy between home and the hospital. That was her sheer bad luck.

One thing that Susan realised was that Sanjay was an honest, upright and straightforward person who had overcome his greed for money and property. In today's world, how many people are there who refuse their father's property? Hardly one or two. The people of this world do not want to take the responsibility of the parents, but they want the share of their properties. What a heinous attitude! Sanjay was miles away from this greedy nature. That is why, in spite of all the odds and all the torture, Susan had love and respect for Sanjay in the deepest core of her soft mind.

Secondly, Susan was highly impressed by Sanjay's scholasticism. Out of one lakh, only one is there who has academic affairs, the rest of the lot just goes through books to get a meagre job. So, one thing is very clear. Sanjay was an odd man out. His positive and negative qualities were uncommon among other gents of society. But, in overall rating, Susan had respect for Sanjay. Only about his HIV status, she was damn dissatisfied.

Sanjay was an ardent book lover, and their whole house was full of books. Susan never protested because she knew if you need to accept a person, then along with his ten good qualities, you will have to accept his four bad qualities too. Susan was known for her reticence and this grave nature helped Susan live independently in this cruel society. The main role of society is only to criticise you. You can throw a party and spend lakhs of rupees, but still, you cannot win the minds of people. At any cost, they would find some faults. If you put a black dot over a white paper then a normal person would enjoy the white background, but a negative-minded person would look at the black dot only.

So, Susan decided never to give a divorce to Sanjay. She was ready to stay by his side till the last day of her life, and she had completely diverted her mind to the design of Andria's career. She did not have any crush on any other person. She did not have an opportunity to enjoy conjugal happiness, but she suffered from conjugal unhappiness due to erratic activities of Sanjay. But, in her life, she could never think of any person apart from Sanjay. Though there is a saying that a man is by nature polygamous, the thought of Susan was of monogamous nature only.

Society did not know about the status of HIV of Sanjay and Susan. Only Andria knew it. Regarding the HIV status, Susan preferred to have an incognito status. Susan's role in the family can be compared to sugar in tea. As long it is present, we do not praise it, and the moment it is absent, people start feeling it. Susan's role was so imperceptible that no one could feel easily her contribution, but Andria and Sanjay knew that Susan was the rock of Gibraltar for both of them.

Sometimes, in the early morning, Susan used to get up and dastardly go to the terrace, and she used to look at the mist soften morning. She used to be submerged in the miasma of the past. But, for her, duty was the first priority. She did not have time to enjoy the beauty of the rising sun with a steaming mug of coffee and the fresh newspaper because she could not wipe away the obligations of her life. For her morning meant starting of series of commitments. It starts from ironing Andria's dresses to polishing Sanjay's shoes.

Once, after a big argument, Sanjay left the house, and he straight away went to Serampore to his father's house. It happened just after Andria's departure to the USA. There was no fault of Susan. While Sanjay's departure, Susan never tried to prevent him from going. She knew his nature, and she knew that after ten days he would return also. But, this type of erratic attitude of Sanjay used to disturb the complete peace of the family. After seven days, Susan received a letter from Sanjay, and the letter was dropped three days after Sanjay's departure from Serampore only. That means after leaving the house, Sanjay realised his guilt and wrote it and dropped it. In the last line, he wrote, "Your tears told me more than words could have conveyed." By this line, Susan was deeply touched. The speciality of mentally ill people is that, due to some reason, these people can read the minds of other people better than the people who are certified as normal human beings by society. Both Susan and Sanjay used to feel for each other, but Susan never made an exhibition of her love for Sanjay. Susan's speciality was that she kept everything inside. She never vented her happiness and unhappiness publicly. Feelings, and especially mutual feelings, are essential in a conjugal relationship. The feeling of care is the beginning of affection.

After a few days, Sanjay returned from Serampore and joined the college. Due to this small change of place, his mental health was slightly improved. He was in a good mood. Though Sanjay was literally bogged down by society, he didn't bother because one thing he knew very clearly: this sad, bad and mad society wouldn't feed his family. So, he fucked the rituals and ethos of the social fabric.

One day, the whole family was invited by the parents of Andria's best friend. Though Andria was in the opposite hemisphere of the globe, Sanjay gladly agreed to visit. Sanjay wore an off-white shirt with navy blue trousers, and he looked impressive. After getting dressed, he practically squirted the deodorant bottle on his entire body, and only a little amount was left. They started. Due to some reason, Susan's mood was off, and Sanjay could read her mind. For that reason, he did not initiate any conversation. Their relationship slowly began to deteriorate as years passed on, but still, Susan decided not to give a divorce to Sanjay.

80

Madness of Her Husband and the Severe Bout of Insanity

Sanjay was a critical patient of anxiety disorder, depression, mood swings and bipolar disorder, but apart from that, he used to face many physical problems, e.g., twitching of eyes and muscles, repeated urination, stiff muscles, tremors, vertigo, dry mouth, loss of balance, allergy from crowds, feeling of collapsing, so on and so forth. Just due to medicines, he was in a state of neutral equilibrium. There was a history of insanity on his maternal side, secondly, his mother was also a patient of acute neurasthenia (weak nerves), and being the second child, Sanjay, too, inherited all the diseases of his mother.

But, Sanjay made a mistake. He discontinued psychiatric medicines without informing Susan. Though Susan was under the impression that Sanjay was taking the medicines regularly. Actually, she was under the wrong impression. Sanjay stopped all the recommended medicines, e.g., Amixide, Ridazine–10 and Oxetol–300. He only used to consume Valium–5 (Diazepam–5) whenever he wanted.

Gradually, he was losing all the energy and hope. He could be compared to a wilting leaf. He used to wear tattered shirts and trousers, and in that haggard condition, he used to go to college. All the staff was aware of his bad mental climate; even the students were aware of it. Only because of Sanjay's fury and rage, no one could mock at him. Sanjay was a person with self-stultification, and he was aware of his weak points and deficiencies and always used to counsel himself.

It was a Saturday morning, and on Saturdays, Sanjay used to have a morning college. He went to the canteen after taking the first lecture and ordered a veg sandwich. Once he nibbled the sandwich, he immediately realised that it was stale. He became red with rage, went to the canteen manager and slapped him. A big scene was created, and that became a very serious matter. The canteen manager wanted to file an FIR against Sanjay, but the college authority pacified him. Sanjay was forced to beg for an unconditional apology publicly. Though Sanjay did that, internally he could not accept it, and that matter triggered all his psychiatric problems.

There were aberrations, which were visible in day-to-day life. Susan used to play the role of a fortification to protect Sanjay from all social taboos. But, luck was bad. Andria was not there, and Susan went to the nearby market. Sanjay was alone at home. In those days, Sanjay's behaviour became very odd, and in spite of having Valium (Diazepam), he used to have insomniac nights. Susan was yet to return from the market. By that time, Sanjay went to the landing outside their apartment in a completely naked condition, sat on the staircase and started masturbating. Suddenly, the neighbouring lady opened her door and screamed loudly upon seeing Sanjay. Sanjay was inert. Immediately, a few people and the security staff of the society rushed to the spot and forcibly put Sanjay in his flat. Sanjay did not have any mental balance about the dos and don'ts.

By that time, Susan returned from the market, and she was shocked and ashamed beyond the limit because of this most unusual behaviour of her husband. This was not an incident to promulgate, but the people of the society spread this news to all the corners. Sanjay did not have malicious intentions, but this world does not accept the unnatural behaviour of any person. This world will not listen to your problems; they won't listen to your sadness; they won't realise your pain, but certainly, they would point out your mistakes. Due to this activity of Sanjay, Susan was in blushing mode.

In the evening, the chairman of the society called Susan and asked about the gross behavioural disorder of Sanjay. Along with other members of the society, he clearly told Susan to send Sanjay to a mental asylum. They had logic behind their suggestion. To date, there were no complaints from the society, but the heinous activity of Sanjay zeroed their social status within a fraction of a minute.

Susan returned home and did not discuss anything with Sanjay. Sanjay was sleeping at odd hours in the evening. The time was 8:00 pm. Susan talked to the psychiatrist who used to treat Sanjay. Even the doctor advised rehabilitation for at least a month. Nothing was told to Sanjay to avoid further insanity and vengeance. But, the next morning, an ambulance came along with a squad. Sanjay was totally unaware of these things. Four strong men were there, and they were properly equipped and trained, too. Two of them went inside the bedroom and caught hold of Sanjay. Sanjay started fighting with them with the energy of a bull and started abusing Susan in Bengali, "*Ei khanki* (prostitute), mother *chod* (mother fucker), *ei saber pichone tui hochhis asol saitan* (you are the main culprit behind all this). *Eta holo tor sarajantra* (This is your conspiracy)."

Those two people dragged Sanjay to the drawing room, and then the other two people tightly caught both his legs. In that condition, he was tied with a strong rope, and for pacifying him, a strong dose of sedative was given in the form of an injection. There was no light. So, the elevator was not in operation. He was shifted from the fourth floor to the ambulance manually. The house was like a frozen star in the sky. For the neighbours and society people, it became a *tamasha* (a matter of merriment), and for the whole day, they whispered about Sanjay's mental state and his shifting to the mental asylum. Even Susan's lips became salty with tears, which trickled down her cheek. Susan could very easily sense a shift in the atmosphere of their society. Only because of her grave personality, no one dared to ask her any questions. Susan could not sleep the whole night. It was nearly 3:00 am., and Susan was still awake, thinking about the beginning of the end.

81

Husband's Permanent Departure to Mental Asylum

After Sanjay's shift to the mental asylum, he never returned home. It was his permanent departure. Due to his blasphemy, the doctors did not want to relieve him from the asylum. The shift brought a permanent taboo to his family. Susan never used to mix with others. She used to visit Sanjay once a week. Sanjay would always be in an irritating mood and was always under the impression that Susan sent her to the mental asylum by conspiring with his psychiatrist. Though, actually, it was not so. But, who would convince Sanjay? It was practically impossible to convince or counsel a mental patient because their thought process is not like common people's. Their thought process is totally different. The doctors, too, cannot bring them to the mainstream. Using modern medicines, they can do just enough so that the patient's condition does not deteriorate further.

One day, Susan was leaving her house to meet Sanjay. The asylum was located at a distance of twenty kilometres from their house. Susan's only weak point was that she did not know how to drive. After purchasing the car, Susan learned how to drive, cleared the exam and got the license, too. But, she could not gather the confidence to drive on the busy roads of Pune. So, mostly, she was dependent on autorickshaws and public transport.

When she was leaving her house, the weather was squalid, and there were gales from the western side, due to the low-pressure region in the Arabian Sea. When Susan reached the asylum, she found a lady moaning outside the casualty in a half-naked condition, and her family members were trying to console her. After inquiring, she came to know that the young lady was brutally raped by a gang of bastards, and right from that day, she lost her complete mental balance. Not a single rapist could be traced because she could not see anyone in the darkness of a rainy night in a desolate area of the locality.

Before meeting Sanjay, Susan met the doctor under whom Sanjay was being treated. The doctor did not talk much. Only by his gesticulation, he made Susan understand that Sanjay's condition was not good. After meeting Sanjay, Susan did not become comfortable. She brought a homemade cake and sweets for Sanjay because he was fond of bakery products and sweets right from childhood. But, instead of accepting them, Sanjay threw the cake into one corner of his cell, and the sweets were not even touched by him. Susan was deeply hurt. Without saying anything, she came out of the asylum and sat over the small green lawn of the campus. Sanjay was morbidly melancholic.

Susan was just looking at the fresh blades of grass over the lawn and thinking, "Why me?" There was no answer. Small children are dying in road accidents for no fault of theirs, innocent girls are raped, and corrupt politicians are surviving with glamour and grandeur. After this, how can one believe in God? At least she did not.

I have kicked the idols of Gods and Goddesses many times in my life. In the Hindu religion, they say, calamities occur due to the sin done by one in the previous birth. But, my question is that why the bad sins done due to bad deeds are not settled then and there in this birth itself? Though from the inner core of my mind, I do not believe in the previous birth or future birth. For that reason, I respect, like and love the essence of Christianity. They do not believe in rebirth. They believe in one life and try their best to enjoy it thoroughly.

Gradually, the evening was enveloping the atmosphere. There was eerie silence everywhere in and around the asylum because it was located at the extreme end of the city. Susan stood and started walking on the tree-lined road in front of the asylum. Once, she looked back and thought, the person who loved her most is shifted there and nothing can be a bigger tragedy than this. But, due to Sanjay's volatile temperament and insane nature, it was not recommended to keep him in a civilised society.

Before returning home, she walked down the boulevard in front of the asylum and came to the main road. Susan purchased some flowers, and after reaching home, put those flowers in the conical flower vase, which was presented by one of Sanjay's colleagues on their marriage anniversary long back in Khamgaon. In every nook and corner of the house, memories of Sanjay were engraved. It was the end of September, and in the same month, the famous *Ganesh* festival was there.

82

Sacrificed Her Whole Life for Her Daughter and Family

In the Second World War, a British soldier was dying, but he had a way to escape. When after being severely wounded, he was shifted to the hospital, one of his colleagues asked him, "Why didn't you escape? There was ample opportunity." He replied and the reply is a landmark reply in the history of human civilisation. He said, "I will die, but my son will live." What does it indicate? It indicates that at least one generation has to suffer and sacrifice for the next generation.

In Andria's life, Susan played the role of that soldier. Susan practically sacrificed her whole life for her daughter and family. She was qualified. She could have opted for a full-time job, but in that case, Andria's career would have been affected. So, at the cost of her own career, Susan designed Andria's career. By nature, Susan was orthodox and puritanical. Susan never went for the reclamation of her ancestral property from her mother. One thing she knew very clearly was that if someone gives you something with hatred and unwillingness then you must not accept that thing.

In the evening time, Susan used to sit on a rickety folding chair kept over the hand-knotted carpet and look at the helm of the mountains, which were a hundred miles away from their residence towards Lonavala and Khandala.

Sometimes, Susan used to think of her old days. How was the time spent from 1991 to 2016? Twenty-five years passed by, and little Andria of that day became a posh lady. True education is to learn how to think, not what to think. Susan always gave maximum stress on this true education. You can see thousands of qualified people, but rarely do you have the opportunity to come in contact with an educated person. Education is different. Qualification is external and education is internal. Sometimes, she used to sob silently by remembering the past and the ups and downs of her life.

One day, she was weeping. It was difficult for her to control her emotion. She straightaway went to the terrace of the apartment. It was raining with moderate intensity. It was raining, and Susan was weeping. Her tears were mixing with the rainwater, and after some time, when she returned, a few society members found her in a completely drenched condition, but Susan was able to camouflage her tears. Because she did not want a showcasing of her sentiments and emotions.

83

Husband's Superannuation Due to Insanity

Sanjay was in the mental asylum, and all his leaves were consumed. He was surviving without any pay. So, both Susan and Andria decided to go for the processing of the papers for Sanjay's VRS. Sanjay was totally mad in those days, and most of the time, due to heavy doses of the medicine, he used to be in a somnolent condition. So, there was no point in talking to him regarding VRS. One thing was sure. His mental health was derailed beyond repair, and he was declared a completely insane person by the panel of doctors.

Susan visited Sanjay's office and brought the required papers from the registrar of the college. Luckily, Sanjay got a government service while working in Khamgaon, and luckily, he had completed more than twenty years of government service. He was eligible for a pension because he served more than twenty years. Though in a severely ill condition, one may get a pension even before twenty years, those procedures are very long and complicated. One thing Susan realised was that if Sanjay took VRS, he would get a pension, and in hand, he would get some lump-sum amount from his savings in the GPF, gratuity, GIS (Group Insurance Scheme) and, last but not the least, the pension commutation value. Since all his leaves were consumed, the question of leave encashment did not arise.

So, Susan filled up all the papers and went to the asylum for taking Sanjay's signature. He was in a very bad mood. Still, Susan dared to give him the papers. After seeing the papers, he became furious and said, "Do you people want to convert me to a mummy?" After saying so, he tore all those papers.

To fill the papers, Susan needed two complete days, and being in Texas, Andria continuously guided Susan for filling all the papers accurately. By seeing this act of Sanjay, Susan was shocked beyond measure, but she was helpless. After some time, the hospital authority told her to leave, because the visiting hour was over.

With a tense and broken mind, Susan returned home and consulted Sanjay's best friend. He was also a faculty in the same college in the same department as Sanjay. He assured her that he was ready to get the work done.

After a couple of days, again, Susan went to the Registrar of the college, and on seeing her, the Registrar asked, "Madam, have you brought the signed papers?" Susan narrated the whole incident. The Registrar was an aged and sympathetic person. For a couple of minutes, he kept mum. Susan broke the silence and talked about Sanjay's friend who was ready to get the work done. The Registrar told Susan, "That will be better because Sir always had good intimacy with Christopher Sir."

The generosity of the Registrar Impressed Susan. The Registrar was a helpful person, but he was known for flirting with the lady faculty of the institute. Once, Sanjay, too, discussed about the Registrar with Susan. When Susan was talking to the Registrar, he was continuously looking at Susan's cleavage, and she had been wearing a low-cut blouse on that day. Susan didn't even get time to select a dress properly, and for that, whatever was available was chosen by her. The blouse was old enough, and with the passage of continuous use, it had faded with time.

Again, Susan collected the same papers from the Registrar and came out of the college. The weather was slightly cold. There was a tinge of cold in the air, and the air was crisp and cold. Susan was depressed and devitalised. She had a lot of dreams about Sanjay's career, but all the dreams were shattered in the last few months.

For a psychiatrist, one good thing is that the patients treated by them can never be cured, at the most, their psychological problems can be controlled to some extent. So, for them, the patients are just like clientele, and with each passing year, the numbers of patients keep on increasing.

After coming out of the college, Susan was slowly walking on the road adjacent to the college, and the dappled sunlight was filtering through the dark green trees. Sanjay did not bequeath anything for Susan or Andria except the flat where they used to stay. To date, Susan remembers how she used to crouch when Sanjay used to assault her mercilessly, Sanjay did not even spare little Andria too. But Susan tried her best to protect Andria, and she used to sustain all the blows for no fault of hers. Susan was thinking about how unfortunate a lady could be if she did not have earnings. Otherwise, Susan did not have any wish to take a single penny from Sanjay. Her only negative point was that she was dependent on Sanjay for two square meals.

With a broken mind, she reached home. She had some last night's leftovers, popped a pill and went to sleep. She did not even know when she slept. It was 11 pm. Suddenly, she got up. She was quite hungry. She prepared butter toast and an omelette. She didn't have the luck to have ready food. From the age of nineteen, she used to prepare and serve food to all the family members in the house of her father-in-law, who was a brut under the cover of a man.

84

Night Sky

The night sky was Susan's favourite, but where was the time to gaze at the starlit sky? Before marriage, both Susan and Sanjay used to sit in the big playground of the college campus and gossip for hours together. Sanjay was a chain smoker. He used to consume one after another cigarette, and Susan used to play with her gold pendant. Then they used to lie on the soft grass and look at the moonlight by which the clouds were bathed. The star-spangled sky could be compared with a platter full of stars, and it was a feast for their eyes. The façade of the main building of the college used to be submerged in the moonlight, and both of them used to be lost in Wordsworthian thoughts. They used to listen to the music of the sphere and the silence of the huddled trees, which used to whisper with each other.

To date, Susan remembers the phosphorescent blue of moonlight, which used to cast a partial shadow of Sanjay on the trunk of the tree adjacent to the ground. Susan used to listen to the wind filtering through the willows. To date, Susan can vividly recall those moments when the strong summer wind used to blow and create a ripple over the grass blades on the ground.

Sometimes before the evening, both of them used to meet at the rear gate of the college. It was a very silent area. At that point, some privacy was there; at least they were able to enjoy a sweet kiss behind the bush near the main water tank of the institute. The cobalt twilight sky used to be the witness of their love for each other. After that, they used to come to Susan's house. Still, Susan remembers the silvery moonbeams peeping through the broken glass panes of their drawing room.

India is a place where forget about open sex, even if you just hug your partner, a thousand pairs of jealous and sex-starved eyes will frown and look down upon you. These senior scoundrels didn't have sexual satisfaction, and they do not want the next generation to be happy from the sexual point of view. For them, sex means producing children, and obviously male children. Because these bastards have a gender bias. But, they forget that their mothers were also ladies. A house where a woman is not respected can be compared with hell.

85

Death of Sanjay

Susan had a suppressed fear of Sanjay's suicidal tendencies, and exactly that happened at the end of 2016. Sanjay used to feel claustrophobic in the asylum and repeatedly wanted to get rid of the asylum, but looking at his mental health, the doctors did not permit him to get discharged from the asylum.

It was the early morning of 16th December 2016. Susan received a phone call from the asylum and came to know that Sanjay was sick. She was advised to report immediately. She guessed perfectly because she had trepidation about Sanjay's acts, and that's why, repeatedly, she requested the dean of the mental asylum to relieve Sanjay. When she reached the spot, already a police van was there. A few policemen were there. Even in that condition one of the policemen was staring at Susan unabashedly. Really shameless person!

Sanjay committed suicide in the wee hours by hanging from the ceiling fan. He used a nylon cord as a rope. No one ever thought in their wildest dream that Sanjay would leave this world so easily and so early. All the inmates were curious. By the time Susan entered the spot, the body was shifted from the room to another room adjacent to the staircase.

When Susan reached the place, she was shocked upon seeing the expression on Sanjay's face who was already dead. The eyes bulged outside the eye socket, and there was a deep mark on his neck on both sides due to the heavy pressure of the nylon rope. His tongue was projected outside partially. There was a one-line suicide note where Sanjay expressed his last feelings to her beloved daughter. It was written, "Dear *Gnyeru*, please take care of Dog in my absence. Bye and Love. Always Yours, *Bapu*". Lovingly, Sanjay used to address Andria as *Gnyeru* and both Sanjay and Andria lovingly used to address Susan as Dog. After seeing this horrific scene, Susan lost the ground below her feet, and she did not know what to do. In his last days, Sanjay became very thin with a conspicuous Adam's apple.

Everything was settled, and one thing was good, they didn't have any relatives who would claim the properties. In the society papers, the apartment was made in Susan's name, and for bank-related papers, Susan was already nominated by Sanjay.

Andria was in the USA, and her 1st semester of MS was in full swing, and that was the time of her examination. There was a grimace on Susan's face. Within no time, the body was sent for a post-mortem at the government-run hospital, but Susan decided not to inform Andria immediately. Because she did not have money to come to India, and secondly, even if she would have come, the person who was no more could not be made alive again. So, there was no point in perturbing her.

Susan sat under a tree. Right since the morning, she didn't even have a cup of tea. Due to an empty stomach and enormous stress, she had hyperacidity and nausea. Somehow, she controlled herself.

Before his death, Sanjay didn't shave for a couple of days. He had a salt-and-pepper beard on the last day of his presence in this world. In the post-mortem, they took adequate time. It was a bleak afternoon for Susan. In the meanwhile, there was a Whatsapp video call from Andria, Susan did not receive the call.

By late evening, the body was handed over to Susan, and the police had a brief discussion with Susan. The weather was cloudy, and a solid shelf of winter clouds was there. Sanjay was cremated in the local crematorium, and most of the neighbours and local Bengalis came to the funeral. Susan had to do all the venerated customs of the Hindu religion just because Andria was not there. Though Susan didn't convert her religion, still she silently obeyed all the rituals stated by the priest.

In the end, Susan heaved a sigh of relief because a great and perturbing chapter of her life was over. Apparently, it seems to be very odd, but in reality, Susan was relieved of great responsibility and mental agony. Only the caregivers of psychiatric patients can feel Susan's condition. For most of the people, colleagues and students, Sanjay was nothing but a nerd.

While torching the funeral pyre, Susan was recollecting Sanjay's favourite dialogue. Whenever he used to be in a good mood, he would say, "Sus, we shall adapt to the curves of life." But, ultimately, he couldn't. Ultimately, he preferred death, and he must have thought about Andria more than a hundred times before taking the final step, but he must have been psychologically collapsed and devastated.

Before starting the funeral rituals, one of Sanjay's office colleagues removed the gold ring from Sanjay's finger. There was a ruby fixed in the gold ring, and the facet of the ruby was still shining like a grain of a pomegranate. The funeral started and the flames were moving upward. Susan was gazing at the burnt logs of the funeral pyre. There was a pall of silence. Susan was standing very close to the funeral pyre, and she was feeling the heat of the engulfing flame. She had a queer feeling that she was being watched by hundreds of pairs of eyes.

A scholar was slashed just like a star from the celestial sphere. Sanjay departed forever. It was the end of a chapter of Susan's life. Due to the heat of the funeral pyre, Susan's glasses became moist. She took them off and wiped them slowly with the corner of her *dupatta*. She had no tears because the tremendous shock choked even her tear glands. She was broken from the inside. Susan had watched Sanjay fall sick and die. Right from day one, she was the witness to the struggle of her scholar husband.

The news of Sanjay's death rippled through the society. Many of his students and colleagues also came to the funeral. Approximately, two hundred people were there. A few ladies also joined to console Susan. When a close family member dies, the society tries to console the other family members. They can't eliminate the grief, but what they can do is alleviate the pain and grief.

At the end of the funeral, a few more rituals were left. Susan was about to break down, but somehow, she fought back her tears. One thing was known to her. With time everything will change. This mental scar would never vanish, but the pain would subside with each passing day.

Sanjay's father was still alive in their native place, Serampore, but Susan didn't inform that octogenarian about the death of his son. Because he was of no use. His father was so selfish that even the news of his son's death couldn't prevent him from taking dinner on time. Sanjay had decided to relinquish the property of his father long back, and he possessed a broken relationship with his father. Susan didn't even have an iota of respect for her father-in-law. So, he was not informed about Sanjay's death. Sanjay's brother was out of reach because his address was not known. He was settled in Abu Dhabi. For the whole family, it was a bizarre incident.

Once, Susan read in a book, "A tragedy is never a tragedy for long until it happens to yourself." That day, Susan realised the inner and deep meaning of that line. Susan was remembering the days when they were just introduced to each other. Susan used to run her fingers gently through his thick hair. Those moments would never come back in her life.

After the funeral was over, she came to the house, and there was no one with her. She strongly decided not to inform anything to Andria immediately, and afterwards, she would think about it. After a few minutes, Susan left the house with an enlarged passport-size photo of Sanjay and went to a nearby shop. She told the shop owner to put the photograph of Sanjay in a wooden frame and deliver it immediately. She took the delivery, and the wooden frame was hung with rope in the south wall of the drawing room of their flat. In the photograph, Sanjay looked very jovial. No one could guess from the smile that he was a patient of deep depression and morbid melancholy. On the ground, there was a peacock blue carpet, which was selected by Sanjay in a local exhibition.

It was 1:00 am. Since morning, except for a few cups of tea and biscuits, Susan did not have any food. The ordeal, which started at 5:00 am, ended at 9:00 pm. In the crematorium, everyone observed her equanimity. There was no emotional vent in public. Now, she was free. No one would irritate her; no one would call her from behind; no one would insult her, and no one would assault her. Still, why was she so possessive about Sanjay? Even she didn't know the answer.

She did not even know when a wife was converted to the caregiver of a psychiatric patient. A psychiatric patient can't survive without his caregiver. Probably, this must be the reason for his death-cum-suicide. Susan, many times, requested the doctors to relieve Sanjay, but the doctors didn't want to take the risk. The next morning, Sanjay's ash was collected, but it was not laid to rest with great solemnity because Susan lost all respect for these rituals. There was a time when they were two different individuals, but their minds were together. But, after knowing about Sanjay's sexual behaviour, Susan lost all respect for him.

Andria was informed about Sanjay's death after eleven days. By that time, her first-semester examinations were over, and there were holidays due to Christmas. In the whole complex, Andria was staying alone. All her friends left the campus. Most of them went to their respective countries, and the rest of them went to some of their relatives within the USA only. Neither Andria had the money to travel to India nor did she have any relatives in the USA. She was totally broken, but Susan requested Andria's best friend to take care of her.

Andria's best friend was a Nigerian girl named Bukky. She was Andria's classmate. Though Andria had shared a rented apartment, most of the time, Andria used to be at Bukky's place. Bukky used to stay inside the campus and belonged to a very rich family. But, her speciality was her down-to-earth nature. Luckily, Bukky didn't shift her coordinates during the Christmas vacation, because her relatives were staying in close proximity to the college. Susan could really rely on Bukky at the most critical stage of their life. Andria was the primogeniture to inherit all the properties of Sanjay, but unfortunately, except loan, Sanjay didn't keep anything for the family. He could only repay the complete loan of the apartment, and he made the apartment in Susan's name after clearing the entire home loan. So, the question of uprooting from the house was fortunately absent.

Susan was standing in front of the photo, and at a stretch, looking at the brilliant and radiant eyes of her first and last love, Sanjay. She, too, couldn't realise when the tear started trickling down her cheek, but now she didn't control herself. A solitary tear trickled down her cheek. Sanjay could see her beloved Sus nodding through her tears.

86

Witnessing the Widowhood and Not Going for Any Ritual

After Sanjay's suicide, Susan became a widow overnight. Truly speaking, after their marriage, neither Sanjay forced Susan to convert to his religion nor Susan was interested. It was not because Susan was a hardcore Christian, but for many other important works, it was not their priority. Though Sanjay's father reminded them more than once to convert Susan's religion, neither Sanjay nor Susan gave any importance to it. Ultimately, she did not convert her religion. Since she was not converted, the question of following the Hindu rituals didn't arise, and secondly, Susan was not even interested in those baseless rituals. Hindus go for rituals, but they don't even realise and understand the meaning of the Sanskrit *mantras.* They can hardly pronounce those *mantras* correctly.

The sudden death of any person in a family (whether by suicide or accident) put the family on an emotional and financial roller coaster. Due to his high qualification and his position as a faculty in an Engineering College, Sanjay always enjoyed a cult status in society, and secondly, he had a background of NIT. But, after his death, gradually, the family started losing that cult status. On the contrary, a group of people made Susan responsible for Sanjay's death. Since Susan was not very social and friendly, people in the society were not happy with her. In Indian society, the easiest thing is to assassinate the character of a lady. Though Susan did not bother. She knew one hard truth, and the truth was that in the hour of need, this society would not feed her family. As lord Christ carried his own cross, in the same way, Susan had to run her family.

It was an evening of a rainy season. The weather was dull. As daylight steadily bleached darkness from the sky, in the same way, Sanjay was permanently removed from her life. Susan was not an atheist, but she didn't show off her religion. She used to visit both churches and temples. She prayed for the well-being of the family both in churches and temples. One important thing she realised while being united with God through prayer was that the place of the prayer is not important; the attention of the prayer is important.

After Sanjay's death, Susan used to feel very lonely. After all, Andria and she had an age gap, and both of them belonged to two different generations. What you can discuss with your spouse, you can't always discuss that with your child. You may be friendly with your child, but you can't be their friend.

For many days, Susan used to feel deeply depressed, and then she used to go to her room and throw herself on the bed. All those days, she used to skip dinner and Andria was told not to call her after the evening. For heavy depression and loneliness, Susan already consulted the same psychiatrist who used to treat Sanjay. She was prescribed tranquillizers and anti-depressants. There was a basic difference between the pattern of the depression of Sanjay and Susan. Sanjay had depression genetically, but Susan's depression was from the family atmosphere, the sudden trauma of Sanjay's death and acute loneliness. It was an induced depression.

Once, there was a marriage in their society, and the whole apartment was illuminated. Susan was invited because the family in which the marriage was taking place belonged to the same building. In the evening, people started dropping in for dinner, but Susan didn't go. After Sanjay's death, Susan lost the old spirit, and most of the time, she used to be morose and used to suffer from deep melancholy. Luckily, Andria didn't receive this depression genetically from her father, though there was a great probability because she was the only child of her parents.

Susan was witnessing her widowhood from close quarters, and internally, she became barren and hollow. She used to be alone all the time, and as far as Andria's career was concerned, everything was done. Her duty was to convert the sliding friction to rolling friction, and she successfully did that. She was tired beyond the limit after this whole tiresome journey, which started on the day of her marriage. From both sides, she was devastated, physically and mentally. For her, there was no charm in survival. Lady-like Susan was losing her inner strength for the time being. But, it was a temporary phase. She had to survive for Andria and the downtrodden of society. Because she took an internal oath, and the oath was that after launching her daughter, she would devote the rest of her life for the downtrodden of society. But, certainly, the untimely and shocking departure of Sanjay created a big hollow in her life.

87

Didn't Want Anything from Anyone in Life

Susan always gave maximum weightage to her self-respect. Even in her whole life she never bargained while purchasing anything. Because her mother used to bargain too much, and right from her childhood, she developed staunch hatred for the people who go for haggling. Her life was over on the very day her father expired. She was very close to her father, and she was the eldest child. She had one younger sister and brother, but her father was most attached to Susan. After the death of her father, new things started popping up. Her semi-qualified mother initially got the job in the same college as a group-D staff because she was not even a matriculate. Then for the need and hunger, that lady cleared matric and was promoted to the clerical cadre, but with each passing year, there was a distinct difference in her behaviour, and she was having very strong gender bias. She used to neglect both her daughters and used to give the cream of everything to her son.

So, from that very time, Susan became unfortunate, and truly speaking, after eleven years of her father's demise Sanjay came into her life, and she tasted love after eleven long years. Practically, she lost her complete teenage without any love and affection. When her other friends were pampered beyond limits, Susan had to sacrifice the merriment of a school picnic for just five rupees. The fee for the school picnic was rupees five, and her thrifty mother was not even ready to spare it for Susan. She was a child who was deprived of her childhood. The only companies of her childhood were depression, melancholy, the anger of her mother, insult, comparison, partial starvation, hunger and pathos. There was no one to ask her about her choice. There was no one to present her with single chocolate. In front of both daughters, her mother used to purchase chocolates only for their brother, and they were told to accept that. What a devastating childhood of a professor's child just because of the untimely death of the professor!

When Susan started growing up, her mother used to convince her about the monumentality of her responsibility because she was the eldest. Her mother wanted Susan to do some job after graduation, not go for marriage and pull the cart of the family and sacrifice her whole life. Susan never expressed her opinion, but she was mentally ready to pull the cart, only the presence of Sanjay made everything topsy-turvy. Except for Sanjay and her daughter, there was no one to give her a gift, and Susan, too, was not in a position to accept any gift from anyone, and due to her high self-respect, she never wanted anything from anyone.

People generally do not bother for self-respect when a crisis crops up, but even in the most critical time of her life, Susan didn't lay her hand on her father-in-law. Sanjay's father was a very thrifty but solvent person. He could have easily sent Sanjay to the USA for higher education, but that man didn't have an iota of attachment to his children. He was a widower and a sex-starved person. Sanjay's mother was a sick-cum-frigid lady. Sanjay's father was not only sex-starved, but he also vented about it to all the near and dear ones, including his office colleagues. He projected himself as a hero and portrayed the image of his wife as an ill and frigid lady. Society took the fun out of it, and by doing so, he did not get anything. He just brought insult to the whole family. After marriage, Susan was an unpaid domestic worker in his house for four long years. Those four years were enough for her to read the mindset of her father-in-law.

So, Susan's speciality was that she didn't want anything from anyone in her whole life. It is not so easy for all the ladies. Most housewives criticise their husbands behind their backs, but most of them can be purchased with a few good *sarees* and a few gold ornaments. One of Sanjay's classmates was working in Indian Railways. His wife was from a poor family, but that lady didn't have an iota of self-respect. Her father-in-law openly insulted her parents in front of her husband. Even her husband didn't protest. Her husband knew very well that this poor beggar spouse could be controlled by just a few *sarees* and ornaments. She didn't have the self-respect to boycott all the money given by her husband in protest of the insult of her parents. Most of the housewives are of the same character. They criticise their husbands and in-laws behind their back, but in front of them, they do all kinds of sycophancy. But, Susan didn't belong to that cheap category. Her genre was different, and it is not possible for an ordinary person to understand Susan. For understanding Susan, one needs intelligence, common sense, vision and respect for women.

88

Why does She Hate Dowry System — Her Idol Khokan da

Right from her childhood, after her father's death, Susan was the victim of gender bias, and her mother used to scold Susan and her sister for no reason and pamper her brother also for no reason. India is a country that doesn't have a proper culture as far as marriages are concerned. Here marriages don't take place between the bride and bridegroom but between two families. It is a country where, to date, the dowry system is very much present, and practically, people purchase their sons-in-law by giving a huge amount of money and gold. I have seen all the Bengali communities where the dowry system is very much present.

Right from her childhood, Susan was dead against this age-old system. Two of her aunts (mother's sisters) remained unmarried just because their family couldn't afford the amount of dowry demanded by the family of the boy. How shameless this community is! On the contrary, they are proud of it. I would rather praise the backward classes of Maharashtra where there is no dowry system. Even among the Maharashtrian Brahmins dowry system is not seen. Even my father was in favour of dowry, and he wanted both his sons to be established by their fathers-in-law. A person who supports the dowry system is nothing but a person without a backbone. A greedy person is the cheapest person.

Susan's role model was her neighbourhood brother named Khokan. Fondly, he was addressed as Khokan *da* (*da* is the abbreviated form of *dada*, and in Bengali, *dada* means elder brother). He was not only against the age-old dowry system, but he was keen to marry a widow. Due to this reason, there was a lot of turbulence in his family, but he didn't deviate from his commitments. He married a widow; the question of dowry didn't arise. Secondly, he didn't have the financial ease to throw a big party for five hundred people. He did what was possible for him. He presented a box of sweets to all his neighbours, and afterwards, he refused his father's property. After a couple of years, his father-in-law expired. Before his death, the gentleman wanted his daughter (Khokan *da*'s wife) to give her share of the property to her brother. That means his father-in-law wanted to give the complete ancestral property to his son, but without the written consent of her daughter, he couldn't do that. When the gentleman came to his daughter, she asked Khokan *da*, "What to do?" Khokan *da* gave a crisp answer. He said, "Just sign wherever he needs it and finish it off." This was the character of Khokan *da*, the rarest of the rare. In Sanskrit, they say, *'Shada Ripu'*, and they are *Kam* (Sex), *Krodh* (Anger), *Lobh* (Greed), *Maad* (Pride), *Moho* (Illusion) and *Matsarjya* (Jealousy). Man is made of these six vital enemies. It is even difficult to win one of the six, forget about getting rid of all the six enemies. But, Khokan *da* had the capacity to get rid of *Lobh* (Greed), and that's why he became a role model for Susan. Even Sanjay had the same quality, and that's why Sanjay and Khokan *da* had a very close relationship and deep intimacy. Khokan *da* was three years senior to Sanjay.

But, the ultimate conclusion is that these types of good people who go against the so-called framed rules of society suffer a lot. Probably this society salutes those who take a good amount of dowry and insult the in-laws and wife. The world is a peculiar place. We respect them and try to be close to those who don't even count us, and we never bother about those who really love us.

Susan witnessed Khokan *da* satiate his hunger during lunchtime only with a loaf of bread. The poverty was so stringent that he didn't have the money to buy even rice. From his face, Susan could make out that her Khokan *da* was starving, but never did he compromise with his self-respect. That's why Susan doesn't search for her role model among Swami Vivekananda, Netaji Subhash Chandra Bose or APJ Abdul Kalam. Her role model is Khokan *da,* who is an unknown Indian and will remain unknown for the rest of his life.

89

Suppressing Sensuality (In India, It Is Considered a Quality)

To date, in India, if a widower goes for a second marriage, it becomes an occasion, but if a widow goes for a second marriage, it becomes a question mark. The problems of widows are to date disconcerted. Neither there is a settlement of problems nor can we come out of the confusion. People frown at them. It is a male chauvinist society, and for males, there is a seven-murder excuse policy. A rapist can be scot-free if his crime isn't proven in court, but an innocent lady, who is raped for no fault of hers, is side-tracked by society. This is really a peculiar society. These are those people who use original lemon to wash their hands after having food in a hotel and use the artificial flavour of lemon in drinks.

So, like all other widows, Susan, too, was leaving a barren life, and the struggle was so enormous that the question of suppressing sensuality didn't arise because to have sensuality your mind must be relaxed and free from stresses. But, as far as Susan was concerned, she was overburdened with the mental and physical workload. Especially, after the sad demise of Sanjay, she became a single parent. It is true that Sanjay used to contribute very less. On the contrary, sometimes, his presence itself was a horrifying thing. But still, physical presence does have some value. After the death of Sanjay, Susan didn't have anyone to talk to at home. Because all the things cannot be shared with Andria, and secondly, she was in the opposite hemisphere of the globe.

Her sexual desire was microscopically small, and that can be compared to shuttered wooden cottages of a village. It was shut forever. For diverting her mental attention, she always focused on Andria's career. Mother's love is like a sea, abyssal and endless. Andria was blessed to have it.

90

Seaside Seclusion for a Week

Being fed up with life, Susan decided to have some change for one week. So, she decided to visit a desolate and less crowded beach in the Konkon area, and she chose Dapoli Beach. It was a Saturday morning. She hired a cab and started from Pune. The distance was around 250 kilometres, and it generally takes six hours to reach Dapoli.

By late afternoon, she reached Dapoli. The room in a standard resort was already booked, and she checked in. It was a visit to some place outside Pune after a few years. Last, she visited Kolkata in 2015. It was a strange feeling. The docility and courtesy of the resort staff impressed her. The panoramic beauty of the atmosphere was beyond description. She had a sea-facing room. She had been feeling exhilarated for years, but there was no one to share her feelings with. Sanjay was no more and Andria was far away from her.

One can say, it was sea-side seclusion for a couple of days. As plants need both light and darkness for proper growth, similarly, every human being sometimes needs seclusion from public life for at least a few days. Then only, they can discover the inner human being within themselves.

It was the month of March 2017. Summer was in the offing. In the afternoon, partially hot air was blowing, and along with that, there was a light sand storm, though you can't call it a sirocco. Susan was famous for her asceticism, though it was not due to religious reasons. It was just self-discipline. Susan had mixed feelings about religions, and for her, continuous working and thinking positively were the main religious activities.

One thing was good in the resort; there was no one to startle her. There was no unwanted doorbell or vexation of the salesman or hawkers as she used to have in her Pune residence. They used to stay in a LIG (low-income group) colony, and obviously, the society was not posh, and there was no one to prevent the salesmen from coming inside the society. The work of the relatively less paid watchman was mainly to operate the pump for lifting water to the overhead tank and maintain the basic cleanliness of the society.

There was the facility of room service, and an electric kettle was already there in the room for preparing tea and coffee. Susan was fond of coffee. She prepared a large cup of coffee, and with the steaming mug, she sat on the adjacent sea-facing balcony. Still, there was time for the evening to envelope the atmosphere. She was far from the maddening crowd and traffic of Pune. She was deeply impressed by the unfolding panorama of nature. She witnessed the butterflies; she witnessed the innocent grasshoppers who would hide under the grass, and she enjoyed the series of waves followed by the celestial blue horizon and good seafood. She was thinking of the spacious imagination and latent talent and capacity of Sanjay, which didn't get proper recognition. She was looking at the series of stupendous waves. The surfy water was playing with the sand grains of the sea beach.

The sky was scattered with cirrocumulus clouds, and she was enjoying the refulgent beauty of the sun. Gradually, the crepuscular darkness of the twilight enveloped the whole surrounding, and Susan had the opportunity to enjoy the marvellous beauty of the shell-pink sunset.

Gradually, the evening started pouring in, and in a corner of the sky, the dying moon was visible. Its diapered light was being reflected over the water of the ocean, and the beauty was beyond description. It could only be felt. Susan was looking at the screen of her mobile, and Andria's photo was her screen saver. Andria was wearing her graduation robe and hat along with her certificate of MS in her hand. Susan used to keep her mobile in her sling bag, and the bag was not nicely arranged. It contained a few very important things, e.g., mobile, money, a few coins, an Asthalin pump, a credit card, a photocopy of her Aadhar card, a family photo in which all three of them were captured in a happy mood, a few biscuits and chocolates, her glasses, a key of the house, two small handkerchiefs, a pen, a tube of Boroline and a few tissue papers. This sling bag of Susan was an inseparable part of her life. She was sitting for a long time. Suddenly, she noticed that it was 9:30 pm. The atmosphere became dark, and only the beams of the crescent moon were the source of light on the beach, which was absolutely less crowded and less trodden by.

Around 10:15 pm, Susan came to the room and decided to go for dinner in the restaurant, which was located on the ground floor. She took a corner seat and quickly flipped through the menu card. She ordered chicken soup and prawn *Biryani*. It was difficult for her to consume the total quantity of the *Biryani*. She was done with half of the quantity. Andria had a severe allergy to seafood, but Susan was missing Sanjay. Sanjay was an ardent lover of seafood. After dinner, she returned to her room. The atmosphere was stone cold at night, and due to the whole day's hectic schedule, she felt sleepy and her eyes were sunken. She didn't even realise when she fell asleep.

The next morning, the chirping of the birds helped her to get rid of her deep slumber. It was around 5:30 am. Through the window, she saw that dawn was creeping into the sky and only a handful of stars were still visible. Gradually, the sun rose thinly out of the Arabian ocean, a soft vermilion red at first, turning into an orange disc. It was a feast for her eyes.

Again, she went to the balcony attached to the room and sat comfortably. There were very few visitors to the beach. She decided to enjoy the beauty of the sea from the balcony itself. She ordered the breakfast and just wanted to have one omelette and four pieces of butter toast. It was her favourite breakfast item. Nearly after twenty-six years, she was enjoying readymade food, and that, too, was served. It was just like a dream situation.

After a few minutes, breakfast was served. The omelette was slightly runny inside, but she didn't mind. There was no point in complaining when you are in the mood for vacation. The complaint won't solve the problem, but certainly, it would dampen the mood of vacation. She was quite satisfied with the service given by the staff of the resort, and secondly, she knew, after one week, she would have to start working. So, why create a problem by complaining? Susan felt cocooned by their hospitality and care. After completing her breakfast, she switched on the electric kettle to prepare her coffee. She had a cup of coffee, and after some time, she poured herself another cup.

The bathroom was clean, but small. All the basic amenities were kept there along with a set of fluffy towels of different sizes. She enjoyed a good time there. During the whole week, she didn't go to the beach even for a single time. On the last day, she visited the beach but didn't touch the seawater. She enjoyed the beauty and serenity of the sea just by standing at a distance from the sea.

Throughout her life, she learnt one thing, and that is, if you want to live fully, then you have to live fearlessly. She gave the same teaching to Andria also. Bad days always seem to be very long, and good time vanishes very quickly. It is nothing but relativity. The same thing happened with Susan, too. She couldn't even realise when the whole week was over and the time of departure was at the doorstep. She really had a good time after around two and a half decades. There was no one to disturb her. Really, it was a meaningful seaside seclusion for one week.

91

An Ideal and Real Mother Who Executed Women's Empowerment in True Sense

Susan is one of the very few mothers of this vast sub-continent who implemented and executed women's empowerment in the true sense. Susan never thought of redemption; she was the last person to try to please God. For Susan, the highest form of worship was to discharge her duties towards her family. The world is such a place where if a lady wants her rights then her attitude is considered insolent, though, in reality, it is an absolutely false allegation. Though we have developed much, so much of women's empowerment is there. Still, somewhere, there is a lacuna as far as women are considered, and it may take another hundred years to bridge this gulf.

Susan had devoted her complete life to promoting a girl child, and she didn't do an exhibition or showcasing of her hard work. She did it in a very subtle way. Her steadfastness is even praised by her critics also. She never deviated from her duty, and to do the duty in a perfect way is also a duty. Andria's career was her dream, and she realised that Andria had hidden potential. For creating fire, you don't need fire, you just need a spark, and that spark becomes the motivation. For Andria, Susan was that spark. In spite of mountable difficulties, Susan always possessed flaming enthusiasm.

Susan always gave importance to Andria's apparel. The world won't respect even a scholar if he appears publicly with tattered clothes. The most important thing one learns for being successful is professionalism. There was unimaginable grief because of Sanjay's mental health and his untimely demise, still, Susan performed all her duties. She possessed steely determination coupled with distilled experience and that helped her groom Andria in a proper way.

Her age was around fifty, and it was the time of hormonal shift for most of the ladies. Even Susan had to undergo that hormonal shift. Many ladies complain that they suffer from hot flush, vertigo and many other things during this period. But, Susan was so busy that she didn't even notice the hormonal shift, only sometimes she used to be irritated for small reasons. That may be the manifestation of her hormonal shift.

She always tried her best to give Andria the best possible things in the market. Susan used a smartphone, but that was not very costly. For Andria, she went for a pricey cell phone, and that was nothing but a recent model of Apple.

Susan's father-in-law possessed a fissiparous tendency, but in her life, Susan never entertained that. Susan used to get up early in the morning. She didn't have the habit of dreaming of the future; she was a lady who made her dreams true through hard work. In the early morning, after getting up, she used to look out of the window and greet the mist-softened morning and the fresh dew drops rolling off the blades of grass in the adjacent lawn. Mother Nature used to be the silent witness to the start of her day.

92

Visiting West Bengal after a Few Years

After Sanjay's death, Susan was left alone, and it was really difficult for some time to spend time. Mainly, after the evening, she used to feel very lonely. Just after returning from Dapoli, she was thinking of visiting West Bengal for a couple of days. They left West Bengal in the year 1990, and it was 2017. Andria didn't have the scope to see West Bengal. 2016 was the year for the family, which was lucky as well as unlucky. Lucky because Andria went to the USA for her MS and unlucky because Sanjay left this world.

Susan decided to visit West Bengal for one fortnight. She didn't have any sort of connection with her mother, brother and sister, but she had formal relations with her maternal side. She booked the ticket, and she preferred the journey by rail after a long time. There was Duronto Express, which used to run between Pune and Howrah. On the day of departure, Susan embarked on the second AC compartment of Duronto Express. The train was running smoothly and literally speaking the train was tearing through the dark night.

She preferred to travel in the second AC as it is quite comfortable. It was the month of November. Durga Puja was just over and Deepavali was about to come. Susan had chosen the time between Durga Puja and Deepavali because that time is soothing to visit West Bengal. She preferred to stay in the house of Khokan *da*.

Both Sanjay and Khokan *da* were brought up in the same colony. Both Sanjay's father and Khokan *da*'s father used to stay in rented accommodation under the same landlord. Right from childhood Sanjay, Khokan *da* and many of Sanjay's friends were brought up together. It was a big colony, and there were twenty-eight tenants. There were many houses. Sanjay's father used to stay in the same building in which the landlord used to stay in the first floor. The landlord used to occupy the first floor, and on the ground floor, there were six tenants. All the families of the tenants were just like a big family. But, there was not a single tenant from East Bengal. Basically, all the tenants belonged to the district of Nadia, Birbhum and Bankura. Though Sanjay's father was very much alive, Susan decided not even to inform her father-in-law about her visit. Because she didn't have any sort of respect for her father-in-law whom she compared with the Claude Frollo of Hunchback of Notre Dame. Even Sanjay's father was not informed about Sanjay's death.

It was the month of November, and the day was 5th November 2017. Susan reached Howrah station. Khokan *da* knew about her arrival, but due to his office, he couldn't come to receive her. It was not needed also. Susan was just supposed to go to Serampore and ample numbers of local trains were available. Only she had to come with her bag and baggage from the new complex to the old complex of the Howrah station. She needed to visit the ticket counter for purchasing a ticket for the local train. She had a habit to take her weight in the weighing machines in Howrah station twenty-seven years ago. Old habits die hard. The same trend continued. Here also after purchasing the ticket for the local train, she approached a weighing machine and put a one-rupee coin in the slit, the machine gobbled the coin and the ticket came out and her weight was 60.8 kilograms. She was slightly overweight.

She embarked on the local train. She got a seat. It was morning and not rush hour. Because, in the morning, the rush was there in all the Howrah-bound trains. But, she was travelling in the opposite direction. Susan found no change in the atmosphere and infrastructure even after so many years. The windows of the local trains were equally irritating; it was not possible to roll down them, because due to lack of maintenance, all the windows were jammed. There were a lot of hawkers and beggars within each compartment. There were beggars with their eyes popping out of their eye sockets due to severe malnutrition. From the train, the glistening line of sewage in the adjoining areas was clearly visible. Due to unplanned industrialisation, everywhere, the air was polluted and an acrid smell was present. Though it was November, in these twenty-seven years the weather pattern had changed a lot. Though there was no bone-scorching heat, at the same time, the nip in the air was absent.

Within half an hour, she reached Serampore. Along with her bag and baggage, she crossed the subway and came to the local cycle rickshaw stand. She found a change, and the change was that the number of four-wheelers had increased to a great extent, though the road width was the same as it was twenty-five years ago, and the health of the roads deteriorated further. On her last visit in 2015, her stay was confined to Kolkata only. She didn't visit Serampore, so it was a visit to Serampore literally after twenty-five years. She left Serampore in 1992 after the birth of Andria. Everywhere there were potholes. The roads were overburdened everywhere, and the population also increased to a great extent. Seeing most of the old shops, Susan went down memory lane. There was continuous honking of the cars, and practically, all the vehicles were thrashing through the traffic. There was no civic sense. One person lowered his car window and spat the blotch of *paan* (betel leaf) on the road itself.

She took a Rickshaw and reached Khokan *da*'s house on S K Mukherjee Street in Serampore. Khokan *da*'s wife, Priya was there, and Susan was a close friend of Priya even before twenty-eight years. Priya and Khokan *da* were the witnesses of the struggles of Susan and Sanjay. Susan found that Khokan *da* and Priya refurbished their apartment, and it became more comfortable. The drawing room was sparsely furnished, and for that, there was ample space in the drawing room.

It was a journey of twenty-nine hours. Susan was tired enough. Priya told her to freshen up, and she came with a plate of sweets and water. Priya knew about the untimely departure of her Sanjay *Da*, but immediately didn't raise the topic because it would unnecessarily intensify the fog of depression within Susan.

After freshening up, Susan enjoyed the sweets of West Bengal after so many months. She could visibly notice that Priya became aged. Twenty-six years ago when Susan saw Priya, both of them were in their early twenties, and now, both were on the wrong side of fifty. Ageing is a process, which doesn't spare anyone. After having the sweets, Susan went for a bath, and after that, she straight away went to the kitchen to help Priya. It was nearly 12:45 pm. Someone pressed the doorbell, and Priya told Susan, "*Jao, darja kholo. Tomar khokanda eseche*" (Go, open the door. Your Khokan *da* has come). Susan rushed to open the door, and upon seeing her beloved Khokan *da*, she tightly hugged him. There was no such change in the appearance of Khokan *da*, only he had become totally bald.

It was a half day for Khokan *da*. He used to work in the local cooperative bank. The bank office hours were split into two divisions. In the morning, 9:00 am to 1:00 pm, and in the evening, 6:00 pm to 9:00 pm. That day, for the arrival of Susan, her Khokan *da* took a half-day off in the second half. After that, all of them had a sumptuous lunch followed by endless gossiping. All of them were sitting in the bedroom of Khokan *da* and Priya. Their flat was on the ground floor. From the window of the bedroom, the sky was visible, and the blue sky of November was dotted with clouds. Susan was thinking about how many yesterdays of her life were buried in Serampore where every brick knew about her past and her struggle during the span 1987-1990. For the time being, Susan was lost in the miasma of the past.

In the evening, Susan and Priya went to the other side of the railway track to purchase fresh vegetables. Susan was fond of the vegetable market on the other side of the railway track, and that's why Priya took her there. Otherwise, the vegetable market of Serampore was at a stone's throw distance from Khokan *da*'s house. Susan chose the vegetables and, forcibly, didn't allow Priya to spend anything.

After the marketing was over, both of them crossed the subway. For crossing the subway, they had to travel through platform number three. Suddenly, Susan stood and looked at a cabbage-green butterfly, which was resting on the wall of the platform. Even decades ago, she had seen many multi-coloured butterflies on the same platform. The same tradition was being continued, only due to urbanisation the numbers of butterflies and birds were reduced to a great extent. There were a lot of hawkers on the platform who were selling fruits. Some of them were selling lottery tickets, and there were a few tea vendors. Susan looked at the stained cement benches under the wan tube lights in Serampore station. She remembered that during Sanjay's post-graduation, he used to come to the station and read there comfortably by sitting on a corner bench. Throughout the platform, a lot of papers were there in a trampled condition. They were nothing but newspaper cones in which the people enjoyed *jhalmuri* (a snack item of Eastern India, mostly popular in the state of West Bengal), and after finishing it, they trampled the paper and threw them randomly in any corner of the platform. Indians don't know the effective use of a dustbin.

The next day, Susan was at home only, and after that, Khokan *da* and Priya planned for local sightseeing. They decided to travel to Ghatsila. There were four members — Susan, Khokan *da*, Priya and their daughter, Surabhi. It was a thrilling journey by train. Susan enjoyed the beauty of miles of vacant flat land under a soft blue sky. Mist-softened green expanses were a feast for the eyes. Susan had the opportunity to come across wafer-thin butterflies in the jungles of Ghatsila. They went for a picnic near a hillock. The whole atmosphere was very healthy for a picnic and any sort of merriment. At the end of the day, when they were winding up for returning to the hotel, Surabhi told Susan to look at the scarlet-coloured sun, which was visible on the western horizon. The sunlight was flickering through the leaves of the tall trees, and within a couple of minutes, the sun slipped into the forest.

93

A Lady Who Is for the Ladies and Who Really Wants the True Liberalisation of the Women Folk

In a country like India, ladies are the biggest enemies of ladies. Most of the mothers-in-law want their daughters-in-law to produce a male child. This gender bias is there in our blood, and this is deeply ingrained in our thought process. I don't understand the logic behind this obsession with a male child. In today's scenario, the girls are more caring about the family. In previous days, too, all the girls were more loving and caring, but they were not taken seriously.

Susan was a lady who really wanted the true liberalisation of the women folk. It is not that she did some movement or joined some political parties. There is a saying, "Each one, teach one." If all the mothers of the country follow the footprints of Susan then the future of the country will be changed. Just make your child a good citizen, and the rest of the things will automatically fall into place. Susan's faculty of thinking was far advanced and she had the vision to foresee the future. Whatever the situation was, she always maintained the Catholicity of mind, and in every deed, she used to maintain pristine purity. She was an eternal source of motivation.

Sometimes, in summer, the electric supply used to be closed for high demand and relatively less supply of electricity. In the evening, when the electric supply used to be disrupted, Andria would read in the light of a hissing paraffin lamp. Susan used to sit by her side to motivate her and used to take out the snippets of onion and garlic for cooking. The bars of the low-intensity light used to slash across the face of Susan and Andria. Susan wanted to do many things in life, but Sanjay's psychological condition messed up everything.

Sometimes, she used to think how quickly thirty-one years passed away. In these thirty-one years, many good things could have been done, but only because of Sanjay's mental health, the whole family suffered. They couldn't even enjoy a single week in a proper way. Sanjay and his mood both were unpredictable, and being the spouse and child, both Susan and Andria were the victims. Still, Andria had a social life due to her school, college and office, but for Susan, it was forced captivity within four walls, and there was no variety in life. People say variety is the spice of life. But, in Susan's life, neither there was any variety nor any spice. It was a monotonous life with mountable responsibilities and monumental work.

Sometimes, even before preparing tea, she used to think about whether to prepare it or not. Because preparing tea meant the task of cleaning all the utensils used for preparing tea. Work pressure used to dangle just like a sword on her head. Never had she gotten relief from the work. Sanjay practically used to do zero work. Andria hardly used to do ten per cent of the household chores, and the rest of the work, e.g., cooking, cloth washing, sweeping and mopping the floors and shopping for vegetables and groceries, were done by Susan only. She used to work like a machine, and there was no holiday in her life. She used to work like a perpetual machine and both Sanjay and Andria were served beyond imagination. Susan's role could be compared with sugar in the tea, and she was taken for granted both by Sanjay and Andria. In spite of this Susan used to promote Andria, and it means, she used to promote the girl child.

94

Changing the Continent for the Time Being

The year was 2018, and by that time, Andria was mostly settled in the USA. After her MS, she joined a good consulting organisation. She used to send one thousand five hundred dollars to Susan per month through Xoom, and she was very dutiful to her mother. Andria didn't have the opportunity to gift anything to her father. Sanjay left this world before the completion of Andria's MS.

Andria was settled in the Fort area of Dallas, which was one of the poshest areas of Dallas. After joining the job, Andria was requesting Susan to come to the USA for some change, but Susan was not very serious. Because a trip to the USA was not an easy task for Susan. Even if Andria would have spent for the whole thing, it would have been pressure on her. But, due to repeated requests from Andria, Susan decided to go at least once to her.

Susan always wanted Andria to be wooed by big companies eager to sign them up and exactly that happened. Andria got five jobs in five famous American Companies. She rejected four and chose the most preferred one. Susan's passport was ready; she just had to go for the basic formalities of the tourist visa for the USA. All the paper works were done by Andria; she even took a back-to-back appointment and mailed all the details to Susan. Susan just needed to visit Bombay for two days.

On the very first day, all the required formalities for the biometric data were done, and on the next day, she had to appear for the visa interview at the US consulate (visa office).

There was a rush, but multiple windows were there. Susan's officer was a lady. She just asked the purpose of her visit and the name of the consulting firm where Andria was working. Within no time, the interview was over, and the officer kept Susan's passport. Susan was told that, within a couple of days, she would receive her tourist visa.

The city of Dallas belonged to one of the largest states of the USA, which is nothing but Texas. Susan knew about the megalopolitan Dallas and other famous cities of the State of Texas, e.g., Houston and Austin. Bukky was settled in Houston, and Susan made it a point to visit her.

Bukky was a real friend of rainy days. She was always there by Andria's side, whether it was exam time, time of illness, time of Sanjay's demise or time of shifting from college station to Dallas. More than once, Andria took a loan from Bukky and repaid it in due time. Bukky was from Nigeria. Andria had a number of friends from Pune, but the contribution of Bukky to her life is simply unimaginable. There was no Indian friend who could do as much as Bukky did for her.

Susan got the visa and booked a to-and-fro ticket with a credit card. She requested the concerned bank to spread the whole amount into thirty-six EMIs. Then she had to purchase the required things. The month was June, and for that, she didn't have to buy garments for winter because, in June, it was scorching summer in Texas. Susan booked the ticket for Qatar Airlines. The flight was via Doha, and in Doha, there was a layover for three hours. It was Susan's first international journey. Susan was smart; still, some amount of nervousness was there.

The date of her flight was 17th June 2018, and the flight timing was 2:45 am. Susan started on the morning of 16th June and booked a hotel near Chembur just for spending some time after reaching Bombay. Susan never wanted to do any work at the eleventh hour. She had one big bag and one small bag with her apart from her handbag. On the 16th, after breakfast, she started by an intercity Uber cab and reached Chembur by 1:00 pm. After reaching the hotel, she had light lunch and slept for a few hours. The packing was already done. So, both the bags were not opened. Around 10:00 pm, she checked out and proceeded towards Chhatrapati Shivaji Maharaj International Airport by an Uber cab. After reaching the airport, she immediately went inside, completed the paper formalities, dropped her luggage and, after the security check, went to the lobby where all the other passengers were waiting.

In due time she started and, after reaching the USA, went for the formalities related to immigration. After all the formalities of immigration, Susan came out of the airport. Andria was waiting for her. Both of them were happy beyond measure. Andria rushed towards her and hugged her tightly. It was a meeting nearly after two years. Andria told her, "Mummy, finally, you made this possible." Susan didn't find much impact of Westernisation in Andria's behaviour and attitude. Andria was totally exhilarated by seeing her beloved Mom. Andria still remembers a poster in which a bear was shown, and on its back, there was a teddy bear. Under the poster it was written, "Home is wherever Mom is."

They came out, and Andria straight away took her to the parking zone where Andria's Toyota Camry was parked. Susan was amazed by Andria's driving skills. Even in India, she used to drive her Victorian vintage, an old Maruti-800. But, here the scenario was totally different. Though this Toyota Camry was also second-hand, it was in very good condition, and the size was much bigger compared to Maruti-800. Susan asked Andria, "How do you control such a giant car so easily?" Andria told her, "Mummy, it's nothing. If you would have learned to drive at the right age, then I would have shared the driver's seat with you."

While going to Andria's apartment, Susan was amazed by the beauty of the city. In between, there was a big and famous church. Andria wanted Susan to see the church from the inside. Susan was highly impressed by the nave of the church and the beautiful chandeliers placed in the different locations of the big church.

They reached home within half an hour. The weather was hot and sunny. The house was made of wood. She used to stay on the first floor. All the houses had similar looks, and all were two-storied. After entering the house, Susan felt very relaxed, as if she was seeing her dream in three dimensions. She knew what an enormous struggle was there behind this small settlement of Andria in the USA. But, it was just the start. Susan was confident enough that a day would come when Andria would illuminate the technical landscape of the country with her hard work, intelligence and honesty. Susan always taught Andria to adopt the honest path. It is tough, but it gives permanent results.

Susan sat on a sofa, and an oblong patch of sunlight was coming through the window panes. Ordinary guardians of India can't even think of this struggle in their foggiest idea. Susan had a credit card, but for her safety, she had two thousand dollars with her. The wad of notes was kept in her handbag.

In the evening, Andria took Susan to a nearby Italian restaurant. Susan was confused by the tongue-twister names of the dishes. She couldn't understand anything except for the varieties of pizza and pasta. She told Andria to place the order, and Andria had a complete idea about Susan's taste. She ordered some non-spicy and delicious items as the main course. They didn't go for starters and only ordered soup as an appetizer.

As Rabindranath Tagore gave his life and love for the Vishvabharati, in a similar way, Susan devoted her complete life and love for the sake of Andria's academic and professional career. There are many people who are academically stalwarts, but on the professional front, they fail miserably. One must know how to convert one's knowledge to money. Then only professional success will be there. From day one, Susan was serious about Andria's professional success, and that was the main reason why, upon sensing her stagnancy in the MNC in India, Susan advised Andria to go for MS and leave India permanently. If a person with a strong academic background fails in the professional world, then no one will take them seriously. After a few years, people forget that once the person was academically good. This crude world doesn't want to see your old biodata; they are interested in your present biodata only. Great personalities work for the nation, but lesser-known personalities like Susan works for the family. If all individuals work like Susan, every family will be successful, every family will add some value to society and, in this way, thousands of families will be changed. What is a nation? It is nothing but the collective integration of all the families. If there is only one Susan in each family, the meaning of the whole nation will change, and it will be a successful nation. If you do just your work sincerely it is more than enough.

After dinner, they returned to the house, and till late at night, they were chit-chatting, and obviously, the central point of their discussion was Sanjay who was no more.

95

Women's Empowerment and Women's Liberty

Women's empowerment and women's liberty — these two terms are small, but one thing we must understand is how much empowerment is there, and in the literal sense, do women really enjoy liberty? India is known as the rape capital of the globe because of its loose administration. After a rape, even if the rapists are caught, it takes seven to eight years to punish them, and till the end, the culprits try their best to get rid of capital punishment. In the name of democracy, we have damaged the whole system. It is surprising how all of us are still alive in India. It's a country where even on the one-way road, vehicles come from the opposite side, and if a license holder kills you, you will die on the spot, but the license holder will be scot-free. He only needs some manipulation and lubrication of the hands of the authorities who decide the punishment. In this country, there are two kinds of women. 99.999% of women are totally suppressed by their husbands and in-laws, and in the name of wife, they are nothing but unpaid domestic workers. They are always frightened. After the whole day's work, they can't even sleep properly. The brutal husbands behave like beasts, and in the name of lovemaking, these anaemic ladies are raped by their husbands day after day, month after month and year after year. Their only fault is that they are not qualified and can't earn.

Now let us talk about the rest of the 0.001% ladies. They are qualified. They earn a huge amount and treat their husbands like domestic pets. They don't have any sort of respect for their in-laws and family members. They are snobs; in the name of spending they practically splurge with money. These ladies are having real women's empowerment and women's liberty, but they obverse it and don't do the needful for the needy women of the society. On the contrary, they take the benefit of being a woman. So, ultimately, the cross sections that suffer are in no way benefited or helped. This is a serious issue.

There are many welfare projects by the government for needy women, but how far are they benefitted is a big question. Does the grant reach the end or is diverted to another's hand in between? Corruption is there in the veins of the people in this country. The hobby of maximum women is juicy gossip about neighbours and society. Since they are relatively less free, they are more suppressed, and this suppression leads them to be jealous. These are all interrelated. This can be a very important topic of research for the subject of psychiatry. Most women waste their lives just by cooking, chopping vegetables and separating coriander leaves from the bundle of springs of fresh coriander.

I personally witnessed four semi-literate women, chopping vegetables and criticising the fifth woman who was absent that day. This is their regular life. Criticising others is an inseparable part of their life, and woman is the biggest enemy of woman. When a man is married and produces a girl child, his mother becomes the first person to be upset the most. Every lady wants a grandson, not a granddaughter. Being a lady, if you don't want a granddaughter, society is bound to go to the dogs. This is nothing but a lack of proper education. Even within highly qualified males, there is gender bias. Why? To be qualified is easy, but it is difficult to be truly educated, and unless one becomes truly educated, they are bound to have a gender bias. Qualification is nothing but a superficial outward coating, but true education changes one from the inside.

So, it may take another hundred years to change the mindset of the people. There must be a kink in the path of thinking, which is nothing but a straight line. Women's empowerment and women's liberty are just two terms. A woman like Susan doesn't have any record of doing any government or private service. But, her daughter knows and her husband knew what Susan is. She is the burning example of women's empowerment and women's liberty. Is it easy to launch your girl child and place her in the global coordinate being a single parent? It needs hard work, vision, sacrifice, intelligence, wit, money and, last but not the least, great common sense. Fortunately, Susan possesses all these qualities, and that's why Andria's career path was smooth, and she has a chequered career.

For Susan, initially, life was nothing but sorrow, death, hate, cruelty, disease and starvation, but she had begun with all these odds, and gradually, with efforts, intelligence, smart attitude and hard work, she reached her destination. Her destination was nothing but to place Andria in the global coordinate. She only taught Andria to win by inches, not by miles.

96

Joining an NGO and Working for HIV-Infected People

After the departure of Andria to the USA, Susan became very lonely. In the morning, it was okay, but it was really difficult to spend the barren afternoons. Sanjay's memories used to corrode her from the inside. Andria gave her a standing invitation for coming to Dallas, but Susan knew that she could visit Dallas for a few months, but couldn't stay there permanently. Already, in her recent visit to Dallas, she experienced it. Because at that age, it was really difficult to change the coordinates permanently. When a person is young, the mind is like soft clay, and you can mould it in any shape, but once the age crosses fifty, the mindset starts becoming rigid, and the flexibility of the mind starts dying and decaying. Sanjay's untimely death was a cause of brooding for Susan. So, thinking from all points of view, Susan decided to join an NGO that was working with HIV-infected people. It was on the outskirts of the city. Susan came to know about the organisation through the internet and called them. She got an appointment, and on that day, she reached there half an hour before the scheduled time of the meeting.

After nearly forty-five minutes, she was called by the organisers. After entering the board room, she greeted everybody pre-set over there with folded palms. She got a brief introduction about the scope of work, and she was supposed to do mainly two works. One was to teach some soft skills to the patients who were being admitted there, and the other was some administrative work in the accounts section. Susan agreed, and they offered her a minimal salary. She accepted that without any negotiation. After the interview, she came out of the room and had a round within the campus. It was a small campus of seven acres. She sat on a sun-bleached rock in front of the cafeteria on the campus and had one coffee. There were lots of trees on the campus. She observed a squirrel darting up and down the trunk of a tree. There were internal roads, and due to lack of maintenance, tall grass flanked the road from both sides. There were lots of jungle flowers on the whole campus. One can say it was a Kaleidoscope of wildflowers swaying in the wind.

Nowadays, it is really difficult to get land in the cities like Pune and Bombay for some social cause. Because due to the software revolution, even the villages located on the outskirt of cities like Pune and Bombay are converted into high technology paradise. After having the coffee, Susan came out of the campus and tried to cut through hundreds of vehicles on the road, but she couldn't take the risk. She waited till the signal became red. After a few minutes, she got a bus and took her seat and started thinking about the condition of this unfortunate country.

It is a country where with each passing day the rich becomes richer and the poor becomes poorer. And, this gulf between the rich and poor will be an ever-widening gulf, which can never be bridged. Politicians are also in favour of poverty as it is the best tool to use to beg for votes. Politicians don't give us anything. They take back our things like water, electricity and ration and, during elections, promise to give the same things back. It's a country of hypocrites. Today's condition is that there is no labour law. A diploma engineer is working from 8:00 am to 10:00 pm, and their salary is just six thousand rupees. Apart from that, they get free lodging and food. Conditions are so bad that if they refuse, the next candidate is there, ready to accept a salary, which is even lesser. The greatest curse of this country is population, pollution and politics, and India will slowly get rid of these three parameters.

97

Joining the Vagrant Home Where Poor Girls Are Taken Care Of

When all the duties of Susan were over, and Andria was completely settled in the USA, she decided to dedicate the rest of her life to a social cause, and by contacting an NGO, she joined a vagrant home near Pune. Susan was aware of Buddhist Monastery. A monastery is nothing but a place occupied by a community of monks living under religious vows. But, there was a difference between a monastery and a vagrant home. With a vagrant home, religion was not related. It was open to people of all religions and mainly used to help those who were dumped by all (even relatives and close family members).

Working in a vagrant home was a totally new experience for Susan, and it was unprecedented. The atmosphere of neglect and abandonment was almost tangible. With her act of humanitarianism, she wanted to do her best for human welfare. The vagrant home was mainly occupied by very poor people who didn't have anyone to look after them. Most of the workers there were nothing but semiliterate masses. The vagrant home belonged to the government, and it used to get aid from the government, but that much aid was not sufficient for comfortable living for the inmates. Most of the workers used to come by cycles, and most of the cycles were old and weather-beaten due to continuous use. All the faces of the inmates had forgotten how to smile. Hunger, poverty and diseases erased smiles from their faces for a lifetime. For society, the inmates of the vagrant home were nothing but a burden, and they could be compared with nullity. Unless you contribute something to society you are practically of no use. The whole atmosphere was very depressing and working there was a challenge.

Susan first decided to teach the street children who had their shelter within the vagrant home, and she started from scratch. With her own money, she purchased notebooks, pencils, erasers and scales for the children and started teaching them very rudimentary English and Mathematics. Gradually, those children got interest, and within a fortnight, they became big fans of Susan. Apart from this job, Susan used to help the authority in admin jobs. Susan used to donate fifty per cent of her salary to the children of the vagrant home.

Apart from these teaching and admin jobs, another routine affair was to talk to Andria every day around 9:00 am for fifteen to twenty minutes. Obviously, it used to be a Whatsapp video call. Andria was settled in Dallas. By knowing about the progress of the poor kids in the vagrant home, Andria became so happy that she immediately sent five hundred dollars for those children, and that was more than enough for them. Susan kept four hundred dollars and just used hundred dollars to purchase some good colourful books for the children. The whole day, she used to wait for her class, and there she used to see smiling faces. Those faces were semi-starved, but they had an inbuilt desire to learn. In today's scenario, there is a dearth of devoted faculties in every country. Even in developing countries like the USA or the UK, professors are mainly doing research, and in the name of teaching, they go to their classes with PPT, present them, but don't share them. Students can't take notes so quickly, and secondly, all the subjects can't be taught by PPT. Subjects like Building Construction can be taught by PPT, but topics like Fourier Series, Laplace Transformation and Schwarz Christoffel Transformation can't be taught by PPT.

Many times the teaching is done by the MS/PhD students who are the Research Assistants (RA) or Teaching Assistants (TA) of a professor. In those countries, for a professor, earning IRG (Internal Revenue Generation) through consultancy is more important than teaching. They need to generate their own salary.

Humanity is God, and social service is real religion. Susan realised the meaning of this sentence while working and serving the poorest of the poor in the vagrant home. The people were poor, and the quality of the food was not so good. For those poor people, the only thing available to enhance the taste was chilli, and most of them used to nibble the chillies while eating.

Susan used to return home in the evening, and then, after having a cup of coffee, she used to sit on the open terrace of her apartment. Sanjay departed permanently from her life; Andria was at a distance of fourteen thousand kilometres; she didn't have any socialisation, and viewing television was not a solution. So, she just used to sit on the open terrace and submerge herself in old thoughts. The old thoughts used to appear one after another like the waves of an ocean, and the broken yellow moon used to be the witness of those silent moments of a mother thinking of her past, her motherhood and women's empowerment.

In this world, no one will learn about Susan. Only one person will realise her contribution, and she is none else than Andria. Through the work and volunteering of Andria, Susan will reach the masses in a subtle way. Christ was not a Christian, Buddha was not a Buddhist, Muhammad was not a Muslim, and Susan, too, didn't receive any award for her motherhood and women's empowerment, but through the work and creativity of her daughter Susan's ethics, ethos, determination, devotion and direction will be reflected and remain immortal for a long time.

98

Sun Never Sets

We say that Sun sets at the end of the day, but it is a wrong concept. Actually, Sun never sets. It's the earth, which rotates. It is purely relative. Due to the continuous motion of the earth, we see the wee hours and the evening. When a child grows, we say the dresses are becoming small, but actually, the size of the dresses never changes, it is the child who grows. Here also the case is the same, and it is nothing but relativity.

Susan can be compared with the Sun, which is active 24X7. Life is like an ocean; the ocean is not just what you see on the surface. The same is the case with Susan. People used to see a very active Susan, but no one could see her inside. The entire to-do list used to be programmed in her brain. The direction given by Susan for all the small and big works can be compared with the direction of the philharmonic orchestra. It is not so easy to direct an orchestra. For Susan, the series of works from morning to evening was just like an orchestra. It was a challenge for her to bring up Andria and groom her properly in spite of all the odds.

Sometimes, in the evening, she used to visit the nearby lake. Today, she remembers how she casually used to fling stones into the lake. For any achievements of Andria, Susan's glassy eyes used to glow with pride. Her daughter was the main support to her livelihood. For helping Andria, Susan used to have indefinite energy, and that energy and enthusiasm used to be created just out of passion and affection.

99

Looking at the Western Horizon in Crepuscular Darkness

Andria was sent by Susan to the USA for having better education and a better atmosphere. It was the Western civilisation. Sometimes, in the evening, when the sun used to drop behind the far mountain seen from the window of Susan's apartment, she used to be engrossed in her thoughts. Twilight used to grasp the whole atmosphere, and aged Susan used to look at the western horizon in the crepuscular darkness. She used to think if a line were drawn straight from her window for infinite miles then that line would surely intersect with the point where Andria was located. Only the angle must be correct.

With the advancement of age, gradually, loneliness and depression started occupying her mind. Andria was at the far land of the USA, fourteen thousand kilometres from Pune, and Sanjay was no more. The whole house was filled with a mummified silence. In every nook and corner, Sanjay and Andria's memory used to be there. Sometimes, Susan used to stand in front of the dressing table of Andria. All the cosmetics used by her were kept as they were. No one even touched them. The brimming bookshelf of Sanjay was not opened even once after his death. The glasses were having thin layers of dust over them. Susan did all her duties. She successfully launched Andria on the global coordinate.

Andria used to do extra work as compared to others. She used to do a lot of volunteering, and there was no payment for that. On Sunday mornings, when other Indians used to gear up for a picnic or party, Andria used to go for lake cleaning work. This extra work didn't pay her anything immediately, but with the passage of time, she could realise a marked difference between her life, and the life of other Indians and Americans who used to work with her. Everybody used to complete only the assigned work, but no one was ready to go the extra mile. But, these extra miles beautified Andria's resume, and within three years, she was known to all the experts related to her field. She visited most of the states of the USA, and she interacted with experts who were settled across the USA in different states. She got more than one scholarship for attending seminars and conferences.

Susan taught Andria that if she prepares a cake, then she must not forget to keep a cherry over the cake. Mother's teaching paid her. Due to her mother's counselling and hard work, she could see and experience a sea change in her professional career.

Susan was done with all her commitments, and she was ready for ultimate emancipation, but Andria's thoughts always loomed over her head. Susan was a luminous woman. Susan never wanted Andria to work in a corrupt country where money is transferred under the table.

In the evening, she used to be alone. After a brief evening walk, she used to return home and relax on the plush leather sofa. Her whole life could be compared with a crushed and crumpled used tissue, but still, she didn't leave hope. She knew one thing that life itself was her teacher, and she was in a state of constant learning. There is no end to learning. After a certain age, everyone should stop reading books and read only the human characters and nature. Susan used to do that, and out of this, her thought process was widened beyond limits.

100

Accepting the Courier Sent by Her Daughter from Dallas

Since it is the last chapter of the book, I am supposed to write the epilogue, but I am leaving this part to my beloved readers. Let them go through the book, and each of them will look at the book from his or her own angle, and due to that, all the epilogues will be different. Actually, those epilogues will be the individual feedback of the readers. It will be in the form of different shades and colours.

This was the month of December 2018, and Christmas was on the doorstep. Andria had a veneration for her mom. She used to witness the journalistic precision of Susan in all her works. After discharging all her duties to her family, it was the time of salvation for Susan. People in India say that the marriage of the child is the responsibility of the parents. But, Susan never thought so. For her, designing a career was much more important than a so-called marriage. From her own life, Susan realised that if a lady is not financially independent in each step of life, she faces problems and insults. That's why Susan gave main importance to Andria's academic and professional career. Though Sanjay never insulted Susan for not doing any job, her father-in-law, many times, passed sarcastic comments and remarks about Susan before her graduation.

Regarding marriage, Susan had left that to Andria completely. Susan was ready to accept the boy chosen by Andria, and Susan was confident that the struggle of Andria's life would help her to select a genuine person. The husband must not be a liability. Susan didn't have any reservations as far as caste, religion or nationality was concerned. She only wanted her daughter to be happy after marriage. She never believed in grand marriage; she gave emphasis on a grand married life. Susan was not xenophobic. On the contrary, she wanted Andria to be a global citizen. Susan wanted

Andria to beautify the academic landscape of the world with her skills, prudence and thoughts. She was sure that with each passing year, Andria would go places and enthral the audience wherever she would visit as a speaker to give the keynote address. Susan was sure that in future, just by providing consultancy, Andria would earn oodles of money.

America is a country where a real rose is praised for its beauty. It is a land of equality without any kind of bias. That means irrespective of nationality, caste and creed, if anyone excels in any stream, they will be definitely rewarded for their hard work. There is no dirty politics or nepotism along with political interferences. India is a country where even in university matters the politicians interfere. If one wants to be the Vice Chancellor of a famous university in India, his academics alone will not be enough; he must have some political support. What a shame! That's why the education system of India is going to the dogs. America is a country where they are open to the whole world, and even if the child of the American President wants to pursue MS, they will have to appear for GRE and TOEFL, and only based on the score, the child will be admitted. There is no concept of management quota in American Universities. Their transparency and openness made them big and successful.

I am sorry for deviating from the main topic. The month was December, and the wind was needle cold. Since Susan was prone to allergies and Asthma, she had to be doubly careful. There was an invisible organic bond between Susan and Andria. Susan was doing the regular domestic work. Suddenly, someone pressed the doorbell. Through the peephole, she could see a parcel delivery boy. She opened the door and took the parcel from the delivery boy. It was a parcel sent by Andria from Dallas. The weight of the box was very light. Andria didn't even talk about the parcel when she talked to Susan in the morning. It was a great surprise.

Susan opened the parcel with deep curiosity. She found a small photo album. On each page, there was a photograph of Susan and Andria, and all those photographs were captured during Susan's recent visit to the US. Below every photograph, a quotation was written along with the name of the person who quoted that. In the end, Susan noticed a small gift pack in one corner of the box. She opened it and found a beautiful wristwatch, and with blue ink, on a piece of paper, it was written by Andria:

Dear Mummy,

This is for you. I thought a watch can be the best gift for you because I always found you respect time, and I, too, inherited the same quality from you. I was sent to the US just because of your motivation, dedication, determination, hard work and vision. I always felt cocooned in your company, and I know your invisible shadow is always there by my side to protect me from all odds.

Bye and love.

Eternally yours
Andria

Mother's love is always abysmal. Susan was touched. The gift was ordinary, but it possessed an extraordinary value. Because to be ordinary in the world is the most extraordinary thing. Susan again started flipping through the album. She was touched by the soft gesture of her daughter. Only the silence of the room and Sanjay's photo mounted on the wall were the witnesses of the smile of a mother through her tears.

www.ingramcontent.com/pod-product-compliance
Lightning Source LLC
LaVergne TN
LVHW091148150826
845672LV00005B/1067

* 9 7 9 8 8 8 9 3 5 9 5 9 3 *